About t

CW01510910

Robert Verity grew up in Yorkshire, one of three brothers. He read sociology at Nottingham University and then gained a master's degree from York. Most of his working life has been in the Probation Service which was both challenging and satisfying.

He won the poetry prize at the Tonbridge Arts Festival in 2012 and has had a poem published in an anthology of contemporary work entitled *Links in the Chain*.

He was involved in various writing groups in Kent before moving with his partner to live in the Medoc area of France.

French Leave is his debut novel.

French Leave

Robert Verity

French Leave

Vanguard Press

VANGUARD PAPERBACK

© Copyright 2024
Robert Verity

The right of Robert Verity to be identified as author of
this work has been asserted by him in accordance with the
Copyright, Designs and Patents Act 1988.

All Rights Reserved

No reproduction, copy or transmission of this publication
may be made without written permission.
No paragraph of this publication may be reproduced,
copied or transmitted save with the written permission of the
publisher, or in accordance with the provisions
of the Copyright Act 1956 (as amended).

Any person who commits any unauthorised act in relation to
this publication may be liable to criminal
prosecution and civil claims for damages.

A CIP catalogue record for this title is
available from the British Library.

ISBN 978 1 83794 012 7

This is a work of fiction. Names, characters, businesses, places, events
and incidents are either the product of the author's imagination or
used in a fictitious manner. Any resemblance to actual persons, living
or dead, or actual events is purely coincidental.

Vanguard Press is an imprint of
Pegasus Elliot Mackenzie Publishers Ltd.
www.pegasuspublishers.com

First Published in 2024

Vanguard Press
Sheraton House Castle Park
Cambridge England

Printed & Bound in Great Britain

To Colin, for your patience

I would like to acknowledge the help of Sarah Salway who welcomed me to her writing courses, and the encouragement of The Trading Post Writers in Tunbridge Wells.

1

France, last summer

Martha was determined to keep going even though she felt emotionally and physically drained. She had driven up the French coast that afternoon to Erin's house in Saint-Cyprien, and now in the early evening they had come out to Chez-Madeleine to eat. The anonymity of a restaurant was perfect. She needed to explain, and would be able to do so here.

She had followed Erin in through the busy, noisy bar, humming with activity, concerned it was so crowded they might not get a table. If they had to go back to Erin's house, to Claude and the children, she would lose this chance to explain.

The patronne, a statuesque lady who missed nothing, saw them and gestured to one of the waiters. A recently vacated table was cleaned and re-set. When they were seated, the large lady bore down and spoke to Erin slowly with the strong, guttural accent of south west France, asking how she was.

'Tres bien, et c'est ma chère amie, Martha, de l'Angleterre,' Erin replied, introducing her friend to Madeleine. Martha felt odd hearing her name pronounced Marta.

Madeleine looked at her intently with eyes outlined in black, and said that any friend of Erin's was welcome, 'Dans la famille Chez-Madeleine.'

'J' étais ici l'année dernière avec mon mari,' Martha said slowly and distinctly, pleased she had found the correct words to say that she had been here last year with her husband.

Madeleine smiled and made a reply Martha's French was not quick enough to catch. She departed to arrange for an aperitif to be delivered to their table.

Erin put her hand reassuringly over Martha's, a mark of their friendship which went back many years.

'Martha, I know I wrote saying come anytime, but I didn't think you would. Not so soon, anyway. I'm so glad you have.'

They remained silent like that until Martha withdrew her hand and pushed her neat dark hair back from her forehead.

'Thanks for taking me in, Erin. Thierry always wanted to return here. In fact, he suggested it the last weekend before... Oh, well, I saw on the map Saint-Cyprien was on the coast south of Sablette, so I decided to make it a detour on my journey home. I longed to see you, to see someone I knew who wasn't part of... part of any of it. Actually, Erin, I didn't know where else to go, who else to turn to.'

'You did the right thing, Martha. Claude and I have been so worried. So, does that mean you're actually on your way home?'

'Maybe. I'm playing truant, putting things off. Here I am, Martha, the one who always knows her mind and organises other people. I don't know what I'm doing or where I'm going right now. It all feels so... so... pointless, so futile.'

She looked defiant. She was not weak, and would not cry, even in front of her old friend. She realised Erin would be wondering what to say and how to help, but there was no way she could help apart from just being with her.

'This place brings back happy memories of being here with Thierry...'

She was forming the words to say the rest when they had another interruption. A young waiter arrived with two glasses of white wine and cassis, which delayed the moment.

The kir was beautifully cold, and hit the right spot in her stomach.

'Your friend Madeleine has a lot of good-looking young waiters.'

'Yes, she rather specialises in them,' Erin replied as she tried unsuccessfully to secure her mop of curly fair hair away from her face. 'Most are students on summer vacations. She has less staff the rest of the year. The family do most of it themselves out of season.'

'Do you realise we could have children the same age as these waiters?' Martha said unexpectedly. She had, in fact, no children, and Erin's were young because she had settled down late. 'Ah, well…'

Erin remained silent, perhaps wondering where Martha's mind was taking her. She decided to approach the main subject obliquely.

'How are Thierry's parents taking it? she asked.

'To tell you the truth, it was dreadful. I felt shut out. It seemed somehow… maybe because I'm English… they blame me.'

'That's ridiculous, and unfair!'

'Yes, but there's a history to it. I don't think they ever got over his going away to study in England, and then marrying me rather than returning to a local girl.'

'Was there a local girl?'

'Perhaps. I've always wondered. In the family's plan, not Thierry's. His mother had aspirations for him which didn't include me. But Thierry wanted to break free and didn't intend to return. As we began to commit ourselves to each other he confessed he had been involved with someone when we met, a girl in London, not in France. I suspect she didn't give him up lightly. The family probably didn't know about her. They think I'm the reason he settled in London, whereas he loved London and his career there, and having got away, had no intention of going home. We didn't have a lot of contact with them over the years, usually just a yearly visit, and that was often Thierry alone. I never felt welcome.'

She toyed with her place setting. Erin smiled to herself remembering Martha always tidied and rearranged things.

She remained silent, sensing Martha had more to say about the visit.

'I'd hoped I could talk to them and settle misunderstandings. I wanted to know more about Thierry's history. I thought we could remember him together. It was a chance for me to feel close to him again, through being in the farmhouse in Gers where he grew up. I wanted his parents to open up so we could share the pain and make it bearable.

'But... his mother was icily polite. His father was remote. They locked their pain away and froze me out. I tried to break through. God knows I've got enough social work skills, but they were no match for their Gallic intractability, and this is all too personal. So I cut the visit short. Wish I hadn't gone! It made matters worse. Another avenue cut off. I shan't be going back, but I'm not ready to go home yet either.'

'They can't hold you responsible for him being—'

'Killed! There's no point just saying he died, Erin. He was mown down in a London street, that's the dreadful truth of the matter. I don't know why. I can't understand it, couldn't stop it, couldn't save him. I wasn't there! Sorry.'

Erin waited.

'The irony is,' Martha laughed, 'I was having coffee with the chief constable and other do-gooders, and we were all sitting round thinking how important we were, discussing crime prevention in suburbia when it happened.'

'Oh, how awful! Well, I mean…'

'Yes, it was awful. I knew something was wrong when an officer in uniform came in and whispered to an aide, and he whispered to the chief constable, and I realised they were all looking at me, trying not to be seen to be looking at me. The chief constable muttered we had better adjourn the meeting for tea, and I remember looking at my mobile, out of habit I suppose, and thinking there's no text from Thierry. He often let me know what train he would be coming home on, in case I could meet him at the station.

'I found myself being led into a little room, and there was Martin, my boss from Social Services, looking embarrassed and out of place. He shouldn't have been there, and he said, "Martha, I'm awfully sorry," and he was fidgeting with coins in his pocket. He didn't know how to tell me, but I knew.'

She came to a halt, so after a while Erin said encouragingly,

'You knew?'

'Yes, I knew. I don't know how.'

Erin looked her in the face to see if she was back in the restaurant again, or still half removed, recalling something far away.

'Something terrible had happened to Thierry. Was he dead? Had he just… disappeared? I was so cold. Everyone seemed to melt away. I was taken home. Martin organised someone to drive and stay with me for the evening, and it was so quiet, so unreal.'

Martha came to a complete stop. Erin guessed her head was back there.

'You don't need to tell me any more, not unless you want to,' she said quietly.

'He died alone on a crowded London Street. Why? I'll never see him again.'

She was silent.

'I'm sorry, Erin. I didn't mean to burden you…'

'It's okay.'

'And since then, it's all been strange, so lonely. I'm really sounding selfish.'

'No. It's natural.'

'His life ended in an instant.' She paused. 'Mine was over too. I wasn't ready, I wasn't prepared, do you see? And now I feel we wasted so much precious, precious time. If only we could have it over again, live it differently. I'd make sure he didn't go to London that day. Keep him away from danger. Oh, Erin, other people cope with bereavement. I'm finding myself becoming illogical, flying off in different directions. It isn't me! I was so independent, yet without Thierry I've lost it all.'

'I can imagine… No, I can't really… I've tried to think what it would be like if Claude died suddenly and left me alone, but I've not had to face it. I do want to understand.'

Chez-Madeleine was busy, popular and noisy. They sat in silence for a while watching people. Martha could discern no theme to the décor, as there often is in modern restaurants designed to evoke an impression. Madeleine's idea of a colour scheme seemed to be lots of everything. There was also the clutter of many years. Big old furniture lined the walls, looking as if it had been pushed back to make space for extra tables for summer visitors. Wine was stacked higgledy-piggledy, and the young waiters rushed around in tee shirts and jeans, skilfully avoiding collisions, collecting glasses and cutlery from one place, drinks from the bar and food from the kitchen, all in separate directions. Martha dismissed her urge to do an efficiency study. It seemed in its crazy way to work, but people smiled happily and shouted above the noise, and none of it was her business anyway. Like so much else it did not matter.

Although she had lost her appetite since she had lost Thierry, the aromas were beginning to make her hungry. There was a pizza oven just inside the restaurant and a counter open to the village square, serving both customers inside and take-aways. The smell, mixed with wood smoke from the oven, combined with fish, herbs and garlic sauces, steaks and French fries dominated the room.

It was the end of July, six weeks since Thierry's death, and the weather should have made up its mind by now that it was summer and settled down. But there was an edge to the evening breeze, as there often is on the west coast of France, and although some diners were braving the terrace, waiting for the jazz pianist and his ensemble to start, many were eating inside. Martha and Erin were at a table near the unlit fire, with a view across the village square through open glass doors. They could see the jazz group setting up their instruments outside, coming in to collect drinks, taking them back outside while they arranged their stage.

'It'll be ages before they begin,' Erin told her. 'Everything takes its time here.'

Martha had said enough for now. She realised Erin was probably hungry, and asked her what she recommended they should eat.

'It's all good, but try the salade Landaise first. It's got Bayonne ham and gésiers in it, and of course bidaou, their local mushrooms, and it's always fresh. It's so filling you might not need anything else.'

Erin paused while they gave their order. Then Martha asked, 'And the Patronne, I've forgotten her name.'

'Madeleine. I gather her father used to have a café in Bordeaux,' Erin said, 'before they moved out here to the coast. Madeleine inherited it and made it the success it is today, and she's been a good friend to me when I've needed one.'

'Do you think that's Madeleine's father in his café in Bordeaux?' Martha asked, indicating a framed photograph which seemed to have pride of place on the wall opposite. An elderly man was smiling shyly at the camera from behind a bar. It talked to Martha of happier, simpler times, if there had ever been such a thing.

'I've often wondered if it is, though I've never asked,' Erin replied. 'Madeleine is such a public figure, everyone knows of her, and yet she's actually very private. No one knows a lot about her, not even her age. It's difficult to know if she'd welcome an enquiry about the photo. I'd have to choose the right moment when she'd had plenty to drink and was happy to reminisce.

'The one thing I know about Madeleine, apart from the fact she runs this place like a benevolent dictator, and you want her as your friend, not your enemy, is that she has a son on whom she dotes, though he doesn't repay her adoration. We've all got our weaknesses and blind spots... But enough of all that! I brought us her so you could talk if you want, Martha.'

'I know, thanks.'

Their food arrived at that moment, but remained untouched. Martha forced herself to pick up her knife and fork and said, 'It's okay, let's eat and enjoy first.'

Erin picked up her cutlery, but paused halfway to using them as Martha unexpectedly started again.

'I'll just say one more thing and then we can talk about something else, talk about you and your family. Thierry's death. It isn't just that the world changed, and I wasn't prepared for it. It's also made me question everything that went before, all the assumptions I had about our life. It isn't only the people who die that are destroyed—'

'Martha, I won't let you be destroyed.'

'I know that. That's why I sought you out. I thought of you and here as a bolt hole.... Erin, don't look round, but I think we're going to be interrupted again. Some people are heading this way.'

Erin instinctively swung round and smiled, maybe with relief.

'Bon soir, Sébastien.' She started to get up, but the chunky man, who looked to be in his thirties, gallantly pushed her down in her seat and leaned over to exchange bisous. Then another, slightly younger man with spikey hair followed and kissed her on both cheeks.

Erin turned to Martha.

'Do you remember Sébastien and his partner Benedict, Bené as we call him? Bené, what on earth have you done with your hair. You're not a teenager anymore.' She changed quickly from English to French and back again. 'Martha, you met them last summer. They came to the picnic party we had on the beach for you and Thierry.'

'Yes, I recall Thierry chatting to them.'

'They claim they don't speak any English, though I suspect Sébastien understands a bit. They'll give you a chance to practise your French.'

Erin reminded them Martha was a friend from university days, and had been married to a Frenchman, living in London.

'Whereas you settled here with your Frenchman.' Bené spoke French with clear diction and Martha was pleased she understood, even if she could not respond quickly. The brief days with Thierry's family had begun to re-familiarise her with the language.

Martha was worried they would ask her why her husband was not here, and although she needed to talk about Thierry to Erin, she was not ready to do so with virtual strangers. Erin must have been alert to her distress. She headed them off from any more personal questions by asking about the progress of their house. Martha thought she understood them to say it was exhausting work, which is why they had decided to take a break and come out to eat.

'And the scenery is good here too,' Bené said. Martha was sure his eyes were following a young waiter.

'Come round and see for yourselves how it's getting on,' Sébastien invited them before he steered Bené safely away to a table in the corner.

'What are they doing to their house?' Martha asked.

'Building it,' Erin replied.

They have a future, Martha thought.

Erin accepted her attempt to sleep was futile. She was wide awake in the early hours. The evening with Martha had disturbed her. She had anticipated it would, which was why she had taken her to Chez-Madeleine after helping her unpack, leaving Claude to get the children's meal. She had not wanted to hear about Thierry's death in this house, with her children around.

Martha had always been brutally honest with herself and still was. Erin had begun to experience some of Martha's shock second-hand which was probably why she could not sleep. She understood Martha was stuck, unable to move forward, unable to make sense of it, in limbo.

'Claude, are you awake?'

'Um, I wasn't, but I suppose I am now. Can't you relax, darling? You've been fidgeting all night.'

'Well I'm worried about Martha, obviously. Claude, can I tell her she can stay as long as she wants, as long as she needs?'

'Erin, ma chérie, you impetuous soul. I think I should wake up properly before I answer that, but I don't want to wake up any more than I've done already.'

He was drifting off again when she turned over, and the movement of the bed woke him fully.

'I think you should simply offer her a listening ear, a shoulder to cry on, although I don't think she's the crying sort. You must give her space and take it at her pace. For heaven's sake, don't make decisions for her. She'll make her own when she's ready.'

'I'm sure you're right. I owe her, you know, I owe her a great deal, but I won't worry you with that now…'

'No, not now, I've got to sleep because I've got to go to work in a few hours, and I'm not as young as you are, as you often remind me. Come on, time to stop worrying and shut down.'

Claude put a protective, warming arm around her and Erin felt cosy and very fortunate to have Claude's protection. She liked the reassurance of his large body holding her. She loved cuddling together like this. She was glad Martha had come to her. It was her opportunity to pay her back, though she shouldn't have mentioned that to Claude. As he was half asleep, he probably wouldn't remember anyway.

Along the corridor Martha was also in that uneasy space between sleeping and waking. The wind had died down and it was warm, almost stuffy. She thought about opening the shutters a bit and letting in some air, but it would mean getting out of bed, and she was too comfortable. She contented and reassured herself by imagining Thierry lying by her side, and rehearsed what she would say to him when he woke.

She was conjuring up his face, alive, alert and smiling. The world would probably have called him nice looking rather than handsome, but to her he was the best-looking man in the world. His hair was still healthily thick and brown. His eyes were always smiling. They were his best feature. In her mind he had hardly aged since they first met as students, though there were creases round his eyes now, happy creases which she liked. She recalled him walking into the early summer breeze, as they climbed Box Hill just a few weeks ago. The wind had given countryside colour to his familiar features. They did not know this would be the last weekend of his life.

Her mind wandered onto Box Hill where they had been at different seasons over the years. She remembered walking up one cold January Sunday with Rajinder and Priya, boots crunching satisfyingly on snow, banging gloved hands together to keep warm, watching her friends' children sledging, shouting for joy, running back up the hill, pulling sledges, and then collapsing in a tired heap. It had been so good to get home, light a proper fire and thaw out, her hands numb and stinging until they came back to life.

They had been back in the spring together, hunting for the first bluebells and later the first wild orchids. Their last trip was at the beginning of summer, this summer, Thierry's last summer.

'It's like London's lungs,' he had shouted to her above the noise of the wind. 'I don't mind being cooped up in the office all week as long as we can come out here when we're free.' He bent and stroked the soft grass.

'It would do us good to get away this summer. What about France?' she asked.

'Do you really want to see my parents again? I suppose I could visit them and you could stop off with Erin, then I'll join you on the way back. She'd be happy to have you to stay for a while.' He took her hand in his. She felt loved.

'I'm sure she will. We should book soon. Let's sit down and plan it Monday evening.'

'Okay.'

But they did not book the trip on Monday. He said there was plenty of time, but he died on Thursday. He had spent all Wednesday evening in his study. She had supposed he was preparing for a business event the following day. With both work and home issues he often spent time methodically weighing up the pros and cons of taking action before committing himself. She now knew he had not gone to work that Thursday. It was one of the complications she had not told Erin.

She wanted to talk to Thierry and tell him she was with Erin now. Erin was looking after her. He would like that. She had told Erin all about it, but not about the police or the mystery of his being in Guildford Street. But then, if he was alive and she could actually talk to him, she would not have to say any of this. She would have known nothing about that day, as he intended, she realised. *Oh, Thierry, why were you there? What were you doing? Where are you now? Can you possibly not exist anymore? Those ashes I took and scattered on Box Hill, are they all that's left of you except for my memories? Why can't we go back to the beginning of June, so I can find a way to stop you leaving that fatal day?*

Martha finally slept, but awoke early, aware of the light streaming in round the edges of the shutters which did not close properly. Dear Erin did not attend to details in the house. It worked, but by default, whereas her own house in London worked with precision.

But then she knew it was not just the light that had woken her. She had not slept soundly since Thierry's death. Her GP had tried to get her to accept sleeping pills, but she had avoided them since the first night alone when he insisted she take a couple. They had made her groggy, not sleepy, but muddled and unable to fit things together properly in her mind. Confusion terrified her. She could cope with complex issues but not muddle. She had thrown the rest of the pills down the toilet. She would sleep better when it all made sense.

She dozed until she heard sounds of people making their way downstairs, and decided to get up when she judged the bathroom was empty. She performed her ablutions as best she could amidst the detritus of Erin's family. She considered it strange how intimate and revealing people's bathrooms are. Erin's children, Lucy and Ethan, were almost teenagers. Although it was only a year ago she and Thierry had been here, they had grown up a lot in the interval. Martha wondered how much Erin had told them. She guessed not a lot. She was sorry about the load of grief she had dumped on her friend last night, and did not want to involve the children as well.

I'm good with children on a professional level, she thought, *but not in my life. How ironic!*

She made herself presentable, went downstairs and stood in a corner of the kitchen, an outsider looking in, feeling awkward, not knowing what to do until Erin pulled her in and sat her down at the cluttered breakfast table and gave her a large mug of tea, the sort they used to drink all those years ago when they were students. The pot even had a Union Jack on it. Here in the Medoc! Reminders of home both disturbed and comforted her.

She was grateful to hold the hot mug, drink the first cup of the day which was always the best, and smile absently at no one in particular. Seemingly un-coordinated preparations for the day continued. She was not upset that Lucy and Ethan mostly ignored her. They would know enough to feel awkward, but not know enough to know how to respond. She was not part of their plans for the day. Eventually the room emptied and fell quiet. The bread smelled good. She helped herself to some still warm baguette, and poured herself a glass of orange juice which had been left open on the counter. Then Erin returned.

'Peace! Well for now at least. Oh, good, you've found some breakfast. The children are on holiday and have their own things to do. I don't work till this afternoon, so wondered if you'd like to take a walk on the beach. We can drive up the coast to where it's practically deserted,' Erin said while she made an ineffective attempt to clear up the aftermath of various breakfasts.

'It's not always like this,' she said, indicating not only the debris of this morning, but also what Martha assumed were the remains of Claude's meal with the children yesterday evening. 'Well, yes, it is I suppose,' she admitted, as if speaking to herself.

'I'd love a walk,' Martha said, so Erin cheerfully abandoned her attempt to clean-up and went to get ready.

'So would I.' Erin's voice was enthusiastic as she raced upstairs.

Left alone, Martha put any fresh food that was lying around in the fridge, loaded the dishwasher which was not dissimilar to hers at home, just less well looked-after, and swirled copious amounts of piping hot water round the sink. She found herself thinking about last summer when she and Thierry had cleaned the house the weekend Erin and Claude took the children to camp and they were left alone.

Stop it, she told herself, that was then, this is now, he's gone… wherever.

She went and fetched her trainers, and found Erin outside navigating her battered Renault onto the lane without crushing the bikes lying in front of the house.

Martha grabbed their handlebars and moved them out of the way, then hopped into the passenger seat.

'I haven't locked up.'

'Leave it, the kids will be in and out. I'm taking you to La Falaise, one of my special places. We can leave the car there and scramble down to the beach. It's a couple of miles, but the tide's out so we can walk to La Dune where there's a shack and have coffee.'

'Sounds perfect.'

'How are we going to get down?' Martha asked as she stood on the wind-swept edge looking over the reeds at the sand below. La Falaise was at the end of a dirt track, the farthest a vehicle could get. Behind them, inland from the beach, there were evergreen woods, planted, she was told, to hold the land and stop it falling into the sea. Around her were dells in the dunes where Erin said she sometimes came to read a book and have a bit of me-time, as she put it. Various grasses, in hues of yellow, grey, green and purple, grew in tufts isolated in the sand. It was a mystery how they established themselves or survived. On the other side was a promontory, then a sharp drop down to the beach.

'Follow me, I'll show you,' Erin shouted above the noise of the breeze and the waves, as she leapt onto a ledge below. Martha feared the drop looked too deep, but Erin held out a hand to help her down and she joined her on the ledge, which she now saw was a concrete path, broken in places, parallel to and under the cliff top.

'It's an old German road from the war,' Erin explained. 'I think it originally ran the length of the coast, but every winter the cliffs get buffeted, and every summer the extent of the erosion becomes apparent. I understand it was some way inland when it was built. Now it's literally on the edge. Shows you the pace of erosion.'

'Some of it's gone over the edge,' Martha observed, feeling giddy, hating the fact she was neither at the top nor the bottom.

'Yes, bits have fallen off. Each year I have to find a new way down. Look, here we can zigzag. It's less steep.' With that she set off and Martha had little option but to follow, stepping steeply down into the holes in the sand left by Erin's feet. It was less difficult than she had anticipated, and they ended up running down the last slope onto the beach as the only way to maintain their balance.

Martha looked up and wondered how they would get back. She had never been good with heights.

'Do you let the children play out here?' she asked, thinking of the obvious dangers.

'I'd have a hard job stopping them. They've grown up roaming the beach and the dunes. They know about tides and currents. The people who get into difficulties are holidaymakers who go out swimming or surfing without understanding the place. Some people think they can defy nature. They underestimate how treacherous the undercurrents can be. People should only swim out to sea in designated areas where there's surveillance, but they don't and we have drownings every year.'

Martha was thinking about the thunderous power of the water. Walking along the shoreline she was stunned by how vast it was, with nothing between them and America except the ocean. The salty breeze beat against her cheeks, cold and fresh, exhilarated her. The sand stretched for miles both north and south.

'Did you want children? Do you have regrets?' Erin shouted above the noise. The question caught her unawares. It was as if Erin had taken her role, being the straight talker.

'Well, it's too late, isn't it,' she managed to say, catching her breath.

'That's not what I asked.' Erin pursued her point. 'I knew you were never keen, but did Thierry want a family? Did he say?'

'I don't know,' she said, thinking it was absurd to admit it. They had not married for that. Thierry had rescued her… from being too serious she supposed, and from her strict humourless parents she did not want to think about at the moment. She and Thierry had both been

31

keen to establish themselves in their careers. They developed a good life. The right time for children had not presented itself, and she had not sought it out. That was probably unusual, especially as her job had centred on children, placing children for fostering and adoption, taking children into care and places of safety, rebuilding bridges with disconnected families. She had always kept that separate. She and Thierry had attempted conversations about whether or when to start their own family, but they had been inconclusive, probably because of her ambivalence. She had an inkling he had wanted children more than he admitted, certainly more than she had. He would never have bullied her into it. In later years they had rarely talked about it, and unconsciously gravitated to making friends with couples who for various reasons had no children.

It all passed through her mind in a flash and for whatever reason she fought shy of sharing it all with her friend. Erin had fallen into her maternal role late, and unexpectedly, with Claude who was almost old enough to be her father. Erin, who had not had an easy time before, seemed happy with her life now.

'Thierry? I think maybe he did,' she said at last, 'but it just didn't happen.'

When they were halfway between La Falaise and La Dune she said what was really on her mind. She hesitated because she had told no one, and wanted to deny it, even to herself. She thought if she never spoke about it, but kept it a secret, it would go away. Instead it was growing bigger, taking over. Her head was a pressure cooker needing to let out steam.

'He shouldn't have been there that day,' she announced.

'What? Sorry, who?' Erin asked.

'Thierry, of course. I don't know why he was in Guildford Street. It's near Russell Square. Everybody thought he was at work. He worked in London. It's a reasonable assumption. You know his office was off The Strand. But he wasn't at work that day. I thought he was. He went off as usual for the train, dressed in one of his smart accountancy suits, as if he was going to the office, but he didn't go in. He'd taken a day off to meet someone.'

They had stopped by the water's edge. Erin stared at Martha open-mouthed.

'Who?' She was trying to take it in.

Martha was playing with the sand, futilely smoothing it with her left foot.

'I don't know.' She sounded wretched. She squatted down and picked up a pile of sand and let it trickle through her fingers. She was thinking of the myriad possibilities. It could have been someone connected to his work, wanting to trade information. It could have been someone from a rival firm, but this implied Thierry was capable of double-crossing Benton's, which was unthinkable. Perhaps it was a government representative who didn't want to meet him at his office. But why? Or it could have been another woman, and this went to the heart of her anxieties. She could see no good options.

'Are you sure he was meeting someone? How did you find out?' she asked, and Martha wondered if Erin thought she had become unhinged. She decided to tell her how it had emerged accidentally during Rajinder's visit.

It was the day after Thierry died. She was grateful to Rajinder for coming to see her at home in Chislehurst. Many people had offered sympathy by phone, email and tasteful cards, from a safe distance. Just as Martin, her director, had arranged for a colleague to take her home and stay the evening, so Thierry's CEO, Hugo, had written, but sent Rajinder to deliver his letter. Hugo's letter said that the head of HR would personally visit her at home, she assumed to sort out finances and the pension or death in service award. She was surprised Hugo had actually handwritten the letter, which she admitted was a nice personal touch. She imagined him sending a minion out to a stationer on The Strand to buy ink and fill one of the several expensive unused pens which adorned his imposing desk. Normally he used a ball-point to sign letters typed for him on a computer. In this instance he had despatched Rajinder with his missive.

Hugo knew Rajinder was Thierry's protégé, his favourite, one of the new generation of accountants he had mentored, and whose career he had fostered. Thierry always trusted Rajinder in contrast to some of the others whom he considered capable of sticking a knife in his back in order to climb the corporate ladder. Such professional treachery was not unknown at Benton & Powell, auditors to international business and government departments.

Thierry and Martha had been invited to Rajinder's arranged wedding in the Punjab, but had sadly not been able to attend because Thierry could not find the time to get away. They had, though, been honoured guests at long ceremonies in the temple in London when Rajinder's children had been named and introduced to their faith. The genders were segregated. She had sat with the women, which went against the grain, but she had accepted it out of respect for Rajinder and Priya. She saw Thierry looking uncomfortable on the far side of the room, his head covered with a piece of borrowed cloth, no doubt in agony because he had to sit cross-legged for so long, and be careful which way to point his feet.

Rajinder had phoned the evening Thierry was killed.

'I wanted to be sure you're all right,' he said and it was only later Martha understood he thought she had been with Thierry that day. They talked at cross purposes, and he asked if he could come to see her.

'Are you up to visitors?'

'Yes, Rajinder, but the others are staying away. They send notes and flowers. Anyway, you aren't a visitor, you're family. Can you come down in the morning? I've been banned from going into work for the time being.'

'Yes, Hugo has allowed me time off to come to see you.'

'He'll assume you're acting on his behalf.'

'He assumes everybody does everything on his behalf, as long as it's successful. But I'm not coming for him. I'll let the powers that be sort out things for the firm. He's written you a letter, and I volunteered to deliver it in person, but I'm coming as your friend.'

'Thierry would have been pleased. He was very fond of you.'

She spent that first night on her own, understanding and frightened she would be alone for evermore. She was staring into the abys. Thierry had no close family within calling distance. They still lived in France, in the village where he had been born. Martha was an only child, her father was dead and her elderly mother, now dependent on her, was in a nursing home in Bournemouth. Martha had been adamant with the doctor she would be fine on her own. If she did not face it now she would never be able to do so. She was awake and disturbed most of the night despite, or because of, the sleeping pill. She was up much too early, and was glad when the doorbell rang just after ten, because it was Rajinder as she anticipated.

She opened the front door to find him standing there looking young, handsome and apprehensive, with a lovely bunch of flowers, well chosen, and definitely not the sort that can be picked up on a garage forecourt. The sun was behind him because it was morning and the big house faced east, and he was beautifully dark in the shadow it cast. She looked at the curved drive edged with laburnum trees which gave it privacy from the road, and had a stab of pain knowing how much Thierry loved it and would not see it or walk down it again. The sun shone directly into her face, which she knew must reveal the strain she was under. She was facing the day without make-up. Today it did not matter, and she wondered if it would ever matter again.

Because he had visited so often, he automatically followed her into the kitchen and made their coffee while she arranged the flowers in a vase. They went through to the sitting room. He asked if she was okay, and she responded that she was, but then confessed how she actually felt, which was numb. She could be honest with Rajinder.

'I was so worried. We got a call from the Met Police because they found the Benton & Powell ID in his case. I was surprised he had his briefcase with him. When I asked about you they said he was on his own.'

She turned to face him. 'Why did you think I would be with him? I was at work, at a meeting in Bromley as it happens.'

A look of confusion passed across his face. In the silence that ensued Martha saw he was embarrassed.

'What is it, Rajinder? You've got to tell me.'

'I must have made a silly mistake, jumped to conclusions, that's all. Forget it.'

He turned away to look at the flowers which Martha had put on a side table.

'I had to bring you something. Priya chose these. I can't claim to be so artistic.'

'Rajinder, don't change the subject, you're not very good at covering up. What is it? I don't think it was a silly mistake, and I don't think you think it was either. I need to know.' She was older than him, and found herself bossing him as usual.

He squirmed on the settee.

'I shouldn't have said anything. I'd just assumed. I'm sorry.'

'Assumed what? Please tell me.'

'Oh, dear. Thierry said it was a special day, an important day. He was excited about it. I tried to question him, but he teased me, and said it was his secret. No one knew.'

'He was meeting someone?'

'I don't know. I wondered if it was your wedding anniversary, or if he was taking you somewhere special. He'd never booked a single day's leave before, oh, except that time you won the Wimbledon tickets in the draw. It was hard enough suggesting he needed to take proper summer holidays as he did last year. He was convinced there would be crisis if he wasn't around.'

'So he took a day's leave and told you it was special,' Martha interrupted. 'That's why you thought I would be with him. That's why you were surprised he was carrying his briefcase.'

Rajinder looked at his shoes.

'It started as a normal day. He didn't tell me what he would be doing, now I come to think of it, but then he didn't usually say whether he would be in the office or out visiting clients. He was in a good mood when he left home'

There was silence.

'Maybe he was planning to surprise you with a special holiday, and had taken time out to arrange it...' Rajinder's voice tailed off. He knew it sounded weak.

'Rajinder, do you think he was having an affair?' She always came straight to the point.

He looked shocked. 'No, I'm sure he wasn't.'

'Would you have known? Would he have confided in you?'

'I don't know. No, I suppose not. We were close, I think, I hope, in a way, but we didn't discuss very personal things, not that much, not in the office. Sport? Yes. politics? Perhaps. Relationships? Well, I probably unburdened myself more than he did. My jitters over the wedding and worries about the children. We sometimes went for a drink after work. We'd go down to a bar on the Embankment and enjoy watching the world go by before we got our respective trains home. I assumed he was happy. I never heard him say a word against you.'

Martha imagined Thierry would not have said much about her at all. People assumed they were the perfect couple, and they offered no contradiction. But were they? Or more correctly, had they been? They jogged along without tempestuous upsets or public arguments. Had they been soulmates, best friends, or had they simply fallen into a pattern over the years of taking their marriage for-granted?

'Rajinder, who knows he had a day's leave?'

'Um, I did, obviously, and HR will do. I think that's all.'

'HR will do?'

'When they get his leave request. B&P is old fashioned in some ways. Leave requests aren't emailed, they're written out on a card. You have to get the agreement of your pair, although of course he was too senior to be paired. I assume he wrote a card. It's probably still in his desk tray. I was going to ask your permission to go through his personal things at the office, and bring those you might want on my next visit; photographs and such like, and ditch the rest. Hugo will be relieved if I offer to do that. I can also brief him on Thierry's projects and reports. It won't be difficult. He was so up to date and meticulously organised. Oh, dear, I'm sounding so matter of fact, and I'm certainly not trying to jump into his shoes. Oh, I'm sorry.'

'It has to be done. Rajinder, I would be eternally grateful if you could go through his things and sort them out. I'd prefer you looking through them than anyone else, and I'm sure he would have too. But Rajinder, do you have to hand in the leave request, or can you just lose it?'

'Lose it. What do you mean?'

'Does it matter now? Did Hugo know he was on leave yesterday?'

'Probably not. Thierry didn't have to explain his movements. Apart from Hugo we're all electronically self-supporting, so although there's a PA for the executives as a group, I doubt if he'd have told her. I think his decision to have the day off was taken spontaneously. You could say impetuously, earlier that week in fact. I'm probably the only one who knew.'

'It might be better if people don't know. It only complicates matters. Also, I don't want questions, and I want to protect his reputation. Would it be wrong to simply tear up the leave request?'

'I don't suppose so. As you say, it's immaterial really.'

By the time Martha had told Erin about Rajinder's visit, they had arrived at La Dune, a camp site up the coast. Holiday makers were queuing up at the patisserie to buy baguettes and croissants for their breakfast. Erin guided her to her favourite shack where they sat at an empty rickety table, semi-shaded by a frail umbrella which had lost its red colour. It was a pale pink and seemed as if it might take off at any moment in a gust of wind.

They ordered a second breakfast, as neither had eaten much of their first one. Erin had coffee, which came quickly and was hot and strong. Martha ordered hot chocolate which was a mistake because it came tepid and sweet. They asked for juice, croissants, honey, fruit and yogurt to follow. The walk had stimulated their appetites. They talked while they waited for it.

'You're sure Rajinder thought you would know about Thierry's leave? I gather he's a good friend, but he wasn't trying to drop Thierry in it, was he?'

'Drop him in it?'

'Sort of double bluff, if you know what I mean. Sounds nice, but could it be a cover?'

'Oh, no, no! If you knew Rajinder, you wouldn't suspect him of anything like that. I've thought of it from every angle and I'm positive he was relieved when he found out I wasn't hurt. He had thought I was with Thierry, and might have been hurt too. I'm convinced he had no idea Thierry had kept his leave day a secret from me.'

'Thierry's diary? Was it in his briefcase?'

'Yes, he had an electronic one. Contacts, appointments, all of it, and that was in his case and it survived. His smart phone was in his jacket pocket and that got smashed when he was hit. Oh, sorry,' she said as she saw Erin wince. 'The police gave me back his diary after they'd been through it. I haven't told you that bit yet, have I? There was nothing in it to suggest what he was doing that day.'

'Martha, what do you mean, you haven't told me the bit about the police yet? I assume they were involved because it was a hit and run.'

'More accurately it's an open case. We all assumed at first it was an accident. Thierry for some reason stepped off the pavement into the path of the van. There was the fact the van was going far too fast, according to eye witnesses, and didn't stop. That can be explained by it being very noisy with traffic and it wasn't the impact with the van which killed him. He was apparently thrown and hit his head on the kerb. The driver may not have realised what had happened. Or it could have been an assassination.'

'What! Oh, Martha!'

'The Met contacted Benton and Powell first and then me through the local police. I had a visit from the Met the following day, not long after Rajinder had left. The two detectives were very sensitive, very trained, you could say, but I sensed something wasn't right. His diary was empty for the day he died. Well, there was just the initial "J" in it, which meant nothing to me. There are several Js in the office. The atmosphere changed when they asked, ever so carefully, if they could look in his study. I challenged them straight away as to what they were looking for. "Wasn't it an accident?" I asked. Very calmly the nicer one of the two officers said they had to eliminate that it wasn't anything more serious.'

'Anything more serious!'

'I was asked if he had any enemies, inside or outside the company. At first I thought that was crazy, but then wondered if he could have been targeted for knowing too much about the confidential financial affairs of any of the multi-nationals Bentons deals with. All sorts of conflicts of interest are possible. He'd been a witness at serious fraud trials, but never told me anything. He said it was best for me not to know. I simply told the police he didn't involve me in his business life. I began to fear what his real job might have been.

'I'd already quickly sifted through his papers in the study at home. I did it straight after Rajinder's visit. I'd had to steel myself to do it. But I was looking for *her*! I had to see if there were any clues, but I could find nothing. I was both relieved and frustrated.

'So, I stood there powerless while the two plain clothes police officers rifled through his desk. It had seemed a betrayal of trust when I had done it. But this was far worse. It was vandalism. They weren't careful and I was desperate to take things out of their hands and say, "This was personal, it goes over here." But of course I couldn't interfere. They said oh so politely I didn't need to stay and watch, but I begged to differ. They turned everything over. I was trying to discern what was in their minds. They weren't telling me. The possibility of mistaken identity was one of the muffled phrases I wasn't supposed to overhear. There were coded asides to information and secrecy. I assumed it all had to be considered because of B and P's powerful position and the sensitivity of Thierry's work. Otherwise why this attention to something which was probably an accident? It was frightening.

'There was a change of tactics when we returned to the sitting room. The nicer one was apologetic. The bullish one sat there looking uncomfortable. I guess his colleague must have told him, "Leave this to me." I concluded they were frustrated because they mustn't have found anything incriminating or interesting in the study, but they were still fishing. There were questions about his state of mind. Was he depressed? "No," I said, "and it wasn't suicide!" How could I be sure? I realised I had no choice but to tell them about his day's leave from the office. I didn't say Rajinder had told me and I had asked him to destroy the leave card. I simply said he had private plans for the day. They took that better than I expected, but were definitely interested. I caught the look between them. Was I aware of any unusual contacts he had made? Had anyone visited the house? Had Thierry's behaviour been different recently? I told them I knew nothing. I'm sure they marked me down as difficult and defensive. Maybe they were used to questioning women who were compliant, and I didn't intend to be unless it helped solve my mystery. It seemed they were scratching around without a definite theory, but then again that may just be the way they work, a scattergun approach so people can't guess what they're really interested in.'

'God, what a nightmare.' Erin looked appalled.

'I had to get in touch with Rajinder as soon as they left. I had to stop him tearing up the card. I could see how it could lead him into all sorts of trouble. If there was a formal inquest or such like, I could be responsible for him perjuring himself, or creating more suspicion. I couldn't reach him at the office. They said he was out. His mobile was on voicemail and I didn't want to commit myself to a message. The police had already revealed they were going through Thierry's calls.

'It's amazing how quickly you become paranoid! Yes, a death has to be investigated, but there seemed to be a special interest in Thierry's. In the hours I waited, I racked my brains for every possible explanation of Thierry being secretive about his whereabouts that day. Corporate espionage. Was he a suspect in some way? Had he been disloyal to Bentons... or to the government. I made myself consider it dispassionately, and I couldn't believe any of it. But how many wives have been deceived? Did the police think I was involved? I could be a suspect.'

'Martha!'

'Erin, I'm not being hysterical. There are things I don't understand here, and I began to see my initial suspicion that Thierry was embarking on an affair as suddenly the least bizarre, the least dangerous explanation of his behaviour. It would have been a threat to me and my belief in our marriage, but adultery isn't something the police are interested in. For them there had to be the suspicion of a crime.'

Erin ordered more coffee and Martha decided to have some this time. Erin encouraged Martha to get it all off her chest.

'Thankfully, Rajinder turned up after lunch with Thierry's things from the office. He said he always turned his mobile off while driving. I was so relieved.'

'And there was nothing revealing in the papers Rajinder brought from Benson and Powell?'

'Benton and Powell. No. Rajinder brought all his personal effects. He'd had to show them to the police and get them cleared first. He wasn't going to tell me that bit, but I got it out of him. The thought of anonymous people suspiciously fingering Thierry's personal things, sullying them, ugh! But Rajinder got them safely to me. Thierry had a picture of me in a plain solid silver frame on his desk. Apparently he changed it every year or two for a new one, and labelled the old ones and put them in a scrap book. So Rajinder brought that for me. I was really touched. My life in pictures, over my, what? Eighteen-odd years with Thierry. Student balls, graduation, our wedding, me in the garden, holidays, anniversaries and my MBA ceremony. That's when I moved up into higher management and he was so proud. I looked through them and wondered where all those years had gone. The police weren't interested in our personal life together. It was my story.

'There was a leather desk diary too, but he seemed to fill it in with cryptic notes and codes. It also had the letter "J" in the top corner of the day in question, and some incomprehensible doodling, as if he had been talking to someone, perhaps on the phone, and drawing subconsciously, but that maybe my imagination. It looked like an archway or doorway. There were other initials on other dates, and it was difficult to know what any of them meant.'

'J. He wasn't going for another job?'

'No, I can't imagine that. He was so loyal. Bloody Benton and P was his life, more than I was, I sometimes thought. I'm sure he would have discussed that with me if he'd deigned to look outside their hallowed portals.'

'You sound hostile to the firm.'

'I suppose I am. You see, his firm and my department — they took over our lives, Erin. We considered them so important. We believed we grew and developed through our work, but perhaps it actually took us away from ourselves, and from each other as well. We should have looked up, at the blue sky above the treetops.

'What?'

'Just being poetic. I'm angry. I'm irrational, but his death remains a mystery. I can't make sense of it.'

'So, dead end. Oh, sorry, I mean, no clues?'

'That's how it appears. I've nothing else to go on. The coroner gave an interim death certificate, and I gather from that and the police investigation it's still an open case. I can't believe it was suicide. Mistaken identity; how would I know? I hope they're barking up the wrong tree if they think he was targeted because he knew too much about something, and was going to sell or reveal it. I can't believe he was a traitor in any way. I think it was most probably an accident, but it was out of character for Thierry to be so careless... unless, of course, he was so excited about who he was meeting that he became careless. I've only just thought of that. For me it comes down to what was he doing taking a day's leave and walking up Guildford Street, going who knows where, when he let me think, by default I suppose, he was spending a normal day at the office? I can't get the thought out of my head that he was meeting someone significant, someone I don't know, and someone he didn't want me to know. The police aren't investigating my mystery, though it's always possible they'll find out who he was going to meet, and that might help me, in a funny sort of way.'

'Or not, as the case may be. Martha, how much do you really want to know?'

'I need to know everything, good or bad. Otherwise the meaning of our lives is all up in the air. Yes, of course I'd like to have it confirmed he was true to me, and there was an explanation for his behaviour that day. And if he wasn't true to me, or to Bentons, then I'd rather know. I'd find a way of coming to terms with it. But this not knowing, it drives me crazy, and I can't settle.

'When I'm not feeling depressed, I'm angry with him. There was the clandestine day's leave he didn't tell me about. That's evidence of... I don't know what it's evidence of. Dishonesty? It seems I didn't know him as well as I thought. Apparently, he only told Rajinder, and maybe didn't mean to do that. Was he boasting? The damned frustration is that I can't challenge him, can't ask him...'

'And he can't defend himself either. Martha you may be putting a negative interpretation on this which is unjustified. And you'll always live doubting him, instead of trusting him. You did trust him, didn't you?'

'I thought I did. I took our life together for granted. Now it's been thrown into turmoil discovering this secret. It's the secret I can't come to terms with.'

'It's too early I know, and maybe what I'm going to suggest is crass, but how about concentrating on the good times. He was a lovely man. I can confirm that. You must have special memories? They're also true too, aren't they? They can't be taken away. I'm no social worker like you, Martha, but I think this uncertainty, this desperation to discover Thierry's lover, will be like a cancer in your soul if you let it grow.'

'So what do you suggest I do?'

'Difficult. If it were me, I'd probably stash it on one side, in the part of my brain containing all the mysteries I can't solve. I'd forget about it unless or until some more evidence turns up.'

'But I'm not you, and I can't do that. I always tackle things, and I don't know how to tackle this. There's no logical way. I feel I'm up against a brick wall, and I want to see what's on the other side, whatever it is. Erin, I'm paralysed by uncertainty.'

'And uncertainty is what you can't cope with. That's why I think you have to concentrate on those things you can be certain of, and let time do its job. Fine, if you get inspiration and think of someone who may know something, question them. By all means follow any leads that turn up, but in the meanwhile I'll help you with a bit of diversion therapy.'

'Diversion therapy. What do you mean?'

'You're good at lots of things, Martha, but not at relaxing. You can't just be. You'll have to entertain yourself this afternoon while I'm at work, so try and relax. Tomorrow, I'll take you to see the house Sébastien is building. It's no ordinary house.'

'In what way?'
'Wait and see!'

They began walking from the shack down the sandy incline to the beach. Erin saw Martha was going round and round in circles with the puzzle of Thierry's last day, and just listening was no longer helping. She decided to challenge her.

'Okay, so part of you is angry with him. That's understandable, but it's also unfair, Martha. He didn't deserve to die; he didn't bring his death on himself. Maybe he was just in the wrong place at the wrong time. He was a victim, and therefore so are you.'

'You're right. I have been blaming him for being there that day. I'm supposed to be the one with insight, but you're doing better than me.'

'It's because you're locked in the situation, and I'm outside looking in. Insight's the last thing I'd lay claim to. I live more by my emotions and common sense than you do, Martha. I'm not cerebral, but I do have a certain amount of intuition. And I know you. And I knew Thierry, and liked him a lot, which is why I don't think the worst of him. Apart from that, I don't know what to say.'

'There's nothing to say, it's just such a relief to talk.'

'As long as talk leads to something positive. You remember when I unburdened myself on you, all those years ago. I'd not told a soul until then. I felt dirty and thought it was my fault. You knew something was wrong and encouraged me to talk, and the weight of the world lifted, and though it took time, I can date the start of my recovery from the way you responded and made it possible for me to face up to it. I just feel frustrated I can't help you in the same way.'

Erin skimmed a stone across the water and watched it sink. They had reached the shoreline.

'By the way, what happened to Thierry's leave card? Did Rajinder destroy it?'

'No, thank God. He hadn't found it when he came down with Thierry's things. Maybe Thierry had been so excited by his deception he forgot to write it, or hoped his absence wouldn't be noted. I told Rajinder all about the police visit, and we agreed we couldn't try to protect Thierry's reputation by covering up. I said when the police interviewed him, he'd better tell them all he knew. At least they'd know Thierry wasn't on official B and P business, unless that's another of what you called double-bluffs. If the card ever turns up Rajinder should hand it in.

'Thanks for listening, Erin. I'll try and calm down now. I won't keep inflicting my concerns on you... Erin, what's up, what is it? You look worried.'

'Holy shit. Martha, we have a problem. I read the tide tables which Claude uses, and worked out this morning was the perfect time to walk the beach from La Falaise. I didn't calculate the time for the return journey.'

'The tide's coming in,' Martha said, stating the obvious.

'It's coming in fast. We can't get back safely the way we came. We'd be at risk of being cut off, and it's really dangerous to walk along the cliffs. Damn. If I call Claude he'll get really angry. He'd say it's the sort of thing I'm always warning the children against doing, and he'd be right.'

'So what are we going to do?'

'Hell, let's think.'

'There must be another route inland, surely.'

'Yes, but it's far too long for us to walk. I know! I'll try Bené. He works for an immobilier, that's an estate agent, and he's often out and about. He won't tell me off for being irresponsible, 'cause he's nicely irresponsible himself.'

They had to clamber back up to the shack again because Erin's mobile could not pick up a signal down on the beach. She got through to Bené who was in his office. He agreed to take an early lunch break and drive out to pick them up. They sat back down and ordered more coffee whilst they waited for him, though Martha felt she had had more than enough and left hers to go cold. Erin was correct about Bené's reaction. He saw the funny side of them getting stranded and was laughing when his car roared in, creating clouds of dust, thirty minutes later. He drove them back to La Dune to collect the old Renault.

'Don't you dare tell Claude about this!' Erin warned him.

'Oh, la, la! Secrets. I love them. What are they worth, my dear?'

'I hadn't visualised anything like this.'

Martha was gazing in amazement at the avant-garde building, with all its pipes and tubes on display in primary colours.

'I bet you thought they'd be constructing a house altogether more twee.' Erin poked fun at her. Her aim was to take Martha out of herself to help her relax.

It was the following afternoon, and she had taken her via a short cut to Sébastien and Bené's. They walked across a sunny field of neat new vines, with bunches of grapes hanging underneath like cows' udders. To avoid walking where they shouldn't, they kept to the dusty path, so their trainers had become powdery brown by the time they entered a plantation of young pines on the far side.

In a clearing, Martha caught her first sight of the eco-house. It was in the middle of nowhere, and Erin explained it had been a piece of unused land belonging to Sébastien's family. It could only be reached by farm tracks, and there was no electricity or water out here. The first view was of scaffolding surrounding a timber frame with the wires and pipes in red, blue, yellow and green woven in and out of sections. It was set back from the track. Erin led the way down the side of the house, and although it was still under construction, its scale was impressive. An idea of the finished product could be glimpsed on the parts where the wood cladding had been fixed and the workings hidden.

'Come round the front, or maybe it's the back. I don't know, but it's the main elevation. That's where you get the best view.'

They walked down and saw the house from the side furthest from the track where it rose above a small lake.

'Wow, this is really something. I didn't know what to expect, but it wasn't modern like this.'

They stood side by side regarding the elevation of glass two storeys high, capped off by a flat roof.

'I presume those tubes will be boxed in. It's not going to look like the Pompidou Centre, is it, like an oil refinery with all the workings on show?'

'You'd better ask Sébastien. Each time I see it, it's different, and it's evolving. Let's go and find him.'

They picked their way across the ground, treading carefully over loops of wiring as well as the earthworks of what might become the drainage system. As they retraced their steps and approached the hole in the side wall where a door might eventually hang, a young white man with fair hair in dreadlocks came out carrying tools and smiled at them.

'Sébastien's on the roof,' he told them.

'Thanks, Joël.'

'We mustn't stop him if he's busy,' Martha said.

'He's expecting us. Bené said it would be all right. He loves having an excuse to show off his project. It's his passion.'

Erin called out and Sébastien's disembodied voice said come on up. Martha walked into the space inside and wondered where he was and how they would get up to him. Joël re-appeared, his work boots scraping on the concrete floor, casually carrying a rustic ladder which he propped against the edge of what looked like an open balcony covering about half the central room. Erin was up like a shot. Martha hesitated, until Joël took her hand and led her to the ladder, putting his boot on the bottom rung to steady it while she climbed. She had no option. She was conscious of the proximity of his denim leg as she squeezed past, going up, terrified and determined no one would know how afraid she was. She felt better when she was standing on the balcony, well away from the edge, admiring the view down to the lake through the plate glass windows. She was worried about getting back onto the ladder to climb down. There was a thump which almost unbalanced her, and the floor shook, as Sébastien jumped down through a hole in the roof. He wore dusty overalls, big boots and a ridiculously bright yellow hard hat. He looked pleased with himself.

'Martha's very impressed. I think she imagined you'd be putting the finishing touches to a conventional house to be decorated in chintz and swags and tassels.

'What are these things, chintz and swags?'

'Never mind. I was only joking. They're English and I don't think even Bené would dare to introduce them here. What's the balcony for?'

'It's not a balcony. It will be a mezzanine floor. There will be a living room underneath, and another one up here, and they'll both open out into the full length two storey room with the big windows.'

He described how the house would function when it was finished. There would be no fire, because, with the sealed triple glazed windows, the solar panels and the wood construction, it would generate its own heat in winter and cool itself in summer. Water would be pumped up from the well they had bored, and wastewater would run off to irrigate the food beds outside. They would have a generator and use renewables. Martha got the general idea, but her vocabulary fell short on technicalities. There was a discussion about sewerage and Martha got completely lost. Erin interpreted that the loos would be organic which they both considered a step too far. In relation to the well water, although Sébastien had arranged tests, and it was purer than tap water, it was against the law to drink it, so they should buy bottles for that. Whether they would or not was another matter.

'And you've built it all!' Martha said.

'Mostly. Three volunteers, Joël and his girlfriend and Hugh, are helping. They move around, specialise in these sorts of projects. They're camping in the field, not far from our caravan.'

A car drew up outside.

'That'll be Bené. He helps when he's not at work. If he's got clients to see in the evenings, he sometimes manages to get an hour off in the afternoon.'

Sébastien helped her onto the ladder, and though she was hesitant going down backwards, she thought she could get the hang of it. She was hoping Joël would be there at the bottom to help her off, but he was at the far side of the room sorting coloured wires in a giant fuse box.

Martha saw Erin shoot Bené a quick warning glance as he got out of his car, presumably about the incident at La Dune, but he seemed to ignore it mischievously, smiling as usual. Martha said how impressed she was with their house.

'If you want to come down to earth and see how we really live,' Bené said, 'come over to the caravan and I'll fix some coffee.'

The caravan was in the long grass. It was small and old, but functional. They had rigged it up as best they could to manage until they moved into the house, hopefully before another winter.

'One winter out here was enough,' said Bené with one of his funny facial gestures. Whether he was describing something happy or sad, someone he liked or not, whether a surface was clean or dirty, his facial muscles were expressive enough to communicate without words. Even with her limited French, Martha understood him.

'It's quite cramped,' she said looking round at their living space and searching her limited vocabulary. 'It'll be great when you move into the house. I do admire the two of you.'

'Thanks. It's a partnership. Doudou is doing most of the hard work, and I act as his labourer when I'm here

'Who?'

'Doudou. That's what I call Sébastien.

'It doesn't translate well!'

'No? Well, believe it or not, it's an endearment in French. You don't have to use it, my dear. Anyway, I get to dress up in nice clothes and take clients to search for their dream house, knowing none will find one as wonderful as ours. My wages keep us solvent, and able to go out for nights at Chez-Madeleine.'

Despite her presence he started to strip off his business clothes, so she retreated outside where there was an old plastic table and chairs under the caravan awning. Bené emerged in dungarees liberally splashed with paint.

'You see I'm an artist,' he joked, and set about moving the table onto the grass so they could sit in the sun.

'Coffee?'

Martha asked for tea, and wished she had not, as she was given a herbal infusion which smelled of dry grass and tasted of hot water.

'You don't like it, do you?'

'It's different.' She saw him laughing. 'No, I don't like it!' she admitted. 'I'm not a great coffee drinker, but I'm sorry to say you French can't make tea.'

It had made her so happy when Erin had told her conspiratorially, earlier in the day back at her house, 'I have PG Tips.' It was like university days when someone said they had a joint to share.

'We do everything else better, so perhaps I'll allow you the tea superiority,' Bené said. He took her cup and threw the contents on the grass.

'It gives us the perfect excuse to open some of this,' he said, getting out an unlabelled bottle, searching for some clean glasses and blowing on them. 'Ah, you arrive just in time,' he said to Erin who had been with Sébastien.

'Eau de vie. Sébastien's family has a licence, though it will die out with his father.'

'It's very good, but it's strong, Martha. No, I won't have any this time, thanks, Bené,' Erin said.

He poured the colourless liquid into two good sized glasses, one for Martha and one for himself, and said, 'Santé.'

'Santé,' Martha said dubiously, and felt her head explode as she swallowed the first mouthful. Then she started to experience warmth flowing down and reaching the pit of her stomach. It left a subtle fruity taste in her mouth, and she decided it was very nice indeed.

'Yes, I've drunk it before, and know how potent it is, so take it slowly Martha,' Erin laughed. 'You're helping Claude get the meal later, as I've got to go back to work for a couple of hours.'

Martha found it easy to get Bené talking about himself and Sébastien, and understood most of it. He said he came from northern France. Sébastien was from this area, Les Landes. They had met in Bordeaux ten years ago, and although they had lived and worked at various jobs in various parts of the country, they had gravitated back here because they liked Saint-Cyprien and the beaches of this coastline. Martha gained the impression, though it was not articulated, that Sébastien's family accepted them more easily than Bené's, and so did a wide circle of friends and acquaintances. The Chez-Madeleine crowd were very relaxed, and their social life revolved around it. Their plan was to move into the eco house before the winter, and consider setting up a small business venture. They seemed to have it planned out.

'Can you get married in France?' she asked.

'Yes, now we can, but I'm still waiting for him to propose. We've had something called Le PACS for some time, but it was not as good as marriage. It was one thing the government managed to get right.'

Bené clearly enjoyed female company and Martha realised he was the kind of man with whom she could be good friends. It was not easy to have male friends. Even with Rajinder she was aware of certain constraints. She could be at ease with Bené. He was fun as well, not at all wary of her or intimidated as some people appeared to be. She responded to it by loosening up and feeling mischievous. She noticed Erin watching her carefully.

'I'd better go,' Erin said. 'If you walk back with me, I'll show you where everything is for tonight's meal, if I can remember. Otherwise, you'll be improvising.'

'Well, cooking a family meal is not one of my skills, but I'll try.'

They sauntered home enjoying a perfect early evening country walk, though Martha found the ground less level and the paths less easy to follow than on the outward journey. Bené would have happily detained her longer. When she had gone he reluctantly went in search of

Sébastien to see what work he could do on the house for a couple of hours.

'Why does Erin say "she owes you"?' Claude asked Martha as they set the table. The children were upstairs, saying they were getting ready, but probably watching TV or playing a computer game. The casserole was cooking, and Erin had phoned to say she would be back at eight, which was in half an hour's time. Martha was still feeling the intoxicating effects of the eau de vie, and realised she would have to be cautious how she replied.

'Does she?' Martha queried, stalling for time. The way Claude asked was quite abrupt, but he made a point of using simple French he knew she understood. Perhaps he had been waiting for an opportunity to speak to her alone, and had blurted it out like this because they could be interrupted at any moment.

'Well, in truth she's only said it once. It was the other night as she was going off to sleep, and she probably hoped I was either asleep or wouldn't remember. But there have been hints before. I've wondered. What is it, Martha, what's her secret?'

'It's not a good thing to divulge other people's secrets, Claude. I think she should tell you herself in her own good time.'

'Well at least you've confirmed there is something. I thought so.' As she ventured no more he added, 'I hope it relates to before my time with her.'

'Yes, Claude, I think you can rest assured of that, but please don't press me further.'

Time passed and Martha hid herself away, using up her leave, lingering in Saint-Cyprien. The days turned into weeks, and the weeks passed, and July became August and was about to become September. There were far fewer holidaymakers. Summer was ending, as was her doctor's note, signing her off work. Martha helped Erin by looking after Lucy and Ethan, or at least stayed around with the children so Erin and Claude were free to do things together. She helped out at the eco house, particularly with the fledgling garden, and most important of all, she talked to Thierry every day as she walked the wild desolate stretches of beach between resorts and campsites.

She liked it best when she was completely alone with the sand and the ocean. It was then she confided in him, and felt he was not far away. She could pretend for a while she was on an extended holiday and wanted to tell him all about it. She wanted to share everything. He had taken his leave without saying goodbye, and she still expected him to come back. She ached for him to return.

Some afternoons she borrowed Erin's bike and cycled down lanes she did not know, wondering if she would find her way back. There were ditches, but they were dry at this time of year. She had read Thérèse Desqueyroux and could feel how cut off the woods and marshes would have been a century ago. It was true, Thérèse had lived a little way south of here, but it was much the same terroir, the same presque'île or peninsular. Seabirds still hunted inland as they would have done in her time. It was not exactly a centre of modern life today, cut off from the mainland by the Gironde, but Martha had a freedom that Thérèse could not have dreamed of, and so she felt liberated rather than imprisoned by the primitive landscape. Thérèse had needed to break out of the marriage that confined her. Martha longed to return to the protection of hers.

She went to Chez-Madeleine sometimes with Erin or with Bené, and occasionally on her own or with people she met, and learned all the old French songs that were sung on Friday nights, when Yves, the jazz pianist, set up his group on the terrace. His beautiful daughter, who was one of the waitresses, sang new life into traditional ballads. Martha put off thoughts of going home as long as she could.

'Le fin d'été!'

Madeleine declared it was the end of the summer as they took their places round her table. It was the last day of August, and they were outside on the terrace, but it was uncertain how many more nights they could do this. It was past high season, and the number of tourists was declining rapidly, day by day. The summer was a short season. No more cabaret, no more jazz evenings until next year. Madeleine had kept on only two of her waiters: her favourite, in fact everybody's favourite, the blond Cedric, who was going off to La Reunion for the winter, and a quiet lad who did what Cedric said.

The end of summer for another year. Martha felt she was leaving something behind and it had nothing to do with England or France. It was to do with Thierry. His life had stopped in June. He would never move on from this summer. She could not stop the season turning, not remain behind with him. Her attempt to keep hold of him was being stretched and she did not know how long it would hold before it broke.

'Yes, le fin d'été, for another year.' Madeleine looked round the table. Her extraordinary, piercing, protruding eyes gave the appearance she was staring at them each, one at a time, looking inside their minds, revealing their hopes and fears. She homed in first on Claude and Erin, and then she smiled at Lucy and Ethan who had joined the group this evening, and were conscious of being treated as grown-ups. Madeleine was obviously fond of Sébastien and Bené, and had them seated on either side of her. Martha was sitting between Erin and Ethan, helping him with a crossword. She was about the same standard with French words and spelling as Ethan. Her extended summer here had made her more at ease with the children.

The final two people at Madeleine's table were her son, Philippe, and his girlfriend whose name Madeleine feigned not to remember, as if to say "they're here today and gone tomorrow, these girls". Madeleine paid a lot of attention to Philippe, ignoring the girl. Martha tried to show sympathy to her across the table, through smiling and asking questions. Her name was Nadine. It became evident Nadine was not as gutless as Madeleine wanted to believe.

'So what does the new season, the future, hold in store for us, I wonder?' Madeleine continued, holding court. She had apologised to Martha that in the height of the summer she had not been able to give as much attention to her friends as she would have liked. Now it was easier.

'I'm starting a new school in September,' Lucy, who was never shy, told the assembled guests. She seemed to lose interest when she was asked about where she was going and what it would be like. Perhaps she was not as certain about the change as she appeared, or did not know. She took over her brother's crossword and they both absorbed themselves in it, listening to the adult conversation, but pretending not to.

'We'll hold a party when we move into the house, and you're all invited,' Bené announced, and this was evidently news to Sébastien, though he smiled indulgently and posed no objection. He could not lean across and touch his partner because the imposing bulk of Madeleine's bust occupied the space between them.

'We may hold it just before we move in,' the more cautious Sébastien said, having considered the matter, 'before we finish furnishing it. It'll give us more room for the party.'

'Yes, room to invite the whole village. Room for a dance...' Bené was warming to his subject and Sebastien gave him a look of we'll talk about this together later.

'And you are returning to England, and the fog, poor dear,' Madeleine exclaimed.

'We don't have much fog in Chislehurst, it's not like the London of a Sherlock Holmes movie,' Martha told her. 'But I have to go home. I want to go back to work if the doctor agrees.' She was trying to persuade herself. 'But I've grown to know each and every one of you over the last month, and consider you're my friends now. I intend to come back.'

'Oh, yes you must come back when you are stronger. Perhaps you'll return for a holiday at New Year?' Madeleine asked.

'Madeleine's New Year parties are famous; fancy dress, dancing, fireworks, the lot,' Bené told her. 'The evening of Saint Sylvestre. You will hold a party for Saint Sylvestre this year, won't you, darling? You must!'

'If I do I'll call on you to organise the entertainment, Bené.'

'Oh, I'll do that, and Martha will be back long before New Year, won't you?' Bené said, and though he seemed a bit drunk, he also knew what he was saying, and both Erin and Sébastien had the sense the two of them were planning something they had not shared.

Madeleine asked Philippe about his plans for the future, and Martha guessed this was the main point of the conversation. The rest had been a preamble before trying to pin down her elusive son. His manner was confident and vague and Martha could imagine he was practised in the art of giving his mother the run around. He was probably the only person in the world who could. He said they needed more wine, and went to fetch it, leaving Madeleine marooned with her guests and their plans in which she had no interest.

Because she was not always able to keep up with the conversation, Martha had time to reflect. She had to face her imminent return to England and her mixed emotions about going back. She was itching to resolve the riddle of Thierry's last day, find out what he had been up to. How was she going to do that?

She had enjoyed the last few weeks, in as far as it was possible to enjoy anything under the circumstances. Why did she feel guilty about enjoying herself? Because she was alive and Thierry was not, of course. Saint-Cyprien and Chez-Madeleine had given her a breathing space. They were a different world from Chislehurst. Although Erin often appeared disorganised, she had organised Martha's recuperation, for that is what it had been, and she had organised it well. She listened when Martha needed to talk, but did not impose when Martha needed to be quiet. Martha assumed Erin had said something about her circumstances to friends, and it had only been Bené who had been inquisitive to know more. She had found herself telling him the full story of Thierry's death, the only one apart from Erin she had discussed it with. When Martha had said she would not rest until she knew where Thierry had been going that fateful day, he had said, surprisingly forcefully, 'No, you don't want to know that.'

She wondered if that was how he coped with things, shutting them out.

'That's more or less what Erin said,' she replied.

Mention of a helicopter brought her back to the party from her musings. She could not follow and asked what had happened. Erin explained there had been a rescue from the sea today, up the coast away from the supervised beach. Whoever had been plucked out of the ocean had been lucky, and other people had risked their lives for him or her.

'I'm glad it was a successful rescue. You said the ocean is dangerous.'

She looked up at the bright stars shining down on the terrace. She looked around at her friends, old and new, and was glad she had taken the decision to come here, been accepted and encouraged to stay on.

She had no Thierry to go home to. She could see no future, only a lonely amorphous hole. She dreaded returning to the large empty house and an English autumn, the season of decay. She dreaded going back to her job and how things had been, despite having said she wanted to return. She could see no purpose, no meaningful challenge. The future she and Thierry should have shared had disappeared. She shuddered to think of going through the motions of living a life without feeling, without sharing it with him.

People would consider her so brave, "carrying on", but it would be a charade. Was there an alternative? What was her alternative? She was mentally toying with the idea of opting out. Could she summon up the courage to do something different, something challenging, branching out? Had she the energy to take her life by the scruff of its neck in a different direction without Thierry to steer her? She had used Bené as a sounding board. He had given her ideas, but still Martha had no answers, no certainty, only fear and a sickening emptiness.

2

Escape to Saint-Cyprien

Bené sat daydreaming in the bar at Bordeaux airport. He was nursing a coffee which smelt good and strong, but was too hot to drink. He was waiting for Martha's plane, and had chosen the spot strategically so he could watch passengers and see the arrivals board.

I'm glad Martha's on her way, he mused. *Dying to see her. I've been planning what we're doing today, working out the route and our itinerary. I'm probably the only one who knows why she's coming. Well, I may have hinted to Sébastien, but no more than that. I didn't want him to try and stop us.*

I really, really like her and want to help her. It'll be a bit of fun for me too. There isn't much fun at the moment. I get so tired, working on the house all hours after coming home from work, but I'm giving it my all. Sébastien expects, and I'll deliver. I always have and always will. Does he appreciate the effort I'm making? Does he? Oh, Doudou, please take me seriously and be proud of me for a change!

Sébastien isn't big on fun. Martha is, which surprised me. At least she's learning to have fun with my help. I've got a new friend! I know she's lost her husband, so she's sad and confused, but we do have some laughs together. Perhaps I bring out a different side in her, one that's been buried under that icy professionalism for far too many years. From what she tells me I don't think even Thierry appreciated that part of her. I have this image of them, being cultivated and civilised together, but I can't imagine they let their hair down and just had fun for the sheer hell of it. She can relax with me and stop grieving for a while. A respite. I'm helping her and that makes me feel good about myself. Some people may be scandalised. What do I care? I'm gay anyway. Well, let them think what they want! It doesn't take much to upset some people. They're waiting to be upset, wanting to be upset. Vicariously excited. Neither of us really cares what other people think. That's something else we share in common. As long as the people who are important to us understand, the rest don't matter a damn.

Come to think of it, I don't suppose we'd be friends if Thierry was alive. Well, no, we wouldn't. It's only his death that brought her here this summer. I do remember them here together last year. I was newly arrived in Saint-Cyprien. Sébastien came from here, so he knows everyone. He knew Claude from years back, though Claude is a lot older. Through Claude we got to know Erin last year, and she brought Martha and Thierry into the restaurant one evening. My first thought was, What a glamorous couple!

He was dishy, and she was, and still is, beautiful in her simple and understated way. They matched each other perfectly, seemingly self-contained as a couple, but friendly enough in a gentle, distant way. After that we saw them once or twice. Oh, yes, I remember we had the picnic on the beach. Because he was French, I could talk to him easily, whereas her French was not so good then. It was clear he obviously adored her, so I don't buy the idea he was having an affair behind her back.

Who could have predicted that a year later she'd be back, on her own, very withdrawn, very preoccupied? It's not hard to understand how her life was shattered by his sudden death, and then the questions posed, the mystery of it. Most people are unaware of any of this. It was a shock how quickly she unburdened herself, told me her fears and anxieties, a pleasant shock because it proved at least she saw something deeper in me than the frivolous image I project. She didn't see me as just half a gay couple. I suppose she needed someone completely uninvolved to unburden herself on. She's talked to Erin of course, but Erin had known Thierry as long as she had, so she wasn't outside it.

He had a secret he took to his grave. That is so out of character from what I saw and hear, but people surprise me. I can't help her with the mystery of his death. She doesn't expect me to. I can only divert her attention and give her some amusement. That's me. Bené the clown!

Martha helps me in return. She's like a sister, and I can be myself and talk to her about things, a surprising number of things, most things in fact. I talk to women more easily than to men. Erin's okay, but she's so busy — work, husband, children — and she's scatty. The rest of the village, well, they regard me as Sébastien's boyfriend rather than Bené in my own right. Martha's my big sister, the big sister I never had. She accepts me as I am.

Martha confided in me about her intention to buy a house here. She hasn't plucked up courage to tell Erin yet. That'll be interesting! We're playing Escape to Saint-Cyprien, based on the TV programme. Apparently, they have it in England just the same. She's going to come and live here. I've got to find out what sort of home she's dreaming of. I'm sure it will be very different from our eco house. That was Doudou's idea of course. Don't get me wrong, I love that place, it's ours, mine and Doudou's, our retreat, our refuge. It may look stark, wood and glass and eco high tech, but it's essentially our love nest. Maybe with Martha's place I'll get the chance to do all those kitsch things Sébastien will not allow. Shame on him.

Will Martha take to Pascal? We'll have to wait and see. If she chooses somewhere that needs a lot of doing up she'll need advice, and he's a good architect and he needs more work. I like Pascal. He's hot. And he's straight, supposedly. More's the pity, but you never know. Sébastien doesn't like him. I can tell by the way he pronounces his name, in that "why are you wasting your time with him" sort of voice. Of course, Doudou might be a teensy bit jealous. I do hope so. Not that he has any reason to be because nothing has ever happened between me and

74

Pascal, and isn't likely to. But you never know. Keep everything crossed, or not as the case may be.

No, come to think of it, I'm not convinced Martha will take to Pascal. He's young and arrogant, and can be more than a tad chauvinistic, which the lady won't tolerate. She told me that she and Thierry had always been equals. They each took the lead on different things, but neither dominated the other. Thierry must have been some guy to have won all her love and not be dominated by her. Mind you, Pascal has a way of reading people, of working out how to play them. I suppose he's done that with me. He knows how to keep me hoping. I can see him playing up to her and her falling for his charms. And she'll appreciate his artistic ideas. Oh, would that leave me as a gooseberry? I want it to remain fun and not get too heavy. They've both got a tendency to get a bit serious. But I'm running ahead of myself as usual, let's not worry about that yet, I haven't even introduced them. I hope her flight's on time, I'm not good at waiting… Still there's lots of eye candy to watch… and fantasise about… I've got a talent for that.

Martha had made a decision, and felt better for it. *This is more like it*, she thought, *at least I'm moving forward.* She was excited, but in an agitated way. She was not breaking with her past, at least not yet, but she intended to do something positive and new. It was not going to solve her dilemma. It was not going to tell her who Thierry was going to meet the day he was killed, but at least she was doing something to break the inertia. She recognised its importance. It was a start.

Hysteria was never far below the surface while flying. Bright sunlight filled the plane and kept it at bay. This was the first time she had flown alone. That sounded pathetic considering she controlled a large budget and a lot of staff, but in personal terms she had always been protected. She was glad she had requested a window seat so she could look out. As the aircraft started its gradual descent, she was able to make out the coastline below. She was looking for Royan, with its string of white buildings along the estuary. It had a distinctive post-war grey cathedral. If she caught sight of it, she might get her bearings and identify Saint-Cyprien among the trees to the south across the Gironde River.

This was her personal adventure to keep grief at bay. She had taken Friday off work, booked her flight, but not told a soul at work except for Fran. She had weighed up the issues and decided to trust Fran. She needed an ally at work. Martha had emailed Erin to ask if she could come and stay, and of course Erin had replied yes. She had emailed rather than phoned so she could not get dragged into divulging her plans. She suspected Erin may have misgivings if she knew, which she would soon enough, but not in time to stop her.

It had been dark when she left home. The feathery tops of the laburnums on the drive had swayed in shadow against the sky, tentatively waving goodbye as she stole away. It was as if they were asking whether she knew what she was doing. She considered them Thierry's trees watching over her. She drove through almost deserted streets at first. The roads gradually got busier, mainly taxis, commercial vehicles and delivery vans. She was surprised so many people worked through the night. She merged with more traffic when she joined the motorway which was confusingly busy, even at this hour. Headlights dazzled in the greyness. There was a comforting anonymity once she got accustomed to it. She could only see the silhouettes of other drivers and passengers. They had a common goal. Gatwick was the magnet attracting them.

She phoned the meet and greet company, and waited in the grey mist before dawn for the man to come and collect her car. She saw a parking attendant moving closer, instructing people to move on, and wondered how to stall him when he approached. He was only one yellow light away when a van drew up, and she heard her name being called. The parking attendant melted away as she handed her keys to the meeter-greeter, confirming the time of her return flight on Sunday. It was all so matter of fact. She was about to say her car was automatic and had a funny starting button, but he was gone. He would work it out, he probably drove fifty different cars every day, but to her, her's was special. So far her plan was going well. She was out of practice. Each little step was a first. Each little step was important. Since marrying Thierry she had done very little on her own outside work.

She felt more human after eating breakfast looking down over the Channel and bits of northern France which she saw astonishingly clearly. Then it had all been lost beneath the clouds until they descended to meet the Medoc countryside in its mid-morning glory, one hour ahead of English time. From the darkness of the Gatwick parking lot, she had entered the electric glare of Departures, and spent two hours trying to lose herself in her book, trying to remain calm and ignore the artificial world where it could have been any time of day or night. The real daylight outside the plane window now lifted her spirits. Could she actually feel its warmth? Dawn must have arrived whilst she was in the enclosed in the terminal.

She was glad Bené was meeting her at Bordeaux Merignac. She liked him instinctively because he was fun and brought out a lighter side of her that had not been in evidence for so long. Through him she had made new friends, her own friends, not couples who were friends with an entity called Thierry and Martha. Should she feel guilty about that? With no disrespect to Thierry, whom she would give anything to have back, she did not feel the slightest guilt. Thierry would not have taken to Bené as keenly as she had. They had chatted amicably enough at the picnic last summer, but Thierry had given her to understand he considered Bené pleasant but superficial. Martha knew now that was just surface. Without being intense like some of their colleagues, he was far from frivolous, though for some reason he made a good attempt to appear so. She sensed he had a solid core tucked away and she could trust him, though she did not intend to be fully dependent on anyone ever again.

Bené had agreed to take her to look at houses. During the summer he had unintentionally planted the seed of the idea to settle in France. On balmy evenings she had sat under the caravan awning listening to Bené and Sébastien and begun to fall in love with the place. The plan had grown without her consciously thinking too hard, and on her solitary country walks among the pines, dry and dusty in summer, while Erin was at work, she had found herself looking at places and imagining what a new life could be like. Probably because Thierry loved London, they had never conceived of his going back, and her emigrating with him. Now, to Martha, initially daydreaming and then planning, it presented itself as the obvious path. In a funny way she might feel nearer to him. She did not want to run away but needed to free herself. Because she could not define her motives properly, she chose to keep them secret.

Going to live in Saint-Cyprien would not provide answers nor offer peace in itself. It would not unravel the mystery, but neither would she be returning to her former life on her own, picking up the pieces, as people invariably advised. Picking *over* the pieces, more like. *Forwards, not back*, she told herself. Sitting around in Chislehurst would not solve anything. For some reason she was sure, if she remained alert, wherever she was, clues would present themselves and point her towards the truth. *I will find a lead if I wait and actively listen. I must be patient!*

Thierry had been buried, quietly and simply, in mid-July before Martha's first visit to France. Although the case remained open, the interim certificate had allowed that. When she returned home in September, she learned from the police they had handed their file to the coroner and accidental death had been the ensuing verdict. She had the impression she was supposed to be pleased about that. It still left all her questions unanswered, but it allowed Benton & Powell to recognise and honour him, or, as she thought, tidy up the whole affair. A small memorial service had been held in a smart London church soon after her return. Like her, he had not been religious, and the venue had not been her choice; in fact, none of it had been her choice, she had just gone along with it because it did not seem real and did not seem to matter. It did not have anything to do with the Thierry she knew and loved. Several important people were among the select few attending, including a permanent secretary from a government department. Martha had been intrigued by that. *Was Thierry more important than I realised?*

Hugo had been solicitous, and Rajinder had been kind and accompanied her. He had introduced guests as she "did the room" at the reception afterwards. She was sad no member of Thierry's family had come from France though they had been invited. After she had received pleasantries from the good and the mighty, as she thought of them, a nice looking man introduced himself as Mark, Thierry's friend from university. She realised he had probably been there in the group the evening she met her future husband at the college film theatre. Mark said he and Thierry had spasmodically communicated through the years, and was really upset he had been killed. He sounded as if he meant it.

Rajinder took her home as soon as she believed she had fulfilled her obligations. People would think he had performed the role on behalf of Benton's, but she knew he had done it for her, and for Thierry. She thought he was probably the only one apart from her who was really upset, who felt bereaved. Left alone, as she had requested, she had wandered through the large, high-ceilinged rooms of the empty house. She lay down to rest, but finding that impossible, phoned Fran, her ally at work, to ask if she would go out for a meal with her. Despite there being a sumptuous buffet at the reception, she had not touched it and had eaten nothing since breakfast. Above all, she was afraid to be alone.

Martha chose Fran, the head of HR for the local authority, because she was the nearest thing she had to a friend at work. It was an odd time to own up to the fact she had never courted friends, never had the urge to be intimate with people other than a very small clique of people she liked, which had reduced as years went by to Thierry, Rajinder and Priya, and Erin too, though she was in France. Fran was tall, imposing and straight-forward, with a husky, ex-smoker's voice. She wore straight plain dresses which emphasised her height, with bangles that made a noise as she talked and gesticulated. Her children were grown up, she was divorced, and had an on/off relationship with one of the senior police officers Martha liaised with over adult protection cases. Martha was sure it was Fran's choice to keep the policeman as a lover, not a second husband. She doubted Fran would marry again.

Her relationship with Fran was cordial. Their empires overlapped. They had similar seniority, but in different sections. They did not impinge on each other, at work or personally. She was the ideal companion to spend the evening with after the strain of the day in London. Martha changed out of her elegant black suit. They met at a country pub some miles out. Martha did not want to be recognised near home. She felt guilty appearing to be out enjoying herself.

'I can imagine the service must have been an ordeal for you, but hope it closed a chapter and helped,' Fran said carefully after they had ordered food and got small talk out of the way.

'You're talking about that funny concept closure. I don't have it, Fran. Maybe I'll achieve it in time, but I suspect not.'

Like her other colleagues, Fran did not know about the puzzle of the day's leave and simply thought Thierry had been up in town as usual for his work. For her part, Fran was glad Martha was back at work, apparently in charge of herself again, though she had noticed subtle changes. Fran could not put her finger on it, but Martha was less predictable. It was probably natural, and would pass. People required consistency in others.

Martha felt pressure from Fran and others to fit back in, and it alienated her. It was as if they thought that since she had had her exceptional circumstances leave she should now get over it, or at least not show it, not embarrass them. None of them knew she was considering going back to France. She looked at the menu, glanced around the pub, and wished she were enfolded in the camaraderie of Chez-Madeleine. She had a surge of homesickness, feeling less connected here where she had lived for so many years, than there, where she already felt more affinity. Did she belong anywhere, or was she becoming rootless?

She heard Fran talking about time being a great healer and how important it was to avoid hasty decisions in her state, and wondered what state that was. Perhaps attempting to take her out of herself, Fran went on to talk about the potential career benefits of the impending merger of Children's Services and Education. Restructuring and re-grading could provide opportunities, and Martha would be in line for promotion and leadership if she played her cards right.

Once upon a time Martha would have jumped at the challenge. She knew the game inside out. She had encouraged others to seize opportunities. She intended to ignore all advice, though without revealing her intentions. She heard Fran out, without the energy or will to contradict her. It was comforting to be told her staff respected her and were concerned about her. She did not want to abandon them or let them down, so she would have to give judicious consideration to when and how to announce she was leaving. If the timing proved right, she would not be around to be a contestant for a top post. However, she kept all this to herself for the moment. It was such a muddle and her intentions were too unformed and fragile to reveal.

She was grateful to Fran for trying to help, and hoped to safely confide in her about issues going round in her head. She told Fran how much she had loved Thierry. It was not something she had dwelt upon when he was alive, or articulated publicly. They just got on with life, sensibly and quietly. She felt a sense of loss, of emptiness, but it was not all about herself and her loss. She was sad for him too; sad he had been cut down at what should have been the midway point of his life, so many expectations of a life yet to be lived. They had both been unsentimental in dismissing the God and religion of their childhoods, which left no solace of an after-life. It was a challenge learning to live and confront death without an easy faith.

'I can cope with the big public things better than the small private reminders of him. Well, for example, I seemed to float through the memorial service like a ghost, deliberately making the correct movements, gestures and noises so that people would think I was actually there among them. I felt so detached.'

She had received the information about the Benton & Powell death-in-service settlement with gratitude, but with the same lack of emotion as when she opened the letter and saw the size of the potential life insurance pay-out. Apparently it could not be paid until the final inquest verdict. She presumed this was in case it brought in a verdict of suicide, the one option she was certain was untrue. She had no financial worries, leaving aside her own salary, or potential redundancy, but the unsought wealth did not make her happy. It all felt unreal.

'I was determined to be stoic tackling Thierry's wardrobe, but his clothes still felt and smelt of him. It was a wonderful scent which I can't describe, but oh, so evocative. That was the worst moment. I just crumpled and sat there on the floor in front of the open wardrobe door. I was tempted to put them all back and pretend he would need them when he returned.'

'And did you?'

'No. In the end I abandoned the task and asked Mrs. Lyle, she's my cleaning lady, to remove them all, take what she wanted for her family, and give the rest to Oxfam.'

She did not tell Fran everything. She did not say Mrs. Lyle had come to her with a small, smart, black, business-like case, the type a solicitor might take to court. Thierry used it if staying away for a night, but she did not know what to think when Mrs. Lyle opened it and there was a set of clothes inside: dirty jeans, scuffed trainers, a tee shirt which had seen better days, and a brand new hoodie. Apart from the hoodie, she recognised them as things Thierry wore when gardening. Why a hoodie and how had they got in the case? It gave her a sense of foreboding.

'Shall I throw these away, Mrs. Jolivet?'

'The clothes, yes. The charity shop may like the case.'

Martha did not tell Fran about the old clothes that sparked off a trail of uneasy thoughts. Thierry usually kept the case in his study, which the police had searched. Mrs. Lyle had discovered it hidden at the back of his wardrobe.

Martha was weighing up whether to tell Fran about her forthcoming trip to Saint-Cyprien to go house hunting. She was tempted to go without telling anyone. In the end she confided because she thought it wise to have one trusted accomplice in the office. She understood this was probably the subconscious reason she had asked Fran to join her this evening. Fran looked appalled and asked her if she knew what she was doing, so she uncharacteristically backtracked and made out the house might just be for holidays.

'Or rent it,' Fran said. 'It could be a good investment.'

'You're right,' Martha agreed. Fran understood investments.

Her plane was ten minutes from the airport according to the screen. It was now low enough to see the muddy water of the Gironde before it broke into two rivers just north of Bordeaux. Martha continued to take stock of the last few weeks and make sense of them. She had forced herself to visit May, her adoptive mother, before coming away. The task was done out of guilt and duty rather than love.

The Pines, a nursing home in Bournemouth, was May's home now. It was a large, pleasant, red brick house surrounded by a somewhat overgrown garden, two roads back from the seafront, close enough to smell the salt of the sea and to hear the chorus of gulls. May appeared peaceful and settled after the dramas of the last few years when she had been worryingly unsafe in her own home. Martha had acted swiftly after May's last fall to get her into a suitable place, away from London where she said she was not happy. May had not been grateful and attacked Martha as heartless for having her put away. Martha relegated that to history, and was grateful to the staff for their care. She had never had a warm relationship with her adoptive mother. It was too late to hope for reconciliation.

Martha had taken an embossed order of service from the memorial event to give to May and help their conversation. Martha had to tell May of Thierry's death, but not the mystery of it.

The thick white card, smartly printed and with a grey ribbon, Benton's understated but fashionable colour, sat between them on the table as Martha explained she had some bad news. Under Thierry's pleasant and forever young face were the dates of his birth and death. She helped May read them. Did May understand? Her mother, who had always been hard on her, doted on Thierry, though she could not pronounce his name and simply called him Terry. She smiled a private smile as she gently rubbed her finger across his photograph. Martha was touched and wondered if she was saying goodbye.

It was also difficult to say she was moving abroad.

'I'm going over to France…'

'I'd like some paper… and a pen. A couple of biros would do.'

It was not a request Martha had been expecting. She often asked May if she needed anything, and May usually said no.

'Yes, of course, I'll bring them next time I come, or post them to you. I know you liked to write in the past.'

Martha tried to draw her out. She was aware May had been secretary to the local Labour Party before Stan, her husband, put a stop to it. She knew very little about May and Stan, and their life, which appeared veiled in sepia. As a child she had been embarrassed May was so much older than her friends' mothers.

'And an envelope. I want an envelope.'

'Oh, are you going to write a letter? I could write it for you.'

'No.'

That was all. Martha was allowed no more questions. Would May still be able to write? Martha was unsure.

She made one more attempt to mention France, but May did not seem to be listening. As Martha got up to go, May smiled and said, 'Perhaps Terry will come with you next time. I'd like to see him.'

Travelling had given her time to go over events. It was such a muddle. She alighted from the plane into the cool calm of the Arrivals Hall in Merignac. It was such a different, quieter airport from those in London, Paris or any other city she had visited, and it was not just a case of size. It had been designed to absorb noise and quieten the senses. She had brought everything she required in her hand luggage, supplemented by Gatwick shopping, so she walked briskly past the empty conveyer belts and anxious waiting passengers, and recognised Bené grinning at her and making funny faces from the other side of the plate glass partition. She went through Nothing to Declare, and hugged him.

'Are you okay?' he asked before releasing her, and she knew that unlike the countless people who politely asked her the same question, he actually wanted to know the answer.

'Yes, it's been a strain, but I'm glad to be here.'

'Good. Now you deserve some fun. It starts here. This will be like the TV programme.' Bené smiled as he drove out of the car park heading for the Rocade. 'A scrumptious guy with impeccable taste — that's me by the way — takes people to see various properties that meet their criteria and a mystery one as well. The thousand-euro question is which will they fall for?'

'We have several programmes like that in Britain. *Escape to the Country*, *Escape to the Sun*... they're all about escaping. But you know, Bené, they never do it. Every time I've watched it, people can't make up their minds; they don't seem to find what they're searching for.'

'So this is our very own Escape to Saint-Cyprien, and you are going to find what you're searching for, Martha, I promise. I suggest we have lunch at Sainte Hélène on route, and I'll give you the papers to read on the first three I've chosen for you to look at.'

He took her to a bistro near the market, where they ate inside because the season had turned, and only hardy smokers braved outside. They settled down with a half-litre carafe of local Medoc wine and ordered mushroom omelettes and salads. Martha read the blurb on the properties he had selected. One was a neat single-story house situated conveniently near the centre of the village, another was an apartment in a complex on the coast, and the third was a run-down cottage that had once been part of a farm. It was the only one which caught her interest.

'So what's your heart set on? Is it a lock-up-and—go property you can happily leave, or somewhere you can rent out for income when you're not using it? Do you want to keep your options open with something that could be used either way?'

'No. I fancy a place of my own, somewhere I could live, make my home if I decide to move over here permanently. This isn't just a holiday home, Bené, it could be a new life.'

'Oh! That's exciting. I like the sound of it, but are you sure? Think carefully. Is it wise to pull up your roots so quickly?'

'Don't you start, Bené. I've had too much advice about taking my time to get back to normal, whatever that may be. I wandered round my house after Thierry's memorial service, and thought, if there's any chance of him coming back I'll stay for eternity, I'll wait here for him, and he'll tell me what he was up to that day, and it'll be all right. But it isn't as if he may return and find I've gone and deserted him, because he isn't ever coming back, and I may never know the truth. I might not like it if I did. The finality hit me with a pounding ache. Then I understood that if he's taken his leave, I may as well go too. There's nothing to detain me. He didn't have the chance of living the rest of his life, but I have. I'm not going to feel guilty. Anyway, you successfully pulled up your roots, you got away and made a fresh start.'

'Yes, but I had someone to run away with.'

'I've accepted I'm on my own now. You could say this weekend is a rehearsal for it. Come on, Bené, let's go and play Escape to Saint-Cyprien.'

They called at the apartment in the holiday complex on the coast, because they reached it first. It was the sort of place someone might want as a bolt hole, a hide-away for vacations. It also had the potential to be rented out. It could provide an investment or income. It did not feel right. It had no soul. She knew instantly and did not linger.

'Where's this?' she asked as they got back in the car, indicating the description of the old farm cottage.

'It's what's left of a mas or smallholding in a former hamlet called Cachette. It's very isolated. There's nothing else left of the hamlet, but you can walk to the beach or cycle to the village. I thought you might like it. It's the sort of thing Brits go for, but maybe not the sort of place to live on your own as it's so remote.'

'Take me to see it.'

Bené's description may have been designed to put her off, but she was smitten the moment she saw it. It was on a minor track that went to the coast, but was not signposted so few would go that way. It was camouflaged by trees, in fact darkened by too many, some of which she decided would have to come down. It looked as if it had been unlived in for some time, maybe for some years, though she was aware houses abandoned swiftly take on an air of neglect. The garden was overgrown and the old stone house was crying out for light and love. Bené had the keys and opened the carved oak door with difficulty, revealing its potential, even by torchlight in the gloom. Most of the downstairs was one very large low-ceilinged room, with a former stable butting onto it, accessed through a separate outside door. Up the wonky stairs it had few windows and was dark, heavy and sombre. Martha loved the pattern of the rafters and bare joints in the high roof. She was busy re-designing it in her head.

'This is it, Bené!'

'You should look at some more before you decide. It's far from anywhere and requires a lot of renovation. It's probably got woodworm, ugh!' he said pulling a face registering exaggerated disgust.'

'I'm going to give it new life.'

'If you do settle for it, we'll have to commission a survey because it's so old. There could be termite infestation as well as woodworm, and damp, and we'd better get an architect. However, it's been empty since the widow went into a maison de retraite, that's an old-people's home. She's died since. I think the family would be glad to off-load it, and might all agree, so you could get a bargain. I'd negotiate on your behalf because if they got wind an Englishwoman was interested, they'd hike the price and we don't want that.'

They spent the rest of the afternoon visiting two other properties, including a "mystery house", but Martha had difficulty maintaining interest, because she had made up her mind. She asked to go back and have a second look at Cachette, but Bené was still playing Escape to Saint-Cyprien, and gave her more brochures. He advised her to sleep on it, make notes about her essential and desirable wish-lists and comparisons. He agreed they could go for a second viewing tomorrow if she was still serious.

Erin, Claude and the children were all delighted to see her again, which was a relief, but she could feel question marks hanging in the air. Erin looked at her with a we'll talk later face, which Martha deliberately avoided, as a teenager might, with a sullen air of I don't know what you're on about.

'Martha, I notice you've only got one change of light clothes.' Erin confronted her later as she unpacked in her bedroom.

'I'm only here for the weekend. I'll buy things if I need them.'

'Not out here you won't! We're miles from anywhere, and shops shut out of season. You'd have to go to Bordeaux for the sort of clothes you wear. Never mind, I can lend you some sensible warm things if it gets any chillier, as it's predicted to do… Just an idea, if you're going to come out regularly you may as well bring useful bits and bobs over here and leave them. Save you carrying back and forth.'

'That's a marvellous idea. Until I get the house sorted out.'

'What house?'

'Oh, I'm running ahead of myself. I haven't bought it yet. Bené's going to negotiate on my behalf for the little cottage out at Cachette.'

Erin sat down heavily on the bed.

'Martha, what are you talking about? Cachette is miles from anywhere. It makes Saint-Cyprien look like civilisation.'

'It's near the beach. I can buy a bike and ride into Saint-Cyprien to see you.'

'Hold on a minute. I'm not keeping up with you. If you want to buy a holiday home out here, I could show you better places than Cachette. You don't want somewhere so isolated. We'd worry about you. It would be hard to rent out. I don't know what Bené's thinking of.'

'Bené's not responsible. I am.'

'Well, it doesn't seem so at the moment!'

That brought them up short. Erin had never before talked to Martha as she would to a truculent child. They were suddenly so far apart, and both knew that anything they said or did next would be crucial. One or the other could make a mistake they would regret. Erin made the first move. She stood up, came round the bed, and took Martha's hand in hers, gently pushing her to sit down onto the bed. They sat together in front of the open window. The only sound was from cars on the village street a little way off.

'We seem to have changed places, you and I. I'm supposed to be the impetuous, scatty one.' She laughed and squeezed Martha's hand in a sisterly manner. 'You're the iceberg that keeps its cool and never melts.'

Martha looked down at their hands entwined.

'Martha, please tell me what's going on. Have you found anything out about Thierry? Is that what's disturbed you?'

Martha took a few deep breaths. She did not like being questioned like this, but understood Erin was motivated by concern. Her adventure was fragile and she preferred Erin's support to her criticism.

'I'm not disturbed, Erin…'

'No, I didn't mean that…'

'I know. I'm sorry. No, I don't know any more about Thierry's last movements. Oh, except for something I've told no one, but I know you'll keep it to yourself. He had some old clothes, the sort of things he would never have been seen dead in outside the house, hidden at the back of the wardrobe, in a case he took to London sometimes.'

'That's very odd.'

'Yes, very odd. The police missed them because they only searched the study. I'm glad about that. They may mean nothing, but I keep wondering, what was he up to?'

'The police haven't troubled you again?'

'No. For some reason the police lost interest and closed the case, and I have a hunch Benton and Powell were only too glad. They moved swiftly to pay me off, and to exonerate Thierry with a lovely memorial service. I don't suppose I'll hear any more from them.'

'Why do you think that?'

'It's like Thierry's been expunged. He's disappeared from Benton's website, their corporate lists, their publicity material. I can see they have to take him off current contacts, but I had expected to see more than the briefest of brief notes in their magazine announcing his unexpected death. I couldn't help comparing him to a Russian politician who's fallen from favour and been blanked out of official photographs.'

'I suppose death isn't good for business,' Erin suggested.

'He didn't have the right sort of death for Benton's. But Benton's was Thierry's life, and the machine goes on as if he'd never existed. That may be normal, but it strikes me as ruthless and extreme.'

'His protégé. What's his name, Raj something? Has he abandoned you too?'

'No, Rajinder still keeps in touch, but that's because he's a friend. I get my information, such as it is, from him now. I know you had your suspicions about him, but I'm sure he doesn't do it as an agent of the firm. I trust him. He's the only one at the firm I trust. He even took the initiative to try and get the list of calls made to and from Thierry's extension and direct dial phone before he died, to see if they gave any leads, but the police had been there first and removed them.

'Oh, then maybe they were on to something after all.'

'Well, if they were or are, they won't tell me. You were right when we talked at La Dune last summer. You said don't forget it, but stash it away. Follow up any clues that appear, that's why I'm relying on Rajinder. You said don't dwell on it, and get some diversionary therapy.'

'So that's where the house fits in, is it, diversionary therapy. You're looking for a place over here to escape to when you want.'

'Well, if Thierry was taking French leave, so can I.'

'Oh, Martha! I must admit it'll be nice to have you around sometimes. I live in quite a man's world, certainly at work, and looking after the house and car — or not as the case may be — because Claude can't do it. He's not that sort of man. My best friends are Sébastien and Bené, so I only have Lucy for female company, and she's getting to that teenage 'I don't communicate with parents' stage…'

'Erin, I may as well tell you, I'm not looking for a holiday home. I'm thinking of making a permanent move.'

'Oh! What about your job?'

'I don't need it on a financial level. Thierry's left me extremely well off. He always cushioned me against reality, and he's done so again in death. Ironic really, because I keep thinking that if he was having an affair, and I was going to lose him, I'd have needed to work. The way I lost him made me rich, and if I sold the house in Chislehurst I could live without worry till I'm a hundred.'

'Martha, work has never been just a salary to you. It's always been your crusade, your passion, your commitment; too much so, I often thought, for your own good.'

'Too much so, you're right. I can't pretend to you. The depressing part is that it's been changing for some time, though I haven't wanted to admit it, not even to myself. It's harder and harder to keep the passion aflame when the profession you love is treated like a political football, and the powers that be try to control and micro-manage you. They demand more and more and give you less and less to deliver it. No one's treated with respect. I haven't the qualified staff to deliver a good service. The group I graduated with, we were all so idealistic, so positive. I had some good years, the best I realise, but now I feel alienated at work and lonely at home. I'm getting less and less able to keep up the team's morale. I don't want to leave in a bad way and let them down, so I'm training as many people as possible to protect the future…'

'Martha, I didn't mean to set you off on a rant. Calm down. Forget it.'

'Forget it. Yes, of course. Well, I'll be forgotten. It'll probably be like Thierry at Benton's. Three months after I've gone, it'll be as if I never existed. Still, I can't feel sorry for myself because I'm lucky, and have my escape plan.'

'Is that what it is, your escape plan?'

'Erin, how can I explain this? All I know is Thierry isn't here to support me any more... He's gone. That means I can't support him any more either. I have no personal role. I'm no longer needed, except at work, and they'll get over me. I've worked so hard for so long and... I can't any more. You realise I'm thinking this out as I try to explain it. Martha, the planner, for once has no plan.'

'So, all you've worked for, you're giving it up.'

'No, Erin, I don't see it like that. If I've achieved anything, if I've made anything better, that's fine. If I've improved anyone's life, that's fine. But it doesn't mean I have to carry on. Nothing's permanent. We all have to go eventually. I felt like a wound up spring at the end of the memorial service. I thought I might crack, split, break, whatever. I had to control myself. Slowly I'm learning to unwind. I've never done that before.'

'I can see you need to unwind. You must learn to relax. But this move to France, well, you say you've no master plan. You usually do have everything meticulously planned.'

'Well this isn't planned yet, I'm just toying with ideas, a bit sketchy, but though I call it playing, it's not play. It's too important for that. And how do I say this, I can't get there by my usual methods. I can't *plan* to unwind, I'm just *feeling* how to do it, one turn at a time, and each time check how it feels, and so far it's instinctively right. I'm not running away, Erin. I want to rebuild my confidence and my hopes… and I suppose my trust in life.'

'I take it they don't know you're leaving.'

'That's true, they don't know yet; well only Fran, who I didn't intend to tell, but then I realised I could do with her help. She's sworn to secrecy. Timing will depend on making the house habitable, and that's going to require a lot of work. I'd value your emotional support even if you're convinced I'm crazy and doing the wrong thing. Come and explore the cottage with me tomorrow.'

'No. I can't, I'm sorry. It's Saturday. I have to take Ethan and Lucy to their lifesaving class and then run some errands. I committed myself before I knew you were coming, and I'll be out most of the day.'

'That's okay, I'll give you more notice of my next visit.'

Erin went downstairs, leaving Martha alone in the spare bedroom with her meagre possessions and her anxieties.

Martha sat on the bed feeling lonely. She had been settled in a comfortable life splintered by Thierry's untimely death. Their lives had been so entwined she felt at this moment there was nothing left. She was better off than many, but could not buy his life back. She was sorry for

Thierry. Whatever he had done, he had been robbed of his future.

In her logical non-grieving moments, when she was not staring into the abyss, she knew she had to start reconstructing. She was on the edge of being prepared to take a leap of faith. It may have been simply luck that the cottage in Cachette was up for sale and Bené took her to see it. It was the start of a new dream, but her dream had not included Pascal who Bené introduced into her world.

'I don't need an architect,' Martha told Bené when he raised the subject. They were having a second viewing the following day, the Saturday morning, and their words reverberated around the dark, bare, stone walls. 'I know what I want to do with it.'

'That's good. He'll want to hear all about it. He can survey it and develop your ideas, and suggest the best technical ways of achieve them. How do you propose to manage such a project when you're back in England, or are you going to camp out here like Sébastien and I do at our place? I can tell you it's hard and unlike us you're on your own.'

'Don't remind me.'

'So…'

'Okay, well maybe I should meet him to see how sympathetic he is to my vision of the place. You all think we English are nuts about old properties, and leave our common sense on the other side of the Channel. I'm not like that. It's important he understands. What's he like? Do you know him well?'

'Quite well. We've collaborated before, Pascal as designer and me advertising and selling. He's younger than me, I think he's nearly thirty, and he's got good ideas. Before that he worked in the Dordogne for British people with homes out there.'

'That's not necessarily a recommendation.'

'It means he's acquainted with the two different legal systems, moving money, cultural expectations...'

'Okay, I can see you're probably right. I'm going to need someone to help me who knows what they're doing.'

'I'll call and see if he can fit us in this afternoon.'

'In that case I'll do some drawings to show him what I want it to look like.'

Martha was impatient for the long French lunch break to be over so they could rendezvous at Cachette. Bené had to return to his office at midday to see other clients, so dropped her back in Saint-Cyprien. He texted later to say Pascal would join them at four. She was familiar with the French sense of time and suspected that four meant five or later. After lunch she asked Claude if she could borrow Erin's bike and cycle back to see how long it would take and how easy it would be. He looked vaguely amused but agreed. She took a tape measure, a torch, her camera, sketch pad and assorted pencils, all of which had been part of her carefully selected hand-luggage. She would wander round to get the lie of the land. Bené had hidden the keys in the overgrown garden, so she could get inside the building.

It was a long ride, longer than she had estimated, and as all the flat avenues amongst the pines looked the same, she thought she might be lost more than once. She was relieved to find Cachette as she left it, as she presumed it had been for a long time. There were only a few buildings of the former hamlet left standing, and they were clustered together round the cottage on the left-hand side of the lane. She wanted to savour her first entry into the cottage on her own, so she dawdled and decided to walk past and down to the sands to spin out the time. The trees became sparse and scrubby nearer the beach, with lots of heather and gorse. By the time she got to the old German concrete coastal path there were only bushes, some wind-burned and brown, growing sideways, obviously buffeted in winter when it could be wild. Like La Falaise, there was no obvious way down because of erosion. She would discover one in time, and if not, she would make one. For now, she contented herself with simply looking at the golden expanse which she knew stretched all the way from the Point de Grave in the north to Arcachon and then further on into Spain, the historic route of Saint Jaques de Compostella and the pilgrims. She was going to own a tiny bit of it! She loved beaches, best of all out of season and deserted.

Fearing she was being romantic and getting carried away, she turned round, and approaching the cottage from the west for the first time, began to appreciate how much land was attached. She had been contemplating converting the stable into a garage, but now imagined there was plenty of room for a separate garage on the footing of one of the derelict buildings which would enable the stable to be incorporated into the cottage. Planning permission should not pose a problem out here, especially if built in keeping.

The cottage was blond coloured stone, with a patina, and lichen clinging to cement. This struck her as unusual because stone was hardly used around here. Most construction was either wood or brick, sometimes concreted and whitewashed. She approached the front door. She stood back to look at the old carved wood and the low canopy above, and saw it was rotting. She touched the corner of the canopy and it came away in her hand, dry and brittle, breaking into pieces, depositing dust on her hand. Bené was right, she did need professional advice about restoration. She was weighing up whether the canopy could be saved, when she heard a car approaching, and thought it unusual for Bené to be so prompt. It was not his car, but a sleek black modern Audi, and so she surmised the man getting out must be Pascal, the architect.

As Bené had warned her, he was young. She was starting to notice how many people were younger than she was now she was approaching forty. She thought an architect meeting a client in England would wear a jacket, maybe even a tie, but Pascal was in cords, an open shirt and trainers. He had neat, curly brown hair and looked healthy as he bounded up the steps from the lane. They were overgrown with weeds which could easily trip somebody up, but his feet seemed barely to alight on them, before he arrived eagerly on the path in front of where she stood her ground to greet him outside the front door. There was a faint peppery or nutmeg scent, perhaps from his eau de toilette, made sharper by the heat. He wore shiny metallic sunglasses, so instead of seeing his eyes, she was disconcerted by her own reflection.

'Bonjour, je m'appelle Martha Jolivet,' she said, holding out her hand, preserving her distance.

'And I am Pascal Guilloux,' he replied in perfect English, with hardly a trace of an accent. He shook her hand. 'How very polite and formal we are,' he laughed.

She continued trying to speak French, but his English replies were rapid and accurate, so she gave way.

'So you want to buy this tip!' he exclaimed. Was he arrogant, rude, or just challenging?

'Yes, and Bené said you could help me restore it, but if you're not interested I can—'

'Oh, I'm interested, and intrigued, I must say. It's ugly with all these creepers, and hardly any windows. It could be made beautiful, but it will always be alone here, out of the way, on the route to nowhere…'

'It's on the way to the beach,' she said authoritatively. She did not know quite why she said it, but the beach was very important to her, its wildness, its openness, its timelessness.

He turned to look at her and removed his sunglasses. His eyes were large and brown. He had a self-confident smile. She thought his smile was mocking her.

'Yes, the beach is lovely here. You can be very… private… It's lonely though.'

'I don't mind that.' He was too close. She could smell his breath which was sweet. This was getting too personal. 'Shall we go inside and look round the cottage.' It was not a question. She was used to being in charge.

She unlocked the front door, but had to push because it was caught on the stone slabs underneath. It was strong even though it was falling apart. Irritated, she gave it a shove using her shoulder which provided just enough room to slide past. She felt foolish squeezing through the gap, but for some reason did not want to ask him to open it. It was important to invite him into her cottage. He looked at the door, lifted it slightly and it freed itself and opened wide. He followed her in. She was even more irritated, but had to accept he was the expert as far as buildings were concerned.

There was a window over by the sink, covered in cobwebs. It opened inwards, and having opened it, she was able to unlatch the dusty shutters and throw them outwards, providing a shaft of light into the gloom. It had been neglected for a long time, and nature was reclaiming it. That was good because she would never know the previous owner. She was already thinking of it as her own.

'Only one room down here, though a very big one.' He stated the obvious, as if he were an estate agent preparing a plan of it.

'Yes, but I wondered if it will be possible to cut through the wall into the stable, and maybe move the kitchen in there.'

'Ah, yes... The walls are immensely thick, solid stone,' he said running his hands along the wall, appreciating their strength. 'Very unusual for round here. It would be a big job, and the floors are probably different levels, but yes, it's a possibility. We need to envisage all the possibilities.'

The electricity was turned off. Before she could get her torch out, he took one from his trouser pocket and found the box under the stairs. He opened it and flicked away the dust and insects, mostly dead bugs. He was about to pull a switch, when Martha instinctively put out her hand and pulled his away.

'It might not be safe. I don't want you killing yourself on my behalf.' She let his hand drop as if it were burning her. She could barely see him in the shadows, but was sure he was smiling at her. As he crouched before her she caught the nutmeg again. She told herself to focus on the house, and drew back to give him space to get up.

'It's probably disconnected anyway. We'll have to look for some more windows. There don't appear to be many.' He felt his way down the wall and came across a back door opposite the one they came in by, and a key on a grubby shelf of odds and ends. It was also hard to open, but once achieved, light streamed in from both sides, and they could see the whole room. A huge stone fireplace with seats at both ends dominated the space between the two doors. The walls were of dry irregular stone without mortar, and flat square flagstones covered the floor. They were dirty with age, but appeared to be dry. Nothing smelled damp. The roof was low. It made Martha feel she had to duck although there was sufficient clearance. The overall effect was gloomy. They looked at each other in the stillness, the only movement being dust particles in the air disturbed by their activity and caught by the light.

'It has potential,' he said, but sounded doubtful, and she thought he might be grinning at her, but she could not be sure because he was in shadow. 'It's big. It could be divided.'

'No, I want to keep it open plan… but with more windows, more light…'

'You should think how you'll live in it. Walk about. What will you do where? Where will you sit, where will you eat? Then we plan out the use of the rooms, each area. We need to work out where the morning sun comes from, where's the evening sun, where do you want a veranda. The English always want a veranda…'

She was about to contradict him, when she realised he was right. A French veranda is what the English call a conservatory. She imagined sitting reading in a garden room in the late afternoon.

'We should go upstairs. I think it's just an empty attic at the moment.'

She was aware of his proximity as he followed her up.

'There's enough room for two large en-suites,' he said after they had climbed the rickety stairs, 'one for you and one for guests.'

She knew he was right, but decided to challenge him. 'It's important to preserve the beams and roof structure. They're so elegant.'

'Of course,' he agreed, 'so windows at each end which won't interrupt the roof line, but you must replace the stairs. They should be a feature curving round, and I can picture a tall window behind them to show them off at their best.'

He threw in several suggestions, and as he warmed to the project her spirits lifted. Maybe she did need an architect after all. She heard the sound of another car in the distance, getting closer. Any vehicle had to be coming to the cottage, because there was nowhere else for it to go. *I'll always know when someone's coming, even from a long way off*, she thought.

'That'll be Bené,' Pascal said and they went down and met him as he parked. His hard-working car looked shabby behind the Audi. He was carrying a bottle of red wine and three glasses, 'To celebrate,' he said.

'I haven't bought it yet!'

'But you will. I phoned the son of the old lady who died, and he sounded surprised and pleased when I said I may have a customer, though I added there was so much work to do the price would have to reflect that.'

'He may agree?'

'It isn't as simple as that in France. Laws of inheritance are complicated, and all those in the family with a claim have to agree. I'm sure they will because they want to get rid of it.'

'And not a word about it being an English lady,' Pascal warned.

'No, I'll keep that quiet till we have to sign.'

The three of them sat cross legged together on the long grass in front of the kitchen door, like children playing house. Bené poured out three glasses and they drank a toast to Martha's cottage. She relaxed, enjoying the sensation of playing truant from her cares, infected by the young men's sense of fun. She looked at Bené and Pascal, sitting very close together, and a thought entered her head. *No, I must have got that wrong*, she mused, *Pascal knows Bené's spoken for, and I got the sense he's interested in women… well, you never know. I wonder.*

'Martha's not back then?' Erin asked, having dropped the children off with friends. Lucy and Ethan were at a barbecue evening and staying the night. 'I sometimes think the children have a better social life than I do,' she added.

'Martha went off on your bike looking serious and determined, like an English lady explorer from an earlier age,' Claude replied and Erin laughed.

'I know what you mean. She sometimes gives me that impression too. Head girl and queen's guide rolled into one. If she wasn't so lovely she'd be frightening.'

110

'She's meeting an architect at Cachette. She's moving very rapidly with this house idea. I've no doubt she'll turn up sooner or later and tell us all about it…. Oh, and perhaps more importantly, while you were out, Niall phoned. I got the impression he'd like to be invited for Christmas. He said something about not wanting to go to Ireland.'

'I'm sure he doesn't want to go back there. It'll be nice if he comes, don't you agree?'

'Sure.'

'Good. I'll return the call then and ask him over. Martha knows him, and she'll probably be here too the way things are going. On the subject of Martha, does she know what she's doing?' Erin asked, though it was more a question to herself than to Claude. 'You'll tell me not to interfere, but I am concerned about her, very concerned. She's changed. It isn't that I like her any less, it's just that I don't understand her at the moment. She was always so logical.'

'And buying a house out here isn't logical? Erin, you can't protect her like you seem to want to. She's perfectly at liberty to spend her money how she likes, and—'

'Claude, it isn't the money I'm worried about, she's got more than enough to do with as she pleases. I just don't think she's going to resolve her problems about Thierry's death by running away.'

'Is that what you think it is? Haven't you considered that if you can't resolve something, then getting away may be a smart move… What have I said, Erin, you've gone pale… Are you okay?'

'Yes, yes, of course.'

'Well, you look pale. Stop doing things and sit down here for a moment.'

She did as he suggested, and sat down at the kitchen table. Claude had been concerned by how faint she looked. He put his arm round her.

'Your colour is coming back,' he said after a while.

'Yes, I feel okay now. I don't quite know what came over me.'

As they sat side by side, the normally busy house quiet for once, he thought it was as good a time as any to ask her about the remark she had made when Martha visited in the summer.

'Erin, if you are all right, and while we are without the children, and on the subject of Martha, are you ready to tell me why you consider you're in her debt? Don't I deserve to know? We're supposed to have no secrets from each other. Look, I can see you're not all right.' She had detached herself from him. 'Come here.'

He moved closer and held her because she looked faint again. She gave in and put her head on his shoulder.

'Okay, we don't have to talk about it now if you're not well. Forget what I said.'

Always unpredictable, she came out of her reverie just as quickly as she had gone into it. She jumped up as if she had made a decision,

'Yes, I will tell you, but not here, not in this house, Claude. Take me down to the beach and we'll walk and talk. I promise. I'll tell you everything. I've kept it secret for too long,'

She picked up a sweater and he followed, keeping a close eye on her because he was finding her difficult to predict at the moment. He wondered if Martha's unpredictable moods were rubbing off on her. They did not say anything in particular until they were walking along the sand in the direction of La Falaise. He waited, judging she was uncomfortable with whatever she had to impart. He was getting cold feet too, and was not convinced he wanted to hear it now, even though he had asked. She had slipped her hand into his as they had begun to walk in step, but she removed it when she began to talk.

'Martha bringing her life out here has been quite a catalyst.' She laughed, looking up at the sky and blinking. 'She is concerned about herself, and about Thierry's death, but her suddenly appearing this summer and questioning the past has stirred me up as well. It's as if the past is catching up with me.'

'What do you mean, Erin?'

'Claude, you know about my roots, where I came from, though we don't go back there. I mean we don't visit my family. I've cut myself off. So picture it. Rural Ireland, back then when I was a child. It's changed so much in recent years, I hear, but like Niall, I don't want to go back. It took so long to get over it. It took so long to find you. Out of fear, I suppose, I kept it from you…'

'What, Erin, what are you talking about?'

'What I haven't told you is... I didn't think of it like this, but I... I was abused as a child,' she blurted out, suddenly loud. 'I told nobody. It was my uncle. Does that sound corny? It's true all the same. I'm saying the unsayable. There! It's out in the open.'

She looked at him in fear as if expecting him to reject her, but he was searching her face out of concern, trying to see into her eyes. She was welling up with tears.

They had stopped. He had not expected this. He enfolded her and held her close, because he adored her and wanted to take away her pain. He felt male guilt because another man had done this dreadful thing to her. Irrationally he shared that guilt. He was considering what to say when she pulled slightly away and continued, quieter now. He let go, and they walked side by side whilst she told him her story.

'As you know, we have the farm, the farm the family has had going back generations, Burke's Farm. Back then there was Mam and Dad and me and my brothers, and they're all still there except for me and Niall. I don't know how much you remember of them?'

'Well, I remember your mam and dad from that awful visit we made to say we were getting married. They weren't friendly. I wondered if they thought I was too old for you. I think of your brothers as big and gingery, but I couldn't put names to faces. Except Niall of course, the only one who was friendly.'

'You never met the Reverend Conan Burke. He was my father's brother, the priest in the next town. He was dead by the time we visited. He wasn't married of course, though there were stories, but priests were above suspicion then. I was expected to go by bus and help out at his house while my brothers helped at the farm. I tried to get out of going, I dreaded it, but I was hit if I protested. Mam didn't know. At least I can't believe she knew. Surely she wouldn't have made me go if she suspected? Dad was blind to it. Nobody challenged a priest in those days.

'He began by feeling under my blouse when he had an excuse to give me a hug. Then he began lifting my skirts and he grew bolder. I fought back and he said I would be punished, and I said he'd be punished, but he said nobody would believe me and it was true in those days. So I made excuses not to go, but Dad expected me to go and wait on his brother there, like he thought I should wait on him at home, and Mam called me a lazy hussy. I was so terrified. He was so powerful. I told Niall in my dreams and he protected me, but awake it seemed so dirty and…'

'And… go on.'

'And I thought it must be my fault, so I couldn't confide even in him.'

'Am I right to guess Martha was the first one you told?'

'Yes, but that was years later, when I'd got away. I bottled it up all those years. Do you remember back in the house you said if you can't resolve something it may be best to get away? That's exactly what I did. I got away from the place, though I couldn't get away from the shame.'

They sat down. She began to talk again.

'You know this bit. I got my freedom through education, and going to London. Oh, it was wonderful! Mam and Dad had no choice but to let me go. The authorities said so because I'd won a scholarship. I'd clawed myself out.

'As you know I met Martha. She was in the next room in the hall of residence, and the day I arrived she introduced herself in the corridor. She was trying to get rid of her parents. They were quite elderly, and her father was fussing, and she was saying she'd be all right and they should leave her to settle in. When they'd gone she knocked on my door, and said, "Relief!" and I knew just what she meant. She said we could be friends if we told each other a really important secret. That's how forward she was even then. She helped me unpack and we had coffee, big mugs of coffee as students do.

'It's funny how I remember some details and blank out other things. I'd just bought the mugs. They said LONDON, proof to myself I'd arrived. She told me she was adopted. I didn't get why being adopted was such a big deal. In truth, I'd have been glad to discover my parents weren't my real parents. But it was obviously a big issue for her, and still is though she keeps it hidden, and telling me about it was her way of saying she trusted me enough to be close friends. Things are very immediate with students, you know. Friendships are important. It was like that for Martha and me.'

'You're talking about Martha again. I want to know about you, Erin? I'm more concerned about you than her at the moment. What happened when you told Martha about your uncle?'

'Well, I didn't tell her right away, only much later. That first day in hall, I couldn't bring myself to mention it. It was so big, it was too big to divulge, do you understand? So I made up a secret to keep her happy. Stupidly, I told her I fancied my twin, Niall. Heaven knows why I said that!'

'Oh, come on, Erin. Even I can see there's some truth in that.'

'Really! That's so embarrassing. Anyway, Martha swallowed it. Said it probably wasn't as abnormal as I thought. Martha eventually became my confidante, and we discussed all the important things together. Late night chats. Later, when I knew her better, I confessed my secret had been a lie, because I couldn't bring myself to talk about my real issue. She coaxed me to talk and when I started I couldn't stop. It all tumbled out. I described how I loathed myself when my uncle had been touching me, and I got into trouble because I wouldn't undress at school, for swimming and games. I scratched myself and made myself as unattractive as possible. I didn't know what I was doing. Luckily I put all my energy into reading, so I did well and passed everything and began to realise that was how I could get away.

'All Martha did was listen and encourage me. She held my hands and told me it wasn't my fault. I was only a child, and he was the adult responsible for it. I felt a burden lifting. I felt so relieved. She said I shouldn't take it out on myself. I must stop being self-destructive. Be angry instead. I should go to the police, but it was enough at that stage to have begun to talk about it and be taken seriously. I wasn't sure the police would believe me anyway, I wasn't ready for that, and the family would turn totally against me. They'd say I was to blame. Probably cut me off completely. I didn't care too much, but it would give Niall further problems, and I didn't want that.

'Niall visited me in London. He got an exchange programme from his college. He and I were the only ones who got away, and he only partly got away. Mam considered us both spoilt, we twins, the youngest, the babies, she called us. I think she was jealous we had something going between us, a rapport, a sixth sense of each other. I'll never know why Mam's so bitter. Martha said bluntly that's her problem, not mine.

'One evening, while Niall was staying in London, Martha persuaded me to tell him about Uncle Conan, and he was appalled. He went white. He said I should have told him sooner, and I said I'd wanted to, but wasn't certain he would believe me, and worried he'd think it was my fault. He said, "No, I believe you, sis," which made me cry with relief, and also because I'd doubted him. Martha thought my story had connected with something he had been suppressing. She thought Uncle Conan might have tried it on with him too, but he didn't say. Martha has a vivid imagination.'

Claude assumed she had come to the end. Martha had accepted her. Niall had too. She was not to blame. Claude was sure she needed reassurance from him.

'Darling Erin, I'm sorry, so very sorry. You've kept this secret from me all these years. I knew there was something. I'm so grateful you've shared it. Thank you for having this faith in me—'

'Wait! There's more.' Erin interrupted. 'If I tell you this you must never breathe a word. It wasn't long after Niall went back to Ireland that Uncle Conan died. He apparently tripped and fell downstairs. Niall found him and called the emergency services, but it was too late. I've never asked him what happened. I don't want it confirmed. I assume he did it for me, but if Martha is right and Uncle Conan tried it on with him too when he was a child, then he might have done it for himself as well. I felt relieved and guilty when Uncle Conan died. Martha saw me through that patch too. She helped me get rid of all the guilt. She said, "Cry for Niall if you like, but don't shed tears for that hypocrite Conan." So you see, she knows me rather well. She freed me up and that's why I'm grateful to her. Without her, I wouldn't have my life with you and the children. I'd have still been stuck hating myself. I may not have lived up to my potential, because I was never driven like Martha, but I got myself a life which matters.'

'A good life.'

'Yes, a good life, with you, and the children, out here.'

They sat watching the sun going down and remained quiet. She felt relieved. She had fretted over not having told him earlier, and the longer it had gone on, the more impossible it had seemed that she would ever be able to tell him. Again, good old Martha. It was Martha turning up that brought it to the surface. Now Erin was tired, but calmer than she had been for a long time.

'Martha helped me, but I wasn't able to do the same for her. When I asked if she knew who her real parents were, she said she didn't want to know, though I wouldn't be surprised if she fantasises about who they might have been. I suppose that's natural. I think she saw her adoptive parents as a barrier standing between her and her real parents. There was a lot of hostility I didn't understand.'

'You only saw them the once?'

'No, I met them again at graduation. And at her wedding which she arranged without her mother's help. They appeared self-consciously out of place, and Martha was not that sensitive to their embarrassment. I don't think she had a clue how proud they were of her. They were old fashioned, and her mother could be abrupt, probably to cover up her lack of confidence. He was kind and gentle. I became aware that Martha's matter-of-factness was her own way of protecting herself from emotions which she feared could overwhelm. I could see why they found it difficult to get on. I wanted her to be more sympathetic to them, and as I got to know her, I told her she'd been chosen by people who had not been able to have children, and that was a special sort of love. She should think more about that and less about why her blood parents hadn't wanted her, or, more probably, hadn't been in a position to bring her up. She's so bright, and yet she'd been so fixated on the loss, their rejection, that she couldn't appreciate what she's got. She's in danger of rejecting that too. Over the years since then she hasn't spoken much about them, but I know her father died and her mother is in a home now. She does all the right things for May, her mother, but it's as if she does it out of obligation, not kindness.'

'No idea who her own parents were?'

'Don't think so. She probably counselled other people who decided to trace their birth parents, but shied away from discovering her own. She said, "That's the past and I must move on." I know her well. Underneath she's so full of contradictions most people don't see. With Thierry's death, her mother in the state she's in and having no children, she's totally alone. That's why she's fragile and isn't acting logically. It's all stuff that's been buried for years.'

'She isn't acting logically or isn't acting as you expect?' Claude asked. 'There isn't any right or wrong here, you know.'

'Okay, I'll just have to trust she'll be all right. At least we're all right, you and me,' she said and put her head on his shoulder.

They sat on the beach, no longer needing to talk, not bothered about the time. At some point her mobile rang and brought them back to the present. It was Martha, keen for them all to meet up and eat at the Chez-Madeleine tonight.

'Who's all?'

'I'm with Bené and an architect he's found for me called Pascal…'

'Yes, I've heard of Pascal,' Erin said unenthusiastically.

'We could meet you and Claude there at seven,' she suggested, in a way that made it sound it was all arranged anyway. 'We must remember to pick up Sébastien on the way.'

'Yes, don't forget Sébastien,'

'Time to turn back,' Claude said, helping her up. 'Why don't you like this Pascal fellow?'

'I haven't said anything against him.'

'I could tell from the tone of your voice.'

'You'll say I shouldn't interfere, but I don't want to see Martha hurt even more. She lost all her sense of certainty along with Thierry. Last time she visited she was obsessed with where Thierry was going the day he died and who he was meeting. I could see that was a dead end, although it's still there, buried not far under the surface. Now she seems to want to leave the memory of Thierry in London and May in Bournemouth, blank out what she can't understand, and play the recluse in a cottage in the middle of nowhere. She's chosen Bené to help and abet her. He's no problem, just a bit silly sometimes, but Pascal's got a reputation. He's a charming bastard who leads people a merry dance, so it's a potent cocktail. She won't listen to me at the moment. I can see what may happen, but don't know how to prevent it.'

'Suppose for once you don't do anything, but stay friends, and then when she needs you, you'll be there, just as she was for you. It isn't in your nature, but you'll have to be circumspect for the time being,' Claude advised as they walked home along the shore, at peace with each other.

Erin thought Sébastien looked awkward, but she could not go over to him without drawing attention to the situation. They were inside at Chez-Madeleine, at a long table in front of the picture windows, which were partly open as the October night was mild. Madeleine had lit coloured fairy lights outside along the terrace. Two big yellow citronella candles burned on their table to ward off mosquitoes, making the air fragrant with the smell of lemons. It was the season insects came out of the forest to bite. The others did not seem to be aware of Sébastien in the corner, hardly contributing to the conversation which was becoming animated as more wine was imbibed. He looked sad each time Bené's voice and laughter became more raucous.

Martha was avoiding Erin's glances. They were quite a little gang, the three of them in the middle, Martha, Bené and Pascal, brought together by a common cause, excitedly discussing what the cottage would be like when renovated. They seemed to have forgotten the need for secrecy, but the restaurant was empty. Erin saw Madeleine put her hand on Sébastien's shoulder as she leaned forward to set down the coffees. Her staff of student waiters had left along with the summer and she attended to the tables herself now. A look was exchanged. Erin realised Madeleine had probably known Sébastien all his life. She would have been a grown woman while he was still a child in the village, before he went out into the world and returned with Bené. Erin thought she caught the look of sheer affection and concern on Madeleine's usually inscrutable face.

Erin was tired and ready to go home, but Madeleine offered everyone *un digestif* on the house, so she was stuck for a while longer. She eventually saw Martha get up and leave the table, but recognised Claude's look of don't follow her, and knew he was right. Now was not the time to try to tackle her. Erin assumed she had been to the loo, but when she returned she had settled the bill saying tonight was her treat. There was some half-hearted protest, but the deed was done and she was thanked. Someone suggested a walk around the village before they went their separate ways, and somehow Claude ended up with the gang of three, while Erin and Sébastien trailed behind.

'A merry evening for some.' Erin opened the conversation, to see if she could coax him out of his melancholy.

'But not for everyone, you mean,' he replied. 'It's true, I'm sorry, I've been a bit morose, haven't I? Bené will tell me off. He'll tell me to lighten up, when we get home.'

'He does keep everyone amused.'

'I'd be quite serious without him, you know. He tends to see the funny side of things. I don't mean he's frivolous or shallow, he just finds it difficult to be solemn. He doesn't worry. He can rely on me to do that for both of us. I don't think he appreciates how much I need him.'

'I'm sure he does, and I think it's mutual… Sébastien, I'm concerned about Martha,' Erin said. 'I don't think she understands what she's doing…'

'She does. The real question is does she understand why she's doing it? She's nothing to lose from buying the cottage and doing it up. I think she'd be better off, though, asking for a year's sabbatical, rather than resigning and making the move permanent, but it's her decision. I reckon she'll come through it…'

'Do you?'

'Yes, she's sensible, if a little vulnerable at the moment. To be truthful, I'm more worried about Bené, but then I would be, wouldn't I? We used to talk about everything, but he seems to confide in Martha now. I don't mind them playing games, playing house, together, I just hope he doesn't lead her astray. Pascal for instance. I can't imagine why he's gone and introduced her to Pascal. Bené's crazy sometimes. He says she needs an architect. Okay, but I know Pascal and his sort. Well, I don't really know him, and don't want to, but I've heard rumours. He may try to fleece her, and seduce her. He's not even Bené's true friend, he's just toying with him for his own benefit.'

'And you can't say these things to Bené, just like I can't talk to Martha at the moment. They'd both think we were… what, jealous? Over-dramatic? I don't know, but we'd be saying things they don't want to hear.'

'Until it's too late. That's the danger.'

'What are you two conspirators talking about?' The voice came out of the dankness. There was a torchlight beam and Bené's shape appeared, having turned back and broken away from the group in front. 'Secret whispers. Can I join in?' he laughed.

They had reached the fork in the road where the others were waiting. Claude, Erin and Martha had to go one way, Sébastien and Bené the other. Erin wondered where Pascal had left his car, or more precisely, which way he wanted to go. Martha looked as if she would like to follow him. Bené was making patterns with his torch on the ground.

'I'll go with the boys to fetch my car,' Pascal said to the group in general. 'I'll be working on the plans and then I'll be in touch with you through Bené,' he added, moving closer to Martha, as if he were conveying more than talk about the cottage.

'Yes, I'm eager to see them,' she said.

'Come on, Martha, let's get you home. You've had far too much excitement for one day, and don't forget you've got a flight tomorrow.' Erin took her arm and began to manoeuvre her away. Voices in the dark said farewells as they went separate ways.

'It's all happening so quickly. I came to look, and it seems I've found what I was looking for, all in a couple of days.'

Even though she had her reservations about the cottage, Erin hoped that was all Martha was talking about.

Martha was lonely and unsettled back home. She found it difficult to sleep in the bed she had shared for so many years with Thierry. Each time she returned to the home that was now so quiet she felt the reality of his death hit harder and deeper. She was lost and looked forward to the next day when she could go to work and loose herself, but work did not satisfy her as it once had.

She was uncertain she had made the right decision to buy the cottage at Cachette and spend so much renovating it. It had all fitted together while she had been out in St Cyprien. Now in her house of memories she was reluctant to make the final commitment to change the direction of her life. She was tired and lacked the strength and purpose required.

She knew how the world saw her, smooth and polished on the outside. People rarely contradicted her. She was articulate and intelligent. She moved with grace. She had seen herself on training videos at work and been pleased. She had cultivated a style and made it her own. Now she saw her image imprisoned her. Facing the rest of her life on her own, she felt the surface could break at any time, like thin ice in winter. Colleagues relied on her. She had a powerful presence at work which she was going to throw up in the air in defiance of those who needed her to remain the same; reliable, dependable, calm — she had heard all the descriptions.

She imagined her skin cracking open, like a china doll exploding. She would emerge a person of blood and bone, with emotions and feelings. They would not like it, would find it uncomfortable, but oh, it would be such a relief. She slept. The night was no time to make decisions.

Martin looked ill at ease behind his desk next morning. Martha reflected he frequently looked like this when she called to see him. She tried not to boss him because he was her boss after all, but it was too easy, and his desire to run a steady ship as he called it was often at odds with her determination to improve the quality of service and do things differently. She was basically kind and if her ideas were successful, she was happy for him to take some of the credit.

He worried when she appeared with that decisive look on her face, as she had just done now. He was alarmed by what she might be about to propose.

'Martin, don't be concerned, this isn't about the department, it's about me this time,' she began, and he relaxed for a second, and then saw this could be even more disturbing. He had given her extended leave when her husband died. Since she had returned to work, she was both energetically busy and less predictable, and he had considered reminding her of the counselling services they could buy in when employees had personal problems. She had referred a number of her own staff to People Matter over the years, but would not dream of seeking help for herself unless directed.

'Martha!' he started and then had to hunt among the mementos on his desk for inspiration to continue. 'How are you now, Martha?' he said with meaning, absentmindedly playing with a model ship he had picked up.

'Fine, well as fine as I can be in the circumstances, but having a lot to do suits me at the moment... Martin, I've come to ask a favour. I've quite a lot of business to attend to in France. It might be best if I booked some Fridays and possibly Mondays off so I could fly over every few weeks to attend to it. Nobody's taking leave in October and November, so it's a good time for me to use up some of mine.'

She stopped. She had decided in advance this was the best way to introduce the subject. The excuse was suitably vague and not untrue, and she knew he would not have the courage to enquire about her business. For his part he was surprised when she came to a halt. He had expected a bigger issue, and knowing her husband had been French, did not think it strange she might have things to sort out over there.

'That shouldn't be a problem. I don't suppose any of the troops will be taking leave at the moment. Let Fran have the dates and agree a rota of managers to stand in for you.' He looked suitably relieved, perhaps reassured equilibrium would be restored.

'Yes, of course, good idea,' Martha said, not letting on she had already done this. 'By the way, we've got an interesting short-list of candidates to run the family intervention project. I'll be glad to hand it over now it's up and running,'

'Oh, good.' She was taking care of another problem for him. It had been astute of her to bring this project, which she had long wanted to establish, forward for funding at just the right moment in the political climate. He could see Whitehall being impatiently interested in the early results. It was disconcerting that she evidently did not intend to take direct line management responsibility for it, but if she found someone competent to do it for her that would be a relief to him. It occurred to him she had begun to distribute her power whereas most managers were anxious to amass and consolidate their hold over whatever they could. It was only after she had presented him with a bottle of Medoc from her recent trip and left him in peace that he remembered he should have raised the subject of bereavement counselling.

'Never mind. If it's not broken, don't mend it,' he said to himself.

It was Pascal behind the plate glass screen at Merignac Airport this time. She had to wait for the carousel to come round, having taken Erin's advice to bring things to leave in Saint-Cyprien. She was not prepared for the hug and kiss he gave her as she emerged from customs. With Bené it seemed so natural, so innocent. This was different and she drew back a little.

'It's lovely to see you, but where's Bené? He promised he would come to meet me.'

'I had to come in the direction of the airport, so I told him I would collect you,' he replied, smiling his confident smile, and she did not quite believe him, though it was pointless to protest. He took her case and led the way to his black Audi in the car park. The sky was grey and it was busy on the Rocade before they turned off northwards. It was a relief to get onto the green tree lined country road. They all looked much the same with pines or vineyards at either side, looking drab and depressed. She thought autumn was an uninspiring season in Gironde. The vines had been robbed of their summer fruit and the evergreens had a tired grey-green dusty hue in contrast to southern England with its splendid trees of orange and burnished gold.

She did not recognise the occasional usual landmarks, and asked, 'A different route?'

'The country way.'

She thought the usual road was the country way, but by comparison this was even more rural, and once they took a corner through a working farmyard which straddled the road.

'I trust we are going to Saint-Cyprien?'

'Of course. I came this way because there's something I want to show you.'

They were quiet for a while. He was a fast and expert driver. She thought of Erin who was invariably in the wrong gear, talking while driving, in the Renault full of family litter. Pascal was perfect; his hair, his clothes, his scent, his driving and his car which smelt new. But for some unaccountable reason she was wary of him.

'It's down here,' he said, turning off onto a track, and driving up to the front of a sprawling building, originally two or three cottages, made into one house, old stone scrubbed blond and shutters in violet, plants around the door, an idyllic sight.

'Your work?' she asked.

'Of course,' he said again. 'Have I got the right idea for Cachette?'

'Yes, but—'

'But this is a bit too pretty, yes? You envisage something more rugged, wilder.'

'I suppose I do.'

'I haven't made an appointment, so we can't stop and see inside,' he began and she had a moment's anxiety he had nothing to do with this house, but just then the door opened and a plump, short woman in a kaftan billowed towards them.

'Pascal, Pascal, I heard a car and saw it was you.'

Pascal kissed her on both cheeks.

'I wanted to show my work to this lady. I didn't imagine you would be in, Clara, but as you are, can I be really cheeky and give her a tour?'

It was clear Pascal could be as cheeky as he liked with Clara. He introduced Martha, but was careful not to mention Cachette. Martha could imagine word would quickly get around that an Englishwoman was interested in buying it.

Clara's house was light and airy, which Martha liked, but cluttered with fussy furniture, particularly ornate chairs and ornaments, which were not to her taste. Although pressed to have a coffee or a glass of wine, Pascal disappointed Clara by saying they had a schedule to keep.

'You youngsters are always in too much of a hurry,' Clara scolded him, affectionately brushing imaginary fluff off his collar. He did not object to her pawing him.

Back in the car he asked for her opinion.

'I like the simplicity of your design, but she has spoiled it with too many bits and bobs.'

'So is your style minimalist?'

'No, I can't say that, but restrained at least. I don't consider Cachette as just an exercise in style. I'm thinking of it as restoration,' she told him. She was aware the word project was one she used frequently and decided to find a better replacement. Restoration was only partially accurate because the house would not be the same as the farm it had once been. But restoration was the best word she could find. She wondered why she had doubted Pascal had designed Clara's house. Who had planted the seeds of mistrust in her mind? Was it Erin, or did it come from somewhere inside herself?

He delivered her safely to Saint-Cyprien. Claude and Erin were both at work and the children at school. She knew where the spare key was hidden and let them in. She made coffee for him and tea for herself while he unrolled several large drawings of thick white paper onto the dining table. They were his architect's drawings of the cottage from various elevations and angles, some as it was now, others as options for the future. The meticulous to-scale line drawings had a computer-generated look, right down to the cut away sections and the stylised trees and plants. He had given her a carved wooden staircase with an elongated window behind, a conservatory, or veranda as he called it, and had raised the floor level in the stable to be the same height as the rest of the downstairs. The kitchen had skylights supplementing the natural light from the small windows. Upstairs he had put bold new windows at each end of the house, thereby avoiding the need to cut into the beams to make dormers which would have looked wrong. It had the clean lines Martha wanted. Pascal was a good reader of character. Martha was entranced.

Ethan and Lucy returned from school. Ethan was excited by the drawings and asked Pascal loads of questions. Pascal gave him some paper for his own ideas. He certainly had a way with him and could even charm children.

Claude was not so easily brought round when he and Erin returned from work. It all looked expensive. Pascal talked about the local materials they would source and knew a sympathetic builder. Talking across Pascal, Claude suggested to Martha she might want to approach two or three local firms to see how they priced it and how they would tackle certain features. Erin agreed and the conversation around the table became strained. It was clear to Martha they thought Pascal had it all stitched up, but Pascal, adept at diffusion, said they could not approach anybody until the purchase had been agreed with documents and signatures exchanged at the notaries' office. It sounded as if he were taking charge, but Martha had to admit that was what she had asked him to do.

Erin asked Pascal to stay to supper as a peace offering. She said the cottage could be made lovely, but she still wished it was not so isolated.

'Someone said buy the view not the building,' Martha said. 'You can alter a building, but not where it's situated, and I like Cachette as much for where it is as for the cottage.'

'We've played out there sometimes,' Ethan said, 'and spooked ourselves by pretending it's haunted.'

'Don't be silly. It's just remote, but it won't seem so when Aunt Martha lives there.'

'Yes, and I want you both to come and see me often,' Martha said to the children.

'Lucy, Ethan, remember you mustn't say a word about this to anyone until it's signed and sealed. You understand?' Erin warned them.

They settled down to eating together, and despite conflicts and differences there was a general air of excitement in the household that evening. For better or worse, something was taking shape.

The purchase went through, and Martha received a registered letter to say she owned Le Mas de l'Ouest in Cachette. She was interested it had a name, and it confirmed it must have been a small farmhouse once. She understood the actual deeds would pass through a number of government departments before she received them. She had opened a local bank account and written her first cheque for the deposit. The purchase price was negotiated by Bené and she paid it by banker's draft. Pascal had tried to persuade her to pay a smaller amount officially, supplemented by cash which he would pass to the vendors to avoid tax, but she refused to do this. He assured her it was common practice. She was, however, grateful to him for going through all the documents, providing a full translation of the main ones, and making sure she understood the rest.

Her second cheque had been to Bené for his immobilier fee, and the third to Pascal for his plans which had been passed by the Mairie. Erin had accompanied her to the bank to organise prélèvements or direct debits for insurance and utility services which had, amazingly, been reconnected.

She now recognised two distinct halves to her life. In England she still had a job and the large house she had shared with Thierry. In France she was making a new life.

There was no overlap, in fact there was a disjunction, a chasm between the two. The tension had initially been stimulating, but was now troubling her deeply, and she knew she would have to stop hanging onto the old, the familiar as if it were a child's comforter.

As a first step she contacted Rajinder and invited him and Priya to dinner on a Saturday when she would not be in France and they could get a babysitter.

Priya arrived with an arrangement of golden autumn flowers and foliage, and Martha was reminded of the time Rajinder called after Thierry's death, with summer flowers of pale pink and blue which Priya had chosen for him to bring. She showed Priya a selection of vases and asked her to choose one and arrange them for her, and asked Rajinder to mix drinks while she completed preparing the meal.

When they sat down with their aperitifs, she asked about them and their children, who were reportedly fine. When they asked her in return she broke the news about the house she had bought on the coast north of Bordeaux, and how she planned to move there. She had intended to work up to this rather than tell them at the start of the evening. They were not expecting this and voiced concern she was making such a big decision so soon. Martha appreciated their misgivings, but said she had considered it long and hard and wanted a fresh start, but also wanted to keep in touch with them, which was why she had decided to inform them first, before anyone else. She wanted to remain friends. Inevitably, Thierry was mentioned as their connection, which gave Martha the opportunity to say Rajinder was also important as her London link with Thierry, and if ever anything came to light about that fateful day he might know first. It remained a vague but important avenue of hope.

'I don't know what I want to hear. It may not be what I want to hear, it may be something I find difficult to accept, but I still need to know.'

'In that case, I promise you will.'

Martha wondered, not for the first time, how such a gentle man had survived and prospered in the bear pit Benton and Powell was considered to be.

They continued to show surprise and disquiet about her plan to uproot, but also acknowledged Martha deserved a fresh start if that is what she had decided.

'I was going to say we'll come over when you are settled and visit, but you won't want all our brood,' Priya laughed, and Martha told her she would have plenty of room.

'There will be two large bedrooms with wet rooms in the attic, and I mean large. I can sleep downstairs when you come, so I'll hold you to it.'

Rajinder wondered if she would be wiser trading in her job for a part time role, rather than severing all her professional links.

'I can't parcel myself up in that way, Rajinder. It's becoming too much of a strain. I need to go and see what I can make of it.'

'Yes, Martha has the chance of an adventure now, Raj!' Priya said.

'But don't burn all your boats,' Rajinder advised, ever the cautious accountant. 'Rent your house rather than sell it, just in case you want to come back—'

'No, I—'

'Well then, sell it if you want to remember it as it is, and buy a flat or something easy to rent out. I will put you in touch with people who can advise you. You may regret it later if you don't keep a bolt-hole back here.'

She took two days off in late November to fly out and go through estimates and choose builders, carpenters and plumbers. She went to see Pascal at his flat and they sat together at his kitchen table going through the papers. She was being assertive following Claude's advice to ask for a selection of potential contractors so he had provided some. She realised she was dependent on him if he were to project manage the venture for her. He suggested a firm as the main contractor who were not the cheapest but who, he claimed, had a good reputation.

'Does Bené know them?' she asked.

'I guess so. They did some work on apartments he sold. Why?'

'It's just comforting to have recommendations.'

'And my word isn't good enough? You need a second opinion?' He sounded hurt and maybe stubborn as well.

'I'm sorry. It's just that—'

'Martha, I've got to tell you something. I've felt your resistance from the moment I met you, from that very first afternoon when you stood your ground at the top of the steps outside the front door and held out your hand like a duchess.'

She was mortified. She did not know how to respond, because she recognised a nub of truth in it, but he was continuing.

'Then you asked me if I was interested in helping you. Why do you always have to hold me at arm's length? Why doesn't Erin like me?'

The last question stopped her in her tracks. Erin had warned her about Pascal.

'I don't know, Pascal, it's a funny time for me... as a new widow.' She had never used the word before, never acknowledged the fact. She did not know how much she should say to him. How close had she and Thierry been at the end? How did that uncertainty relate to her reluctance to engage with Pascal? She wanted to be true to Thierry, she did not want to be disloyal. Was she entirely sure what she was embarking on? Why did she feel this personal pressure from Pascal? She could say, "Pascal, we have a business relationship, nothing else." She knew she should say it, but had not done so.

He was not yet thirty, young and beautiful, and their legs were touching, sitting side by side. They were both tense, and yet she thought it was more romantic than anything had been with Thierry for a long while. Her sane mind told her it was wrong. She was normally able to take the initiative, to say what she wanted and how she felt. She was normally able to say "no". She had approached a barrier she was not ready to cross. She looked at her fingers holding estimates she did not completely understand, and said, 'I want to be friends, but just friends... working together.'

His voice became softer.

'Martha, I can grasp, more than you appreciate, that you are vulnerable at this moment. No, don't shy away because I used the word vulnerable. You may not want it to be true, but it is. I want to get this house right, and not only because it's what I enjoy, and each job I undertake is a professional challenge. I want to get it right for you. This is the one I have to get right. It's become personal. So, yes, let's be friends. Now, let's have some coffee and finish off these devis, and then go out to eat. I'll take you somewhere that you haven't been before, not Chez-Madeleine, where all your friends hang out.' He smiled now, his self-confidence restored after the awkwardness of the moment.

'I've made arrangements to meet Sébastien and Bené there tonight. Claude and Erin want an evening in, so I planned to leave them to it and go out.'

'Leave them all to it and come out with me. You're a grown woman, you can make your own decisions.'

'I'm a grown woman and may I remind you I'm more than ten years older than you are, mister.'

'Then you had better take charge of me as well.' He smiled into her eyes.

She phoned Sébastien and said she could not join them tonight, but would see them on her next visit. He sounded genuinely disappointed and she experienced a stab of guilt. She did not say what she was doing, and said nothing to Erin, leaving her assuming she was going to Chez-Madeleine.

The restaurant he drove her to, Le Caneton Sauvage, was deep in the countryside, one she would never have found on her own, nor retrace her steps back to should she wish to visit again. It looked like a barn in a field, which it probably had been, and it was basic inside. The patronne was another lady who knew Pascal well. Perhaps he brought other clients here. She showed them to a panelled alcove through an archway where there was a table set for two. There were a couple of large family groups in the big room, but their sound was muffled by heavy drapes. A set of tall wine racks provided a room divider and extra privacy.

The menu looked delicious if you liked duck, which Martha fortunately did, as all the main courses were variations of duck, confit, salads and magret. He explained it had originally been a duck farm.

Alcohol had been chosen to accompany each course, from aperitifs to digestifs with various local wines in between.

'You'd better take care as you're driving.'

'I know all the back roads the police don't patrol,' he replied, 'but I'll behave and keep safe for your sake.'

The farmhouse cooking was excellent. She tried to find out more about him, without overtly doing so. Most men, in her experience, were happy, given the chance, to talk about themselves if encouraged. He appeared to tell her a lot, but on reflection told her very little of substance. She tried to set out the ground rules for their relationship, but the smile in his eyes made her aware she had broken the rules by coming out with him in this clandestine way, and he knew it.

'I'd like to come and see you in England when next I'm over. I've several business contacts there.'

No, she thought, *I must confine Pascal to the French part of my life. He mustn't stray across.*

'I don't think it would be appropriate at the moment,' she said, swallowing a mouthful of wine too quickly, attempting to re-erect the barrier he was dismantling. She inadvertently left it open for him to ask when it would be appropriate.

He turned up in Chislehurst a week later, unannounced. She had not long got home from work on the Friday when she heard the distinctive crunch of a car on the gravel. She was not expecting anyone, and most regular visitors such as Fran or Rajinder parked out in the road rather than on the drive.

'I got the right house then,' he exclaimed when she opened the door.

'It's a hire car,' he added, gesturing towards the Fiesta. 'I flew over on business.'

'Are you just passing through on your way to an appointment at this time on a Friday evening?' she asked, but his eyes smiled, confirming this was his destination.

'Business is all done.'

She had no choice but invite him in.

'Where are you staying?'

'Here, if I may.'

'I'm not sure that's a good idea. I'm not ready for this, Pascal.'

'I think you are.'

He shut the door behind him. They were in the hall. She was about to take him through into the drawing room for a drink when the doorbell sounded, causing them both to jump in their excited, nervous state. As he was nearer, Pascal opened it to a young man, less than twenty, who Martha thought looked familiar, but whom she could not place. He had thick brown hair, and kept flicking the fringe out of his eyes. He looked down rather than directly at her. He had a parcel and an electronic gadget attached to his belt, evidently a courier.

'Can you sign for this please?' he asked, looking shyly from one to the other, perhaps to clarify whose house it was, and then at the parcel.

'What is it?' Martha asked.

'Um, coffee, I suppose. It says The London Coffee Company. Was it an online order?'

'I don't remember ordering anything online recently.'

'This is Broomscroft, number 30?' he asked, apparently unable to look at her directly.

'Yes,' she said, thinking it must be a present and wondering who may have sent it. She had better accept it to find out. She took the stylus he offered attached to the electronic clipboard and then saw the recipient's name was Evans.

'Oh, no, this isn't for me, my name is Jolivet.'

She noticed Pascal shot her a quick warning glance. Pascal's tense blocking body language told her he did not welcome the boy's presence.

'Oh,' the young man hesitated. 'This isn't the right house then?'

'It's my address, but it's not for me. Obviously some mistake.'

'Is there a family called Evans at another house in the street?'

'Not to my knowledge. The address and postcode are mine, it's correct, but it isn't for me.'

'Try elsewhere,' Pascal said, shooing the boy towards the door.

'I'm sorry to have bothered you. I'll have to check. I should have a phone number. Yes, sorry…' He seemed agitated and glanced from Pascal to Martha, as if on the verge of saying something else, but then turned and crossed the threshold of the door Pascal had opened for him, and hurried off down the drive with his parcel.

'You shouldn't have told him your name,' Pascal said as he shut the door.

'He's just a boy. He looked harmless. You frightened him. It's strange though. At first, I thought I knew him, but I must have been wrong. Come in and I'll fix us something to eat. You can tell me why you're here and how long you're staying.'

The incident had broken the ice and brought them together, but everything was going too fast for her. She understood she had begun to give in to him, and tried to slow things down. She showed him up to the main guest bedroom. For her, this was still Thierry's house as well as hers. Thierry stood in every corner, sat in every seat, and still inhabited her bed with her until she woke and found she was alone.

Most of her meals were meals for one these days. She was not finding it easy adjusting to cooking and eating on her own, and frequently bought too much. She found she had plenty of pasta, and made a sauce of shallots, bacon, tomatoes, olive oil, garlic, herbs and cheese. He had brought a good Bordeaux, 'To remind you of your new home,' he said, so she asked him to open it to breathe. He mixed the gin and tonics, and she gave him some English elderflower cordial to add to them, and they drank while she cooked, laughing through the steam from the pasta pan. She was happy to have someone in the house, someone to cook for. She quizzed him about the English side of his business, and his answers sounded genuine. They were both aware without mentioning it that she was still testing him out.

That night she slept fitfully, disturbed by his disquieting presence in her house. She thought she heard him moving about and went onto the landing. There was complete silence. He had not got up, but had left his door ajar. She leaned against the doorpost, looked in and watched his face in repose on the pillow in the moonlight. He was breathing gently, and she thought he was sound asleep. After a moment she moved to go, but he was not asleep. He opened his eyes, smiled and pulled back the duvet. His smile broadened and he said, 'Come here, Martha.'

3

At the turn of the year

Pascal was at the airport waiting for her plane once more. He had taken his position in the Arrivals Hall where he could be seen to advantage. He was thinking about Martha, particularly in relation to himself.

I like the fact she's classy, Martha, the "English lady", as the locals refer to her. She leaves a lingering smell of expensive scent wherever she's been. I'd be interested to hear what they call me. Lots of things. Some rude. I don't mind as long as I'm talked about. Hopefully I'm an enigma. But cool, classy Martha. They don't know how hot she can be.

'Je m'appelle Martha Jolivet,' she said to me, holding out her hand like royalty. Cool, but she wasn't as in control as she thought she was. I know she's lonely, and I've taken advantage of that, but I do find her fragility attractive. There's something very chic being a young man, having an older woman as my lover.

What did she think of me when we met? I knew she'd fancy me secretly, because all ladies do, especially those of a certain age, which Martha is approaching. She wasn't immune to my charm, or my body, I could sense that straight away, despite her alluring and challenging "don't touch" defence. She was on guard from the start.

I brought out her maternal instinct too, because I'm young. I mean! When I went to switch on the electricity at the cottage, and she stopped me. She pulled my hand away from the lever. Then she dropped it as if it was a red hot, burning rod. And she said, 'I didn't want you to injure yourself.' Come on!

I could see she liked what she saw when I bounded up the steps to the front door, but I'm not sure she liked me. We didn't get off to a good start. I sensed she thought I was beneath her, a tradesman? That smarted. She said, 'Of course, if you don't want to help me...' My God, I fell for that one. 'Oh, yes, I do,' I pleaded. I should have kept her worrying. Instead, I came up with all those ideas for free. She'll need me if she's going to make them real. I know her sort. They think they run the world, but they don't have a clue about basic things, or prices. I've played my cards right and am indispensable.

I haven't had a problem controlling others. She's a challenge, but I'm winning, She's taken longer but I'm gaining control. The lady wants to be loved. And now she knows I'm good in bed as well. I took her to places her gentle husband didn't find.

She's playing cat and mouse about the commission to redesign the cottage. Keeps wanting to ask Claude's advice. I don't need his interference. She's never had to worry about money. People like Martha think things are better if they cost more. I don't want people to get the idea I'm taking advantage of her, but I might as well make what I can while I can.

We've only had the one night of intimacy so far. Let's hope she's not going to regret it, and pretend it didn't happen. I must keep it up, so to speak, while she gets used to it, finds she wants more and finds it hard to stop. She agreed it's important to keep our affair secret. I have to steer clear of Erin. Tell Martha not to confide in her. Erin's protective. Seems scatty and superficially Martha appears to be the stronger of the two. Really, it's not so simple, more the other way round at the moment with Martha's husband's mysterious death. I must create distance between Martha and Erin and Claude. Drop hints, nothing too obvious that she may react against, but enough to lessen her dependency on Erin. Then she won't take it seriously if Erin warns her against me. I'll let Martha think I've been misunderstood in Saint-Cyprien. She's conditioned to champion the underdog. It works every time.

Then there's Bené! So many people to keep happy! I don't want him jealous of my coupling with Martha. I need Bené to get other commissions, big ones. The chateau's the prize. I'll give Bené what he wants if he helps me secure it, give in and let him use my body. Big Sébastien doesn't like me being too friendly with his cute Bené. I've got to be careful of Sébastien too. Keep people apart.

I love this airport. Clean lines, cool colours. Lots of glass. Let's pretend I designed it. It's famous. I'm admired.

I created this beauty! Just look at the planes, how small they are in the sky. Incredible. Martha's on one of those. It's delayed. How boring. I can see myself reflected in the glass. Not bad. Jeans fit well. If I was gay I'd fancy myself.
   Come on! Where's her fucking plane?

In Gatwick Martha tried to read her novel while she watched the monitor, but found it impossible to concentrate. Noise reverberated all around, there was too much activity and she was frustrated by the lack of information about her flight. She liked knowing what was going on and making decisions. Here she felt insignificant. The departure board continued to flicker "flight BA 240 Delayed". Weekends were too short in the first place and she had not considered holdups.

An observer would have seen a handsome woman with well-cut, smooth, short dark hair, wearing a classic black dress, carrying a sensible jacket, confident and poised, unlike many of the passengers in shorts and flip-flops, and they would have no idea of the confused emotions struggling inside. She felt small and alone and was at that moment having difficulty holding everything together. She missed Thierry, but avoided talking to him in her mind now because Pascal, her secret lover came between them. Everything was moving too fast. What madness was she getting herself into?

She had agreed to the trip under pressure from Pascal. He had begged her to come out now because he had family commitments at Christmas She wanted to be with him, but another weekend trip to France had been difficult to fit in. She felt pressured from all sides, and yearned for support. The run up to Christmas was hectic at work, and as she was taking more time off at New Year, she had volunteered to help on the Christmas emergency rota to compensate. It was only when she heard Bené's voice on the phone she relented and agreed to come over. She was drawn by his laughter as he told her, in the simplest French he could find, they were holding a party on the Saturday night to celebrate moving into their house. She thought it strange she felt more support from Bené, whom she had neglected recently, than from Pascal. She did not know Pascal had persuaded Bené to phone her.

Martha fretted about finding the time to see her mother, guilty for postponing visiting so she could go and see her lover instead. After telling May in the summer that Thierry had died, she had asked the care staff to anticipate a delayed reaction. On her subsequent visit to Bournemouth, bearing paper, pens, envelopes and pencils, the old lady had asked her why she had not brought Terry, and had looked sad when Martha reminded her Thierry was dead. It was as if she held Martha responsible.

'Poor Terry. Of course,' May said, not to her, but to the photograph Martha had left on her table. She looked more gentle than usual. Martha believed May was fonder of Thierry than she was of her, and did not like herself for this stab of jealousy. It was not Thierry's fault.

'I liked Terry.'

'I know.'

'You were a professional carer, but he cared with his heart.'

Martha was riveted in her chair, feeling anger welling up. Erin had told her to give May a chance, and each time she saw her she meant to, and tried hard, but May always said or did something that aggravated Martha. She wanted to reject her mother's criticism, but could not because it was true. She still longed for her mother to love her unconditionally. She was an adult, but the child inside cried because she could not fathom why this had never, and would never, happen.

'Why…' Martha began, but the look on May's face did not encourage her to go on. She found it impossible to ask the questions that plagued her most. Why had Stan and May adopted her? Had this undemonstrative couple loved her, or loved each other, come to that? Was she responsible for it all going wrong?

Martha could not ask, so resorted to small talk, stepping daintily around May's feeling, and left hoping she had not upset the old lady.

She contemplated, waiting for her plane, and acknowledged this minefield was the root of her insecurity, insecurity she was expert at concealing. It was why she held back, protecting herself from feeling too much.

She resolved to go next week and take May a present, maybe take some old photographs, to help the stilted conversation and shed some light on their history. Perhaps the past would be more accessible than the present.

She could no longer put off a host of things. It was time to inform the Authority Board she was not applying for the joint chief executive position, hand in her three months' notice to the director, and begin clearing the decks, as Martin would call it when he got over the shock. She was realistic enough to know she was not indispensable, but her announcement would cause upset and some colleagues would think she was making a big mistake.

Would she be able to breathe more deeply and relax when she had tackled the tasks she was avoiding? At this moment she was impotent to do anything, stuck in Departures, wasting the precious weekend. She had already phoned Pascal to say she was delayed. It was Pascal who collected her from Merignac these days. Nobody commented, but it was noted, and assumptions were made which they had neither confirmed nor denied.

It had been another pre-dawn start, without breakfast, and Martha wondered if there was sufficient time to go upstairs in search of lunch, but just then the electronic display board flashed and seemed to go haywire. When the letters and figures settled down, it took her a moment to see BA 240 had a new departure time and an actual gate number. She grabbed her things and ran, deciding to phone Pascal when she got to the lounge. Once she got herself sorted, Martha found herself passively responding to what was required of her as a grateful passenger. She boarded, flopped in her seat and waited as the bored flight attendant dispensed sandwiches.

Pascal took her to his flat where they shed their clothes and went to bed for an hour. She did not resist. She needed it as much as he did. This was her new secret escape to Saint-Cyprien. It was still new enough to be illicitly exciting. The sheets were uncomfortably rucked up under her nakedness as he lay between her legs and entered her. She stroked his smooth young shoulders and back and wondered why she deserved this pleasure. She would pay for it later. Six months in her life had changed everything. She refused to consider what anyone would think if they knew. She banished images of those who might disapprove and surrendered to the moment, wrapping her legs tightly round him to hold him, trying to lose herself in the moment. As he rested afterwards, becoming heavier and sticky, she gently moved him off and straightened the sheet. She understood this was not forever, it was just an interlude, and he would surely leave her and move on to a girl his own age. The sadness of this certainty made the pain and the pleasure more exquisite, and she cradled his damp hair and held him closer.

Eventually she manoeuvred him aside, got up, showered, dressed and repaired her make-up. Travelling without luggage, she was wearing the black dress she had brought for the party. She would accessorise it for the evening with earrings and a big necklace. Her agitation had disappeared in bed, but it returned, making her edgy. She went back into the bedroom and saw he was smiling in his real or pretend sleep. She spoke his name and brushed his smooth cheek to wake him. Maybe he was playing the sleeping prince. She needed him to take her to the village and drop her at Erin and Claude's as if none of this had happened. She went in to the kitchen to fix some coffee, and he followed her, still naked, and poured them each a glass of wine instead. They were new as a couple, if that is what they were, so she was unfamiliar with his moods, and could not tell whether he was serious or playing.

'You must get dressed,' she said, tempted to smack him as she might a wayward boy, but fearing this would only rouse him more. He was stronger than she was, and she did not want to start it again. 'If we go now, I can just about get away with saying I'm late because the plane was delayed.'

'You don't want them to know we've been naughty,' he said as he walked round picking up bread and cheese, over-stuffing them in his mouth as he drank. She was not sure if this was a game or an accusation, so she remained silent.

'You should just let them know you're staying with me,' he said as he carefully, but boldly, moved her towards the kitchen table and hoisted her up onto it.

'No, Pascal,' she said as he stood between her legs trying to lift her dress while she held it down. He was aroused again. They were both laughing, but this was no joke. 'We agreed on secrecy.'

'You go to your friends and deny me,' he started and she decided not to interrupt as she could not read his mood. 'You go to your friends' party, and what am I when I arrive, your lover or just another guest?'

'They're your friends too.'

'Bené perhaps. The rest don't like me.'

Just as she felt at her most defenceless, fearing he might try to take her against her will, he seemed to lose interest, and without further conversation went to fetch his clothes. She did not like or understand his erratic behaviour, and was sad she had disappointed him. He drove her silently to the village, dropping her off outside the house.

'See you tonight,' he said aggressively before driving off in a cloud of dust. She had not meant to upset him.

Martha went in, intending to tell Erin about the plane's delay but not about anything else.

'Why doesn't Pascal come in?' Erin enquired, though Martha doubted Erin really wanted to see him.

'He has clients to visit and said he would leave me to my friends, so I'm all yours. He may put in an appearance at the party. I must meet him for a final site visit at Cachette tomorrow, and then find out when the builders can start.' She was babbling too much.

'Don't forget Claude's taking you back to Merignac at four tomorrow afternoon, when he goes to see his brother. Honestly, this is such a lightning visit. You normally have one complete day.'

'I'll be here for four days at New Year, if you'll have me.'

'Of course we will.' The sharpness Martha detected in Erin's voice had gone and she sounded tender again.

'Oh, by the way, I brought presents for Lucy and Ethan. I'd like you to hide them until Christmas.'

'Lovely. Come upstairs while they're not around, and we'll secrete them away. It's a shame you won't be here at Christmas. Niall was hoping to see you.'

It was almost like old times, but there were things unsaid, issues avoided. Martha was trying too hard.

'I like the dress, by the way,' Erin said after she had put the packages under a pile of shirts in Claude's wardrobe. 'This is somewhere they definitely won't look. Lucy may go through my things when I'm out, but neither of them will venture in here.' She closed the door and went over to her closet. 'I know we're taking the car, but you may get cold, and I'm not even sure how warm the house will be. The system hasn't had the benefit of summer to stock up its energy levels or however it works. You may want to wear this on top.'

She took out a white bolero jacket knitted in angora wool.

'It's so elegant!' Martha could not disguise her surprise.

'Yes, it is, isn't it? It's not me. I persuaded Claude to buy it for me when we spent a weekend in Paris last year.

158

I told him I liked it because it's the sort of thing you look good in, and I wanted to copy your style. Silly really. We went out to dinner, and I was very self-conscious. I've never worn it since. Have it.'

'I'll borrow it for this evening.'

'You are staying here then? I thought maybe you'd go back with Pascal.' When Martha said nothing, Erin continued, 'Please be careful, Martha.'

'I will stay here, if I may. I'll feel safer... Sorry, I don't know why I said that.'

'What's going on, Martha?' She took both of her hands in hers.

'I'm not sure. It's unexpected and wonderful and yet... well, sometimes I feel under his control. He's helped me. He teases me for being so serious. I've been so task-driven, even over dealing with Thierry's death, and he persuades me to lighten up and have some fun. Don't be shocked. Perhaps there's no harm in it. He's so young and—'

'And forceful,' Erin interjected.

'Yes, forceful is the right word. And moody.'

'Martha, with all your education, you must know much more than me about power in relationships. Aren't you concerned you're being manipulated? I don't want to sound alarmist, and being shocked has nothing to do with it. I just don't want to see you hurt...'

'I can look after myself,' Martha told her, but it sounded like a question.

'Well, I've said my piece. Now try this on.' Erin held out the jacket.

It was as if Chez-Madeleine had been transferred to the eco-house for the evening. Very few diners were expected at the restaurant on a cold Saturday before Christmas, so Madeleine had absented herself. Those invited to the party from the village had been drawn by curiosity. Madeleine had left the cook and one waiter behind, but not before they had prepared the party food and transferred it to Sébastien's kitchen. Hot food was keeping warm in the oven, canapés were being handed round on trays by Lucy and Ethan, lured by the promise of extra pocket money, desserts were in the fridge, and Madeleine had cajoled Philippe into acting as sommelier and bar man.

The finished house was all wood towards the lane, and glass towards the fields. It was blazing with light this evening. Blond wood and white walls shimmered inside. It smelled not only new but natural too as if the countryside had come indoors. Sébastien and Bené were showing guests around upstairs, but anyone who did not know would have mistaken Madeleine as hostess for the evening. Alarmingly made-up and dressed colourfully from head to foot, she towered over guests downstairs who she bullied into introductions and talking to each other.

Martha remembered the hippy builder, Joël, who was in his usual ethnic style, but cleaner and brighter. He looked uncomfortable among the bourgeoisie of Saint-

Cyprien. Martha recognised a kindred spirit and went to talk to him.

'So, it's finished. You must feel proud…' she began.

A girl appeared and joined them. She also carried that sweet smell Martha associated with cannabis. Martha assumed this was his girlfriend. Joël told Martha it was time for them to move on now this project was more or less completed.

She wished them luck, and meant it, and stood on the edge of a group of villagers, trying to get a sense of their conversation. There was gossip about the chateau at Saint-Aubin having been bought by an Englishman. She could follow it well enough to understand people were incredulous anyone would want to sink that amount of capital into its restoration.

'Only the English! They like ruins,' the mayor's wife laughed. She looked younger than her husband, whom Sébastien had pointed out. Martha wondered what they really thought of her, not that it bothered her.

When Bené was free, she asked him about the chateau.

'Yes, my dear, you aren't the only English person buying an old property to fulfil their dreams. This man, from a place with the strange name of Powys, has picked it up for a song, but it needs masses of work doing to it. He wants to have his own vineyard. Since the war it's lost most of the land it once had, so I don't know how he's going to do that.'

'Powys is in Wales.'

'It's all the same to us. You're all the English and we love you for your money.'

'Maybe not for long the way it's going. Did the sale go through your company?'

'It's not my company. I only work there. But I wined and dined him, and got him hooked, and rehearsed how he should persuade his wife who was not so keen, so I should get good commission.'

'I'm sure you were very persuasive.'

'Now Pascal chats me up, because he would love to get a contract for restoration work. He wants an introduction to Mr Evans, but I'm holding out.'

There was something about the name which startled Martha. She realised it was just a silly coincidence about a common name, but wondered why the delivery boy's nice but puzzled face had flitted across her mind. She dismissed him and concentrated on her conversation with Bené.

'Why are you holding out on Pascal?'

'It's a game between us, like chess, but with teasing,' he giggled.

'Who's teasing who?'

'I'm not sure. Yes, you've got a point there.'

Pascal joined the party soon afterwards. Martha noticed he was like a kindred spirit with Philippe, and was given a glass from a bottle Philippe produced from behind the bar and put back again. It had a different label from the ones he was serving to other guests.

'What are you drinking?' she asked as he sidled up to her.

'Try,' he said, offering his glass, and she took a taste of wine far smoother and richer than the one in her glass, which, until then, she had regarded as good. The taste did not disappear on swallowing, but lingered.

'I must talk to Bené,' he said, leaving her with his glass.

'About the chateau at St Aubin?' she asked.

'My God, you've got your ear to the ground. Hush, I don't want people to know of my interest.'

'So many secrets. I can keep one more.'

She watched him glide away, smiling effortlessly, conquering people with the occasional word or gesture.

She stood around pretending she was enjoying herself. Madeleine descended on her and took her by the arm to introduce her to the mayor, a handsome man with steel grey hair, who spoke English. He had approved the plans for the eco-house, and thought it would put Saint-Cyprien on the map, though Martha was unsure Sébastien wanted the publicity the mayor thought it deserved. He let her know he had also been responsible for passing Pascal's less controversial plans for restoring the old mas at Cachette, but seemed mystified why she wanted to live out there.

'Yes, its wildness attracts me. I've never had the opportunity to live anywhere like it before.'

'Excuse me, have you seen Bené? I've been looking everywhere.' Sébastien interrupted with an apology to the mayor.

'There he is, coming back in from the garden,' the mayor said.

Sébastien went over and took his partner's hand to pull him into the room, and said, 'I've been searching for you. Madeleine's going to call order. She says we must make a speech together.'

He propelled Bené forward, and they stood on the curving staircase which now connected the main room to the mezzanine floor where Joël had propped the ladder for her back in the summer. Madeleine clapped her hands and hushed the crowd. Sébastien thanked them all for coming and said he and Bené hoped to see them all as frequent visitors, at which point Bené raised his eyebrows quizzically. He thanked Joël and others who had helped them make the house a reality.

Whilst they were talking, Martha spotted Pascal slipping in from outside. He disappeared into the bathroom before coming to join her. By this time the mayor had taken centre stage and was thanking the boys, as he called them, for inviting everyone to see their house. Madeleine was agitatedly searching for someone to take over the bar as Philippe had abandoned it.

Erin decided to take the children home, so Martha said she would accompany her. The experience of speaking French most of the evening had been good for her, but had proved tiring. She thought Pascal would look hurt and object to her going, but he obviously had other things on his mind. He unexpectedly smiled, kissed her on the cheek, and agreed a time for their rendezvous tomorrow.

'Why did you take Bené outside at the party?'

'Oh, do I spy the green-eyed monster?'

'No, seriously. Don't be evasive.'

They were at Cachette the following day. They were tense, mainly caused by differences about money; how and when to pay for things. She caught him off guard, changing tack and questioning him about last night.

It had been necessary to revise some of the plans after a visit by a man she assumed to be the equivalent of a building inspector. She agreed the proposed modifications to the drainage and the siting of the sceptic tank. Pascal had overlooked them, and she could see the additional work might as well be undertaken now as it would have to be done at some stage. She also saw the sense of removing the stone flags in the main room, digging out to give more headroom, which the man said was now the legal standard. Pascal liked the fact it would bring the floor down level with the stable, without raising the floor there, and they could run the same tiles throughout. The flagstones could be re-used outside. Martha was not surprised the costs continued to escalate, but deemed it prudent to put an overall cap on the budget, and said they must work within it. She had expressed concern when Pascal said the builder wanted a sizable sum of money up front.

'Is that normal?'

'Smaller builders without capital for materials often want thirty or forty percent in advance.'

'Really! I seem to remember when we had the extension built at home, Thierry negotiated to pay in instalments as work was completed. That appeared fair on all sides. I'd prefer an arrangement like that.'

'You may have to give me control of the money. We can transfer it by internet. There are new sites avoiding banks and charges'

'Pascal, I'm not happy about that. You've said before there are ways of saving costs, but I must to do it legally through my bank back home.'

'In my experience, some people like cash, and that works out better all round.'

'But if we do things that way I won't get receipts and guarantees.'

He was also irritated because he could not find what he called his lucky pen, one he said his mother had given him. He used it for all his business transactions. She lent him a ballpoint from her bag, knowing it was not the same, and he added up the bill with that.

In the end she agreed to provide him with a cash float of 10,000€ for sub-contractors, which she considered a lot, but stalled him on any bigger sum. She needed time to take advice and consider options.

To change the subject, she had broached the question that had been on her mind since she saw him yesterday evening coming in from outside and going straight to the bathroom, and asked him why he had taken Bené outside when Sébastien had been looking for him. 'Was it just to discuss the chateau?'

'I didn't take him out. He came out for a chat, and we watched the stars.'

'Pascal, you know he's easily led, don't you. Don't do anything that would hurt him or Sébastien, please.'

'I'm not sure what you're hinting at,' he said in a tone that closed the conversation Their meeting moved to an unsatisfactory ending. She did not get a straight answer from him, but neither did she give him the commitment he wanted from her about transferring money his way.

Just before Claude arrived to drive her to the airport, she gave Pascal a small square packet wrapped in red paper and tied with a bow. It was her Christmas present for him. He was not in a good mood and this was not the scene she had contemplated, but she could delay giving it no longer. She hoped the gift might soften the tension between them, and allow them to part amicably until they met at New Year.

'Don't open it till Christmas Day. I'll be thinking of you,' she said, calculating the tone of her voice signalled her desire to end disagreements. She had bought him a smart expensive watch.

'Oh, thank you, I'm touched.' He kissed her affectionately on the nose. 'It's very English to give presents at Christmas. You will get your present from me at New Year. That's the tradition out here.'

She knew that meant he had not bought her anything. She was not upset. She needed nothing. It was the absence of thought or feeling that hurt. She would have settled for a genuine hug. The tension had not lifted.

It was a lonely Christmas, her first without Thierry and his unconditional love and support. She felt empty and kept her fear at bay by immersing herself in work.

Martha missed Pascal too. She developed tactics for keeping Thierry and Pascal in separate spheres of her brain. She thought fondly and often about her unpredictable young lover. Sometimes he was charming, sometimes remote and unreachable. He was professional in his work, playful when not at work, and ultimately elusive. She thought he uncannily understood her, and was able to look inside her mind and emotions, yet he did not allow her near his soul. It was as if part of him was somewhere else, which made her love him all the more in the brief precious moments he was entirely hers. Those were both special and sad. Now he was reportedly with his family in the Dordogne, a life she knew nothing about. They spoke on the phone, but it did not feel they were in touch. She could not see their relationship having a future beyond the restoration of the house at Cachette.

She knew there was no comparison with the deep connection she had had with Thierry. Everything with Pascal was hot or cold, passion or remoteness. With Thierry she always felt warm and comfortable. Even in their early days together, when she was getting to know Thierry and his history, he had been more predictable, or so she thought, which is what made his last day and death all the more unfathomable.

She was often thinking about their life together. Thierry was two years older than her, but had always treated her as an equal. She was fairly sure he had been in a relationship when they first met, at a London University film society event. Whether his affair had recently finished, or he was in the process of extricating himself from it, she could not tell, but it was clear he was committed to her from the start. Her feelings for him developed more slowly but equally deep.

People had seen them as a serious pair, though that was not how they considered themselves. They deemed themselves happy and did not demand a lot of each other. They were each engrossed in their studies, focused on building careers, and were happiest on their own together, or with small groups of close friends, but not in a crowd. They grew into adulthood side by side, and learned to appreciate each other's interests. At the start, he was right wing because of his upbringing in a conservative French village, and she was left wing in defiance of her father. As the years went by their beliefs merged, and they liked to think they shared a liberal outlook on life.

Thierry was always considerate and she feared now she had taken him too much for granted. She had appeared self-sufficient when his invisible hand was there to steer and support her. He was gone, she was his widow, and she groped in the dark for reasons to carry on, and attain what he would have expected of her. Had she spoilt all that by having sex with a younger man, and so soon? She reasoned that her liaison with Pascal could not hurt Thierry, because he was dead. While married she would never have considered having an affair. She was sure he felt the same, at least until her world was challenged by the mystery of his final day.

She was, back at work, cool and business-like, and she hoped, open and approachable. There had been ripples of shock when she had handed in her notice and she was already being mourned by those who could not imagine the department without her. She enjoyed supervising and giving advice, encouraging people to perform well without doing their job for them. She visited her mother, and made contact with old friends, essentially beginning to say goodbye to her past life, as she increasingly saw it. She even dropped in at one of the day centres the department funded, and took presents for the staff and clients, before going home and wondering if she was over-compensating for abandoning them.

She planned to drive to Saint-Cyprien for New Year so she could take things in the car and leave them. It was the first symbolic stage of her move. The start of a new year. She was sitting on the floor in the study one evening, methodically noting what she required, when Rajinder phoned. He asked how things were going. She was unsure, but responded by asking after Priya and the children.

'They're fine, thanks. I rang to find out how you are, and to tell you about a phone call I received. Well, to be strictly correct, I've been contemplating telling you, and putting it off, but Priya said I must…'

'It sounds like you're still prevaricating, but it's kinder to tell me, Rajinder, whatever it is.'

'I answered a call, a few days ago, on the extension that used to be Thierry's. It was a young man, well not much more than a teenager by the sound of his voice. He asked if Monsieur Jolivet could still be contacted through Benton and Powell. I said no, and asked if I could help. Then the voice said, "He's dead, isn't he," and I said "Yes," and then I knew he was going to ring off, so I added quickly, "I'm Rajinder, his friend. Call me anytime you want to talk," but he hung up.'

The world stood still. Martha was trying to visualise the scene and the young man. She was attempting to put a face on this person who knew her husband, but it was a blank face, like the fuzzy image on a television screen when they disguise the identity of an interviewee for security reasons, photographing him from behind in shadow.

'Martha, are you there?'

'Yes, sorry, Rajinder, I don't know what to make of it.

'Nor do I. He sounded sad, and well, desperate somehow, and that is why I spoke to one of our switchboard people, one I can trust, and got her to put a recording facility on that extension. It's something that's done randomly, but can be requested if there is a special reason. This way I'll be alerted if he rings back. I'm sure the police have lost interest, so it won't raise any alarms. Even if I don't speak to him personally, she should get me

171

his phone number. It's not much, but it's something, at least.'

'It's the only thing so far. Thank you.'

From the way Rajinder had relayed the voice saying, 'He's dead, isn't he?' she was more certain than ever the reason Thierry had taken leave that fateful day was personal, very personal. He had not asked, he had stated that Thierry was dead, and Rajinder had confirmed it. She could feel the young man's pain. That much she could empathise with. The rest she did not understand. She recalled going through Thierry's diary looking for *her*. Now, it seemed, Thierry may have been going to meet *him*. This was something she had definitely not expected. She did not feel angry or upset, more like an outsider, scratching at a frosted window, trying to see inside. It was perplexing and she understood why Rajinder had hesitated to tell her. She tried to behave as if she had not been shaken by the news.

It was a relief to tuck it in the recesses of her brain and get away, returning to her own adventure. She packed the car, not just with clothes, but with items including a kettle to keep at Erin's and take to Cachette as soon as the house was ready, if not to live in, at least to camp out in. She was catching the overnight ferry from Portsmouth, so had the day to prepare, and left in the afternoon when she thought there might be a lull in the traffic on the M25 and the A3. It was a sharp turning out of her drive into the lane and she had to do a small manoeuvre to avoid an old blue car parked opposite.

If Customs pulled her in, she would have to explain the odd assortment of things in the car, but they waved her by. It was easier to drive on board than she had imagined and park in the gigantic metal hold, directed by the ferry staff who looked frozen in their orange anoraks. Each task she performed, which Thierry used to do, was a first for her, a step forward in her confidence. She had driven to France last summer to visit Thierry's family, but that seemed a lifetime ago and she had felt numb at the time.

On board she settled into her small cabin, repaired her make-up and then braved the huge, brightly lit dining room, all mirrors and swirly carpet. It was only eight o'clock but felt later, and the boat was due to sail at half past. She strode in, aware of the harsh lights, noisy diners and being alone. She asked in French for a table for one. She knew many businesswomen ate alone in hotel bedrooms rather than sit at a table visibly by themselves. She had done so herself when travelling to conferences. She was not going to be a coward again.

The ship was far from packed, an after Christmas lull. The dining room was barely half full, and so when she was asked if she wanted to share, she said she would rather not. She did not want to have to make false conversation for the sake of politeness, and dreaded someone raising political views she disagreed with, as frequently happened to her in taxis. At least the waiter responded to her in French, proof of progress. She was pleased with herself as she settled into a seat at a table by the window. They were still in dock, and she could see preparations for departure as darkness gathered outside. The window was spattered with raindrops. An ancient couple sat across the gangway and they all exchanged polite good evenings, before returning to peruse menus.

She ordered a drink and chose the buffet rather than a set meal. Because there was no hurry, she took out her tablet and looked at a map of the route as she sipped her wine. She overheard the old couple talking about boats. Perhaps they used to keep a boat moored in France, maybe on one of the canals in the Midi.

'Would you like me to look after your bag, my dear, and that electronic thingy, while you go to the buffet? It's awkward travelling on one's own.' It took her a moment to recognise the lady opposite was addressing her.

'I couldn't help hearing you talking about boats,' she said on her return. It seemed a show of interest was called for.

'Oh, yes, we still sail our own boat,' the lady said. The gentleman appeared a little deaf.

'Have you ever sailed over to France?' she asked.

'Many times. We did so on the first leg of our trip round the world.' She went on to describe the five year long voyage they undertook some years ago, and the book they published afterwards. They had scaled down their traveling with advancing age, but their exploits sounded adventurous, and Martha thought it made her escape to Saint-Cyprien sound very tame indeed. She felt humbled, especially when she saw how frail they looked. Later, when she went to pay, they were ahead of her at the cash desk. Martha noticed the gentleman's pullover was on back to front, but he was attempting to stand up straight and pull his shoulders back. She almost cried for them.

The build up to the New Year's Eve party at Chez-Madeleine was in full swing when Martha returned to Saint-Cyprien. The restaurant had eighty-four reservations, and it seemed not only the village but most of the surrounding commune would be there. The set menu had been published, eight courses with aperitifs, vodka, wine and digestives carefully chosen to match each dish. There were meat, fish and vegetarian alternatives for mains, and all guests had chosen in advance.

'I can't believe anyone can eat all this,' Martha said to Erin.

'It won't start until about nine, and it'll go on until three or four in the morning, so it'll be fine, you'll see,' Erin reassured her, but suggested she get some rest in the afternoon because they would be up most of the night.

'I'll try, but I wish I knew when Pascal was arriving. I hope he comes soon.' She needed him to face the evening. 'I'm sorry Niall had to go back after Christmas, by the way. I was looking forward to seeing him after so long.'

'Yes, he said he hadn't seen you for many years. He remembered you as neat and intelligent, I told him you looked just the same.'

'Oh, God! That's so embarrassing.'

'He isn't happy you know, not really. He got away as well, physically got away, but something still haunts him.'

Martha recalled Niall as similar to his twin sister, Erin, in looks and seeming disorganised, but different from her, having much darker moods and more intense.

'Take time to talk to him next time, Erin, even if he's reluctant. He isn't as lucky as you. He hasn't found what you've found in Claude.'

Martha herself was best talking to people one-to-one. She was not good at parties. She would feel happier anticipating this evening if Pascal returned early enough for them to have a little time together first. She recalled the tension as they parted before Christmas. She hoped he was as eager to meet her again as she was to see him, and wanted reassurance. Over and over she imagined them walking in to the party together and sharing the promise of the year ahead.

Sébastien and Bené called round in the late morning, having taken some produce from their greenhouse to the restaurant.

'How did you manage to grow things so quickly? I know it's an eco-house but it's not magic.'

'We started the greenhouse last year while we were in the caravan,' Sébastien explained. 'We promised Madeleine some fresh organic decoration for the plates tonight, and she seems pleased with them. Mind you, they're all charging round like headless chickens over there, getting it ready. It's mad. I think Philippe got away. He's probably gone down to the beach.'

'Philippe absconding isn't unusual, but the sea is pretty wild at the moment. I hope he doesn't try going out on a board on his own with no one around.'

'Of all people, he knows what he's doing on the water.

'Have you heard from Pascal?' Martha asked Bené.

'Only that's he's due back this evening…'

'Not till then?'

'No, oh, and that he's been in contact with the owner of Saint-Aubin.'

'Saint-Aubin?'

'The chateau. Work on the main building hasn't been agreed yet because there's a big structural survey being undertaken. But I'm negotiating for Mr Evans to lease back some of the vineyards that used to go with it, and I knew Pascal would be interested in re-designing production houses and vaults for the wine. So, yes, I put them in touch and he's been working on ideas for it.'

'He didn't tell me.'

'No. he keeps things separate.'

Martha did not find that reassuring.

It was late afternoon when Madeleine phoned round to ask if anyone had seen Philippe. Apparently, Nadine, his girlfriend, had not seen him since the morning. Nadine was prepping at the restaurant. Madeleine said she needed him there too. When she tried Sébastien's, he caught anxiety in her voice as well as frustration.

He responded by driving round to ask if Erin would go with him to the beach. Between them they knew every cove, the tides and places Philippe would surf. Claude and Martha said they would look after the children so she could go. They set off north in the direction of La Dune. Erin said he may not have come to the beach at all, just gone to see someone he did not want Madeleine, and possibly Nadine as well, to know about. They had all heard the rumours about Philippe and drugs, though that was speculation. Then they spotted his jeep on the dune road, and when they reached it, they saw the back was open and his board and wet suit were not inside. He had gone to the beach after all, but surely should have been back by this time.

They ran down and spread out along the shoreline in opposite directions, scanning the horizon. The water was grey and forbidding, and left white spray like lace on the cold sand as it retreated. Jellyfish had been washed up and lay transparent and dying. Eventually Erin turned back and met Sébastien running towards her.

'We need to alert the coastguard. It may be a false alarm, but we can't be sure. Only a helicopter search will spot anything or anyone.'

'And the light's fading fast,' Erin agreed.

They returned to the car where a signal was possible and phoned the emergency number, giving their location and the jeep as evidence Philippe had gone surfing earlier in the afternoon. Was he experienced? Sébastien told the operator he was, but the conditions were getting worse by the hour.

'Do you think it's hopeless?' Erin asked anxiously, as they returned to the beach.

'It's pretty desperate if he's out there. It's rough and cold and he could have been taken far out or upstream on the currents. And if he's not out there, why is the jeep here?'

Minutes passed, seeming like hours.

'We've got to find him, and alive, for Madeleine's sake.'

'Yes, we must. Philippe's always been a problem, I can't say I care for him at all, but we have to find him for her... Wait! Look, a helicopter... Wave something to attract its attention, and point to the cliff where the jeep's parked. Then they'll have a better idea of where he might have gone out.'

The helicopter circled and Erin took off her coat and whirled it round her head to catch the pilot's notice. Sébastien had written jeep in the sand with his foot and an arrow pointing to the cliff he thought Philippe must have gone down. The helicopter did a reconnaissance of the land, dipped and then turned sharply out to sea.

'Shall we go back?' Martha asked.

'Perhaps we should go back to my car. We can't do anything here.'

'Then what? Tell Madeleine?'

They were thinking about this when a vehicle sped up the track towards them. It was a buggy containing two lifeguards, and they had a brief exchange, giving the little information they had. They were interrupted by a signal from the helicopter, a sequence of flashes.

'They've found something,' one of the lifeguards said. In an instant they were back in the buggy and careering towards a path which it was capable of manoeuvring down to the beach. Erin and Sébastien watched from the top as the helicopter circled and hovered and eventually let down a rope for the co-pilot to climb down. They strained to watch in the worsening gloom until at last it seemed the co-pilot and a bundle were winched up under the belly of the machine and it took off inland.

Sébastien had climbed down and run towards the buggy. He intercepted it as it was about to leave. The lifeguards were in radio contact with the helicopter and said it was taking a body to the hospital in Lesparre. They did not know if the person was alive, but the co-pilot was a paramedic and would do what he could on the way.

'Do you know him?' the lifeguard asked.

'Yes, but I'm not a relative. I must go to his mother.'

'Take her to Lesparre, go straight to Accident and Emergency,' one lifeguard told him before they hurtled off through the sand, leaving Sébastien to contemplate how to break the news to Madeleine.

Claude volunteered to drive Madeleine down to Lesparre. He had known her longer than anyone. They all prayed Philippe was still alive and speculated that if he was, but badly hurt, he may be airlifted to Bordeaux, where the bigger hospital had better facilities.

Sébastien and Erin went over to the restaurant while Claude started his car and followed them round.

'What can I do?' Martha asked, and Erin suggested she stay with the children and keep them occupied.

As they entered the restaurant, they met Nadine coming out, heading for the boulangerie to pick up bread for the evening. She turned back on seeing them, and Erin and Sébastien found themselves facing Madeleine with Nadine behind.

'What news?' Madeleine asked, her eyes sharp but worried.

'We found his jeep near La Falaise, and called out the coastguard.'

Madeleine's hand leapt to her mouth.

'A helicopter found... well, I think it found him... Nobody else would be out there, and he's been taken to Lesparre...'Sébastien continued, but Madeleine had swept up her coat and was already putting it on.

'Is he alive? I must go.'

They did not answer.

'Claude's coming to take you,' Erin said, taking Madeleine's arm. Then she added, 'Don't worry,' indicating the restaurant. 'We'll look after this.'

Madeleine's eyes scanned the scene. She looked devastated. It had been her life's work. She said, 'This means nothing if Philippe...' Then the professional Madeleine reappeared, and she calculated, 'Eighty-four covers tonight. The main night of the year. The chef is prepared. Nadine, you take charge!'

'No. I'm going with you to Philippe,' Nadine said, unexpectedly forceful.

Madeleine turned on her, and looked as if she was about to eat her up and spit her out.

Erin sprang forward. 'Sébastien and I will take charge here.'

Madeleine looked at her and then nodded agreement. She turned to Nadine with a new softness. 'Yes, of course you must come. If he's unconscious, you can talk to him. He may listen to you if he doesn't to me.' She sounded calmer. She took Nadine's arm and together they made their way to Claude's car.

Erin's voice trailed her, assuring her they would look after the restaurant. Madeleine was focused on getting to her son and it was doubtful she heard.

'You told her we'll look after all this!' Sébastien said to Erin. 'We've been through a lot together, you and me, but we've never hosted a Saint Sylvestre party for eighty-four people. How are we going to do it? They'll be expecting the works!'

'And they'll get it!' Erin replied.

Erin was looking at the chaos of the half-prepared party, attempting to get her head in order, when there was a knock at the door. Sébastien went and let in Martha, Lucy and Ethan.

'I saw Madeleine and Nadine leave with Claude, so Lucy, Ethan and I decided it was time to come and help you get ready for the party. I take it tonight is going ahead?'

'Yes, the food's all here, and Pierre's working on it in the kitchen.'

'Well, he'll require some help. Who's good with food, who could act as sou-chef?'

'Bené would be best,' Erin volunteered, falling into her role as aid to Martha who was the natural planner.

'Where is he?'

'Bené's busy making something to wear for tonight,' Sébastien said, and both women looked at him askance. 'Okay, okay, I'll go and phone him and explain the urgency of the situation.'

Martha asked Erin to get Pierre to join them, and Erin explained what had happened. It took a few moments for the chef to take it all in and express his concern for Madeleine, and then, as he took in their predicament, he said it was imperative to carry on. The kitchen was full of expensive perishable food, all the guests had paid a deposit for this special evening, and Madeleine and her business would be in real trouble if they failed to deliver. They could not prevent her losing her son, but they could stop her losing her business as well.

Martha had taken out her notebook, the one she used to write down facts and figures and make lists about Cachette. On a fresh page she wrote down the names of who was missing in one column, and then who could take their place across the page.

'Thanks, Pierre. You need assistance, and Sébastien has gone to phone Bené.'

'Bené's good,' Pierre said. 'Not a professional, but he's good.'

'Who will be host for the evening now Madeleine's not here?'

'Sébastien,' said Erin decisively. 'He knows the whole village. He can introduce people. There'll be some agitation because of what's happened, but I can't think of anyone more trusted than Sébastien to reassure and see the evening isn't a flop.'

'And he will give out the bills and deal with the money.'

'The way it worked last year was people were given their tallies by four in the morning. Some looked settled in as if we would have to give them breakfast before we could get rid of them, but most were starting to drift away. Nobody got past Madeleine without paying up.'

'Right, well Sébastien will quietly issue bills at three a.m., whether people are staying on or not, and after than it will turn into a cash bar.'

'And who can be sommelier now Philippe is…'

'If he gets here in time, Pascal will do it. In the meanwhile, Bené will stand in when he's completed his sous-cheffing.'

Martha laughed. Concentrating on plans helped ward off the tension of Philippe's accident. 'It sounds like Bené's going to be fully occupied. I hope he's got something to wear if he hasn't finished his outfit. Now, you and I,' she said, to Erin, 'we're the waitresses for the evening!'

'Like we did at uni!' Erin laughed too. 'Ethan and Lucy can help for the initial part of the night…'

'Yeah!'

'And then Claude will take you home…'

'Not till after midnight!' Ethan insisted.

'All right, it's a special night, but your old dad will be quite ready to go home too by then.'

Sébastien had returned from the kitchen having used the phone, and said Bené was on his way. Martha asked the chef if there was a list of guests. He had all their names because they had all chosen preferences. She gave the list to Sébastien and asked him to concoct a seating plan.

'It'll be better if we give everyone a designated place rather than have a free for all. Mix people up a bit, but don't put them with those they don't like. It'll make it easier for the chef and Erin and I if we know where people are and what to serve them. I'm going to have difficulty anyway with my poor French. Arranged like this I can just follow the plan.'

'You've never done that,' Erin could not help commenting.

The best thing, in fact the only thing, they could do for Madeleine was ensure the night was a success. The party, to which Martha had not been looking forward, offered her a challenge, and she was in her element organising it. She found it much easier relating to people when she had a task to get on with.

Claude returned from Lesparre saying Philippe was alive but badly hurt. There was concern about a head injury, perhaps sustained when he was swept off his board. He was suffering from hyperthermia by the time he was winched up into the helicopter. It was a miracle he had been located floating unconscious on his board, and had not drowned. Madeleine and Nadine were staying at the hospital, certainly for tonight as he was in intensive care. The doctors would not transfer him to Bordeaux unless it was absolutely necessary because his head had to be kept absolutely still. Nadine would phone if there was any change in his condition. There was no call, and the group of friends hoped no news was good news. At least he was still alive and Madeleine and Nadine were with him.

Martha had not heard from Pascal. She did not want to phone him and appear possessive. She had no right to be. Keeping busy was the best way to allay her anxieties.

They appeared a merry band eating together, making sure the tension did not surface. They ate early before clearing away and attending to the final decorations. Pascal walked into Chez-Madeleine just as Martha was helping arrange a curtain at one end of the main room for a spectacle later on. She was unsure what sort of show it was going to be. He went straight to her and gave her a hug.

'I'm so sorry, my darling, I didn't let you know I'd be late. Don't worry, I know all about Philippe and what we have to do tonight. Bené phoned me and said you were busy getting it all in order. Tell me what I have to do.'

It was instantly all right.

'Come and eat something first,' she said, relieved. 'It's going to be a long night.'

The seating plan and advance food orders made it easier to act as waitress, though Martha found people irritatingly did not remain in their places, but got up and joined other tables for a chat. She smiled to convince herself this did not bother her, but developed the technique of serving food according to the plan which she found enticed the guests to return to their original seats. Erin tried to follow people with their food and got in a muddle, until Martha told her to adopt her strategy. Pascal helped out at busy times ensuring everyone had wine on their tables and helping Martha serve up, and he seemed happy and popular running a noisy bar. He made a fuss of all the women, especially the older ones, and made sure everybody had a glass of champagne when the clock struck twelve.

Midnight found Martha being hugged and kissed by the whole village, mostly perfect strangers up to that point. She abandoned her apron, her natural reserve, and went with it as best she could. She felt a sudden stab of pain and guilt that Thierry was not there, and would never be there again. She left the crowd and went in the back to compose herself.

Then there was a break between courses for the cabaret. Martha re-emerged and settled down with Pascal and became aware there was nothing between them and the bare floor area that constituted the stage. She felt exposed on the front row. The curtains swished open, an old French song from the nineteen fifties started and after a moment of suspense, a spotlight juddered almost into position, and a girl's high-heeled shoe emerged, then a shapely leg in fishnet stockings kicked out, and then a girl's body came fully into view, a riot of colours and a painted face. There were hoots of appreciation.

'I am Marlene,' she uttered in a mid-European accent Martha could not place. When she moved completely into the circle of light she began to mime very cleverly and to move with the music. It was a pastiche, a mixture of Hollywood, Paris and Berlin, and her dress and make-up were a complete rainbow dazzling, sashaying and dancing to the beat. Martha was transfixed by her eyes encircled with glitter. She put out a gloved hand and touched the mayor coquettishly, but as he sat impassively ignoring her, she moved on and draped her feather boa round Sébastien's head. He laughed coyly, and she teased him to get up and join her on the dance floor. Poor big Sébastien came over all shy, and Marlene skipped over and sat on Pascal's lap, which horrified Martha, but he seemed amused and flirted with her. Martha was overpowered by the smell of cheap scent and make-up and pulled away as far as she could. Marlene dragged Pascal up and into her arms as she mimed to the latest song, a slow sad ballad. Martha loosened her tight, white-knuckled grip on her chair and laughed so people would not think her uncomfortable.

'Isn't he amazing,' Erin whispered, leaning forward so Martha could hear.

'Yes,' Martha replied, thinking Erin was referring to Pascal and his smooth dancing with Marlene.

'And he nearly didn't finish the dress because of coming over to help the chef.'

'Oh!' Martha nearly choked as she realised how stupid she had been. Marlene was Bené, or the other way round. She understood now. She watched his hand slide down Pascal's bottom and circle it as they finished the dance. He winked at her from beneath heavy eye shadow.

People clapped as Pascal bowed and returned to his seat.

'You enjoyed that!' Martha hissed into the side of his head. In response he took hold of her and gave her a long deep kiss, oblivious to what any of the villagers might think. Well, it was New Year.

'Now I have to go to do the fireworks. Philippe set them up, so I hope I know where they all are.' He got up to go outside.

'Please be careful.' She could not be sure if he heard her or not.

A little while later, Sébastien drew up the blinds on the big windows which looked out on the terrace, and a Catherine wheel flew into action, letting off golden sparks, as its colours spun. Then several rockets went into orbit in quick succession, and then there was a lull, while Pascal was hunting his next trick. It was a bit slow, hardly a professional firework display, but the audience were well nourished, happily inebriated, and well disposed. Pascal made it into a comedy routine, acting silly. But he knew what he was doing. He located the touch paper and a row of Mount Vesuvius's erupted, first in colour, and then streaming silver white. The smoke took a moment to clear, and when it did Pascal was miming a coughing routine. Then he made a play of being frightened as a number of exploding fireworks shot into the sky and burst into stars. There were oohs and aahs and rippling applause.

Martha was impressed and hugged him fondly when he came in smelling of gunpowder and cold night air.

'Did you bring something warm with you?' he asked.

'I've got a coat and boots for going home after we've cleared up,' she replied.

'Good, you'll need them down on the beach.'

It was very late, or very early if you saw it that way. Martha did not really want to go down to the wet cold sand now, but after they had seen out the last guests, and put away any perishable food, he told her there would be a bonfire down there. He had collected the wood and taken it near to the old sinking concrete German bunkers before coming up to Chez-Madeleine. Claude had long since taken the children home, but Bené emerged in jeans and a thick leather biker's jacket, looking butch apart from the streaks of make-up he had been unable to remove. He linked hands with Sébastien and Erin, and together with Martha, Pascal and a bottle of champagne they set off, leaving Pierre to lock up.

Erin took off her shoes and ran towards the shore and disappeared into the darkness, determined to be the first to get her feet wet in the freezing ocean this new year. Martha wanted to pull her back, but Sébastien put a plastic glass in her hand, and began pouring out the bubbles while Pascal and Bené lit the wood which had kept dry beneath tarpaulin. It created a small haven of heat and a red-orange light in the cold blackness. They drank around the fire, and agreed it had been the best party ever. Martha was genuinely happy as she looked round her friends, new and old. This was the stuff dreams were made on, she decided, unable to believe the promise of the future after the trauma of last year.

She turned away from the group and drank a toast to Thierry, sad that he could not share any of this. The fire began to die down; they quietened, seemingly each one lost in thoughts which the turn of the calendar tends to provoke. Eventually Erin, Bené and Sébastien said they were going home.

'Are you coming?' Erin asked Martha.

'In a little while,' Pascal answered for her. They remained crouching down to benefit from the last of the heat, watching the red glowing embers as the others drifted away, and they were left alone with the warmth and darkness surrounding them.

Pascal put his jacket for her comfort on a ledge of the concrete bunker and gently raised her up onto it. He undid the bottom buttons of her coat. His hands caressed her thighs under her skirt, and removed her pants. She knew what was going to happen as he unzipped himself and pushed his jeans down. He was not wearing underpants and she took hold of him and helped him put on a condom and enter her. She lifted her legs so he could get in deeper, and wrapped them round him and dug her hands into his bottom. She loved the feeling of being completely entered. She wanted oblivion. She did not want to think, only touch and feel. Her hands felt his balls tighten and she knew he was about to come, and she wanted to slow him down so it would last longer. She tingled warm and pulsing inside and let out an involuntary cry which echoed along the beach into the dark void. She kept him inside her as long as she could, and when he got smaller and slipped out, she touched his face, every part of it, looking into his eyes to see what she could see. His eyes looked beautiful, reflected in the firelight. She got down and rearranged her clothes. She gave him his jacket to slip on.

He took off the condom, smelling of latex, and dropped it on the fire where it sizzled briefly and jumped, reminding her of the bangers and firecrackers they used to have on Bonfire Nights when she was a child. Then it dissolved and was gone. They stood looking into the dying fire until he kicked sand over the remains to make certain it was out, and then peed on it, and only then did he pull up his jeans and take her hand, and they slowly made their way back to the village.

'I think Erin and I will drive to Lesparre tomorrow to see how things are and if Madeleine wants to come home,' she whispered to him as they walked along the deserted village street past the dark, boarded-up restaurant.

'That's okay. I have to see a colleague, but we'll catch up.'

He saw her to the house, which Erin had left unlocked. As he walked away to get his car, she watched him retreating. She stood there a long time before closing and locking the door, and going up the stairs to bed as quietly as she could.

Madeleine was sitting in a corridor outside the ward. She appeared shrunken and older. She smiled when she saw Martha and Erin.

'How is he?'

'The same. The doctors say he is stable, whatever that means. They let Nadine sit with him for a while, and then

I took my turn. We were asked to talk to him in the hope he can hear. Now he's resting.'

'And you?'

'No, I can't rest. I won't rest till he's home.'

'And if…' Erin began.

'He's my son, my blood. We are tough. He'll pull through.'

'Where's Nadine now?' Martha asked.

'Her father came, and we persuaded her to take a break and go home for a while. I promised I will wait here until she returns and then I might think of taking one too if… if…' She looked up at them imploringly, lost for a long while and neither knew what to say. Her eyes focused on them, beseeching them as if they could prevent Philippe dying. Gradually, Madeleine seemed to collect herself and her normally inscrutable face revealed the glimmer of a tired smile.

'I owe you such a debt of gratitude, yes, don't deny it. I heard about the party. You made it a huge success. Even if it's the last night of Chez-Madeleine, it will go down in village folklore as the best Saint Sylvestre ever. I would have loved to have seen Bené as Marlene,' she chuckled.

'It can't be the end of Chez-Madeleine. We won't let that happen.' Erin was adamant.

'But if Philippe doesn't pull through, no, I couldn't go on. There would be no point.'

Martha understood, though Erin continued.

'But he's going to pull through. You said yourself he's tough. It's in the blood.'

Then Martha asked, 'Who was his father? Does his father know he's here dangerously ill in hospital? Surely, he ought to know, and have the chance be here.'

Erin looked shocked. Had Martha crossed a line? Madeleine might explode.

'Ha, you're the first who's dared to ask. All right, sit down and I'll tell you. I'll share my secret, but it is to go no further. You have to promise... I don't know where he is now, Philippe's father. I don't want to know; well, that's not quite true, I still think about him often, and wish it could have been different. I won't say who he was, no, I won't, but he came from one of Bordeaux's older families. Well, really, we must all come from old stock or we would not have got this far in evolution, but they considered themselves a cut above the rest.' It was as if she were back in time, back there in Bordeaux forty odd years ago. She told her story, with many pauses for thought, and Martha had to concentrate to understand Madeleine's guttural accent.

'His mother was horrified when she knew he was courting the daughter of a bar owner. He was sent. away to relatives on the Riviera. I don't know if he wanted to go. Was he bribed, or was he weak? Why didn't he stand up to them, tell them where to get off? Money, I expect. I'll never know. I was informed he'd gone, and I was told not to contact him. I did not deign to tell them he'd made me pregnant. I did not debase myself in front of them.'

She was silent, but they did not interrupt. It seemed she was assembling the next part of her story, deciding how to tell it to them.

'I had to inform my own father. He said we won't tell the family. They would try to pay me off, or arrange an abortion. It was better they didn't know. I came to stay with elderly relatives up the coast not far from here. Father sold the bar, and followed. I had the baby and he opened a new bar, which he called Chez-Madeleine after me. This new one was also a restaurant. In those days he ran the bar and I cooked. We explained nothing to anyone. People came out of curiosity, and then they tasted our food, and loved it, and they came back. From slow beginnings it grew into the success it is today. I didn't know, but Father was ill. He died and his legacy was Chez-Madeleine. He knew I'd be all right because of it. He made me independent.

'Philippe grew up. Like me, like my father too, he's strong-willed, but he's also like his father, who had no staying power, and gave in to his instincts and his passions. Olivier was ruled by his heart, not his head. His mother was too strong for him. I was too strong for him. He may have been glad to be free of me. I wonder if he got free of her.'

She seemed unaware she had mentioned Philippe's father's first name.

'Did Olivier know he left you expecting his baby?' Erin asked.

'Not that I am aware. No one knows any of this. It's our secret. Please keep it to yourselves.'

'Of course,' they both agreed.

There was a long silence. Eventually, Erin asked if Madeleine wanted anything as she was determined to stay on at the hospital.

'No. Thank you, my dears. I don't need anything. I'll just wait. By the way, my story, the story I haven't told anyone else, it was nice to tell you. I'm glad I told you. Oh, Martha?'

'Yes.'

'I inadvertently mentioned his first name. They were such a wealthy well-known family. To some that would give it away.'

'It's also our secret. I'll not tell.'

'Thank you.' They looked at each other for a while. They had the measure of each other.

'When Nadine returns,' Martha decided to say what was on her mind, 'I think you should leave her and Philippe together. Give them some space. You've more chance of keeping him if you show you can let him go.'

Madeleine regarded her for some time. Martha returned her stare.

'I understand,' she said at last. 'Now you are really part of la famille Chez-Madeleine.'

'Pascal drove me up this coastal route once, way back in the autumn, what a long time ago that seems.' Martha said. 'It may have been this way we came.'

'It avoids the towns and the main road,' Erin replied.

'That's just what he said. Also, he wanted to show me some cottages he'd renovated. The funny thing is, for some reason I doubted he'd done them, but he had. Oh, and another time, he took me to a place out here to eat, a place I'd never find again, but it was excellent.'

'What was it called?'

'Can't remember, sorry. It was at a duck farm, or former duck farm, and most of the menu was duck.'

'Le Caneton Sauvage, the wild duckling,' Erin guessed. 'It's not far from here. Shall we stop off and have a light lunch if it's open? It may or may not be on New Year's Day. I'll phone and let Claude know.

She took a detour in the battered old Renault which must have been intimate with these meandering roads.

'Seeing Pascal today?'

'Not sure. He said something about seeing a client.'

'On New Year's Day? Sounds doubtful. Martha, it's none of my business I know, but how much do you really know about Pascal? How deep in with him are you?'

'Um, that's thrown me! How much do I know about him?'

Martha settled back in her seat to relax as much as she could with Erin driving in her usual erratic fashion. She remembered last night with a mixture of contentment and embarrassment. She had held his face and looked into his eyes. She had never done anything like that in the open before, even if the dead of night had concealed it. She had been unfaithful to Thierry's memory. However, she was not going to share any of these thoughts with Erin. It was best to consider Erin's question. What did she actually know about Pascal?

'I know he's got style. I know that's important to him. He dresses with style, the houses he designs have style. I don't know how much lies beneath the style. I tried to find out more about him, where he came from, what he believes in, what's important to him, what he wants out of life, when we ate at the wild duck place, but didn't get far. I'm so happy when he's nice to me, but don't understand his moods. Transforming the house at Cachette is our only common goal, but that's as far into the future as I can see right now. He's too young to be my husband and too old to be my son, and I've never been in this sort of relationship before, and I'm not convinced, as you ask, either of us is deeply into the relationship. We've both got other issues. Mine may be in the past and his are more likely in the present or the future, but they aren't shared.'

'So, I take it you're not in love with him?'

'No... No, though I'm fond of him, and he makes me happy... some of the time... but no, I've known love, and this isn't it, it doesn't compare. Whether it could become love in time, well, he'd have to open up to me first, wouldn't he? I don't suppose he's in love with me either, though he does utter intimate endearments when... Anyway, he finds me attractive, which I must admit is nice, and occasionally he acts towards me as if I matter, but he's inconsistent... I'm not giving him a good write up, am I?'

'Well, you've told me enough to make me understand you haven't thought it through, which is unusual for you. I'll give it to him; he has a powerful personality. Some people find him magnetic; others don't trust him an inch. I often think what he wants is to be admired, and he's not bothered what he's admired for, as long as he's noticed. I'm convinced he's not going to give you happiness, so please don't let him trap you. From his point of view, I can appreciate there is a certain glamour in having an older woman as his lover.'

'Oh, thank you. God, what must the village think of me, a recent widow and some sort of femme fatale, a cougar, I think you say?'

'You've never been particularly concerned what people think of you. At least you're consistent there. He doesn't really belong to the village, and you're going to live out at Cachette, so I don't suppose it matters. You can both afford to ignore village gossip.'

'I suppose we are using each other,' Martha summed up.

Erin turned off up a track and they arrived at the straggle of low farm buildings which made up Le Caneton Sauvage. She pulled up rather abruptly under a tree, and they walked across the rough shingled yard to the restaurant. It was open and there were a few diners, but several of the rough oak tables were unset, showing not many were expected. Most people were probably sleeping off the excesses of last night. They were shown to a table just outside the alcove where she and Pascal had sat. The patronne explained they had a reduced menu today, and both agreed that was sufficient. She fetched them each a Pineau as an aperitif, and left them to peruse the hand-written menu.

'We sat in there before,' Martha told Erin, indicating the archway which led to the alcove.

'There's a young woman in there now... long blonde hair. I can't see her properly, she has her back to us. I presume she's with someone, who must be tucked round the corner out of sight.'

Martha raised her glass.

'Happy New Year, Erin. Oh, I wish! Thanks for all you have done for me since last summer. It's been such a difficult time. I may be acting as if I've come to terms with Thierry's death, but you know I haven't. I'm so dreadfully sad about it all, for him as well as for me. The mystery about it doesn't help, but that's not the main thing. It's losing him that's derailed me, makes me feel empty inside.' She was finding words hard, but forced herself to continue. 'It's Thierry who was, is, important, not Pascal. I know that. I really do appreciate all your support.'

'Yes. I know.' Erin found the right words difficult as well.

They both took a sip of Pineau, realising with all their activity neither of them had drunk much last night, which made this drink even more welcome.

'What do you see in her, is it sex or money?' The young woman's voice cut in accusatively from round the corner, out of sight. She had got louder, maybe with the drink, and voices carried in the near empty room.

'My God! This isn't for our ears, but it may be interesting,' Erin giggled, half embarrassed, and half intrigued.

'Yes, of course there's both of those, and I need lots of both as you know. She has lots of money.' There was a laugh. It was Pascal's laugh. It was a nasty laugh. Martha froze. She saw the look of horror cross Erin's face.

'Let's go,' Erin whispered, barely audible. She started to get up.

'No,' Martha murmured firmly, putting her hand over Erin's. 'I want to hear this.'

'They might come out. They might see us,' Erin whispered, desperately uncomfortable.

'Let them!' Martha put her finger to her lip to urge Erin to keep quiet. She wanted to discover if there would be more. She clung to the hope she was not the subject of their conversation. *Please no*, she thought, but as the conversation continued it appeared she was.

'So, keep out of the way, don't go messing it up for me. It's a very profitable commission, with added perks!'

'It's always the same with you, Pascal. You said you'd come back to the Dordogne and we'd live together properly this time. But I guess you're not coming until the English lady's house is finished and you've screwed all you can out of her?'

'That depends on whether the chateau gets the go ahead, and if I can use my charm to obtain that contract too. I've got Bené working on that for me. He's a dunce as well. I'll dump her anyway in due course; it's just a question of when. If I get the chateau job we're home and dry, we'll be rich! It would delay my coming back to the Dordogne. It's possible you might be able to come and live here, but like I say, only when the time's right.'

'When the time is right! When the coast is clear! Pascal, I've heard it all so many times. It's all I hear from you. You're good at deceiving others, so how do I know I can trust you?'

'Oh, come on, darling...' It was a softer beguiling voice.

Martha felt as assaulted as if she had been physically attacked. She was tempted to go round the corner and hit him, but she was certain he would come out of it better. It would be best to leave. She had to get away quickly or she would explode. She put a ten euro note under her half-drunk glass, and nearly collided with the patronne in her eagerness to escape.

Erin said, 'Sorry, another time,' as she passed the lady who looked confused, holding out her pad to take their order.

'The bastard!' Martha swore as she got in the car. For the second time her whole world had changed in an instant. Her loss felt total. This time she knew she had only herself to blame, but preferred to launch her fury onto Pascal.

'Sack him,' was all Erin said.

'Oh, don't worry I will. I'd like to pull his precious balls off. Erin, I should have seen this coming. I've been such a fool.'

They drove in silence. At home, Claude had left a note on the kitchen table saying he had taken the children out for a walk. Martha sat down at the kitchen table with her head in her hands. Erin made her a mug of tea, and said not a word. Her worst fears had been realised. She was so sad for her friend, who may have been silly, but did not deserve this. She loved her, but knew she had to work out her own solution.

'Okay.' Martha looked up, her voice cool and determined. 'I'm going to write him a letter. Whether I send it or not depends, but that's how I'll start.'

Erin silently put a pad and a pen in front of her.

Martha constructed a letter to Pascal informing him she had overheard his conversation in the restaurant, and was breaking off their relationship entirely, both personally and professionally with regard to Cachette. He must inform his builder he would not be required. There would be no more payments. She kept it short and factual. It was written in cold, hard, calculated fury.

She then phoned the ferry company and was relieved to find she could change her ticket to tomorrow morning's daytime sailing from St Malo, when ferries resumed after the New Year break. It was not full. She confirmed it on the spot.

She said she wanted to leave as soon as she was packed, and stay the night up near the port. Erin helped her prepare. She did not pack all her things. She left a few items such as the kettle she had bought to take over to the cottage. Was that a sign she had not entirely given up on the idea of living there one day, or was it too painfully a mark of failure to take it all back to England? She left the question open.

'I want him to receive this, but not until I'm well on the way.' She regarded the letter.

Erin had remained quiet and supportive throughout Martha's preparations.

'Understood. I'll see he gets it, but not till tomorrow. What are you going to do about Cachette now? Are you going to give up the idea of living out there after all?'

'Oh, Erin, I don't know. You were correct in saying I haven't thought things through. I've got to do so now, haven't I? Got to consider a lot of things. I don't want to cut off from you and my genuine friends here, but I need to get away right now, and not make any hasty decisions until it's all sunk in. But to be practical, I would like Claude to keep these safe, in case I need them one day. They're mine. I've paid for them, as Pascal so crudely and cruelly pointed out.'

She gave Erin the maps and technical drawings for the house, together with the letters of authorisation from the mayor and the planning department.

'If he comes for them, say they're not here or something.'

'Don't worry, he won't get them. He'll get your letter, but he won't get in the door.'

'Thanks, Erin, you're a gem,'

Erin hugged her close and then Martha got into her cold car and drove away, clearing the windscreen as she went, more desolate about the future than she had been when Thierry died. The superficial loss of Pascal compounded the real loss of Thierry. She felt selfish and guilty. She had betrayed her marriage. After driving all afternoon past Nantes and Rennes, she stayed the night in a large, once grand hotel near the docks in Saint-Malo, but could not eat. She left most of her meal on her plate, left the dining room and went to bed.

She could feel the façade she had built up all her life cracking, and wanted it to crack. She must accept herself as she was, desolate and alone. There would be no more pretence. She found strength and resilience inside her core she had not known she possessed. She would survive, but bitterly, she could not imagine she would ever be happy again.

The next morning, she drove onto the boat and climbed the open-mesh steel steps from the garage deck, emerging into the brightly lit foyer and found the coffee lounge. She watched the coast of France, and the pretty old town, with its grey walls and fortifications, slide further into the mist coming off the sea as the ship set sail. She rubbed her hand over the window at the stern of the boat to try and clear the condensation so she could see it a little while longer, but soon it had slipped from sight, much as friends do when you leave them and turn a corner onto the main road. She called at reception and hired a daytime cabin. She lay down and slept.

'Yes, Ayleen?' she answered the receptionist who had buzzed her phone. She tried not to sound tired.

She was seated at her curved workstation, with its pleasing modern lines, in front of a plate glass window with a panoramic view of the south London skyline. On a clear day she could see Canary Wharf, but this was not a clear day.

'A gentleman is on the line. He didn't give his name, but said it was personal. Shall I put him through?'

'I suppose so.' She sighed. She was at the office, in work mode, and not thinking of Pascal.

'Martha, I've found you. Look, there must have been a misunderstanding...'

Her heart began racing, her palms sweaty. It was definitely him. She had not been expecting to hear from him here. He was invading the sanctum of her office.

'There certainly was a misunderstanding, Pascal.' She forced her voice to sound level and calm. 'I misunderstood. I thought you were at least my friend and maybe more.'

'I can explain about the restaurant, and what you thought you heard. You see,' he laughed conspiratorially, 'Corinne is an old friend who has personal problems, and I have to chivvy her along. She's got a bit of a thing about me, and if she thinks I've got other people I'm fond of she gets jealous and I don't want to be responsible for what she might do. So, I have to play a game with her and that's what you probably heard…'

Stop, stop, stop. She had to stop him. She could not bear his lies.

'That's enough, Pascal! If I wasn't so mad with you, I'd give you a prize for storytelling. You were *not* playing a game! Well, perhaps you were, perhaps you always are, but if you were, it was not the one you just told me about. I heard the truth, and I can tell you it damn well hurt.'

She dare not give him a chance to talk her round. She had better get it over with. She talked louder to drown out his response and excuses.

'Pascal, I wrote and said goodbye. I didn't intend to eavesdrop, but I inadvertently overheard you, and was shocked to hear you talk about me like that. Whatever we had is irretrievably broken, and I said all I had to say in that letter.'

'Martha—'

'No! It's over. Too many games, Pascal. It wasn't a game for me. My eyes were opened. The scales dropped. I meant everything I wrote. So, Pascal, why have you called? What do you want?' She felt exhausted.

His voice took on a nasty edge she had not heard before.

'Well, if that's how it goes, then I want my money for starters. You owe me, Martha, for all my professional time you've wasted, and you owe severance pay to the builder.'

'Bullshit! I've paid you for all you did, and we hadn't entered into any contract to continue. I had no contract with the builder.'

'It was drawn up.'

'But not signed. Talking of money, you have ten thousand euros of mine. I should like it back.' She considered this unlikely, but made her pitch.

'Don't be silly. I'll be taking legal action unless you pay me a further ten thousand euros within the week. Don't pay it to my firm, pay it into to my personal credit card account,' he continued.

'So, you're threatening me, and you're demanding I do something illegal; pay it to that account so you don't declare it or pay tax. Am I supposed to pay your credit card debt and subsidise your lifestyle instead?'

'That's about it, darling, unless you want things to get very nasty. And I can make it nasty for you.'

She found it difficult to continue. She was relieved this conversation was taking place on the phone. She mumbled, talking to herself as much as to him.

'I didn't fool myself you loved me, but I thought we were friends, and capable of becoming good friends. I made a very poor choice, a very bad lapse of judgement'

'Please, spare me the lecture. I've had enough of them in my time. You sound like my mother! She's always going on like that. Don't forget, I gave you pleasure. As you say, it's over now, but you'll be very sorry unless you pay up. I have a long memory. I know people who will deal with you if I ask them. I'm giving you one last chance to be sensible—'

'Sensible! The only sensible thing for me to do is to say goodbye, Pascal, and put the phone down. I'm very sad for you as a matter of fact, sad for a man who has style but no soul. I'm sad we have to part like this. But threats make me angry. I won't allow you to bully me. By the way, you are aware all the calls into this department are recorded for security and training purposes? Hello?'

The line was dead.

She drove home, parked on the drive and let herself into the empty house. She was seriously rattled. What power did he have? How could he make her sorry? Would he turn up here at her door again? Would he do anything to hurt Erin or the children? No, not even the new, cruel Pascal whose words were reverberating in her head would stoop to that. He wouldn't, would he? The doubts nagged her as she changed into casual clothes and looked in the fridge to see if there was any comfort food she might want to eat. All the same, she had better phone Erin and inform her of the conversation, and warn her to be careful. It would give her a chance to ask Erin how Philippe was getting on now he was out of hospital.

Martha recognised she was emotionally drained, and it was difficult in such a state to think clearly. She would eat a little, drink no wine, and have an early night to start the recovery process. She had to get her life under control.

When did the shadow of the old blue car register in her brain? Was it parked again in the road when she drove in? It had been there several times recently. Without switching on the hall light, she slowly mounted the staircase which twisted round and gave a good view of the drive from the tall window halfway up. She doubted she could be seen from outside as she peered down the drive towards the road. The laburnums were winter skeletons, making it possible to see, and there it was, an old blue car parked opposite her gateway. Her heart thumped. She watched it for some time and felt certain there was the shady outline of somebody in it. She was sure she saw movement. She recalled the afternoon she set off for Saint-Cyprien for New Year and was positive there was a person in the car then, though it had made no impression at the time. It now appeared ominous.

Was she being melodramatic? Hysterical? Was the car anything to do with her? She decided there was only one was to find out, and that involved confronting whoever was in the car, and asking him, presuming it was a him, why he was keeping her house under observation. She hovered on the landing, considering her options. If there was a person in the car, would she feel foolish if he gave a perfectly plausible explanation as to why he was waiting outside her drive, or would he tell her rudely to mind her own business. It was not illegal to sit in a car, but it was strange, in this residential street, and she had to resolve matters one way or the other. She felt better once she had made up her mind not to cower in the darkness worrying, but go on the offensive. She was taking back control. It had something to do with warding off the danger of Pascal.

Martha left the house quietly without using any lights, and walked stealthily down the drive. She saw the outline of a figure in the car, and he saw her coming towards him. He started the engine. Now she knew he had been observing her or the house. She ran across the road, knowing it was a foolish thing to do. He pulled away and she ran alongside the car and extended her hand to try to grab the door handle, but the car picked up speed and practically knocked her out of the way. She reeled, in danger of falling, but just managed to keep her balance and remain upright.

She came to a stop watching the departing car. Her heartbeat was thumping. She was sweating. She stood in the middle of the road, bending forward catching her breath, and then with an effort she straightened and stood up. She was bewildered, and for the first time, frightened. Her hand hurt from its bang with the moving vehicle. At least she knew from the pain the confrontation had been real, and not a figment of her imagination.

Then she did what she had not done for as long as she could recall. She cried, though she did not know for whom, what or why she was crying. Ever since she had been told of Thierry's death everything had gone wrong. She considered going in search of a neighbour, taking shelter and pleading for protection, but realised she did not know any of the other residents in the street well enough. *That's the trouble with bloody suburbia*, she thought angrily. *I'm having a breakdown in the middle of the street and nobody notices from behind their thick curtains.* She ran inside her house which she had left open, bolted and locked the door and charged round the house switching on all the lights.

'He's not going to get me,' she shouted out loud, he being Pascal in her imagination. She went from room to room checking there was nobody lurking behind any door, and eventually fell into a chair. She could not move. After several minutes she felt her pulse returning to normal and her brain calming. She felt silly. She switched off the lights one by one, methodically, and shut all the doors. She put an icepack on her wrist, secured with medical tape, awkwardly made a cup of tea as best she could, took it to bed with her, locked the bedroom door, drank the tea and fell back against the pillows, exhausted.

She was convinced she would not sleep, and did not want to if it involved dreaming of the old blue car and the shadowy face inside. She shook as she grasped the danger she had placed herself in attempting to stop it. She understood she was in shock. Thierry would have been furious with her. She kept letting him down. Luckily, he was not here to witness her disintegration. She needed him so much!

She slept fitfully. She dreamt, not of the blue car but of a much older car, or maybe it was a van. She was in the van, and it was very quiet. All the big people around her were quiet. She was small. She woke up hot and sweating and disorientated. She did not understand the old van or where it had come from. It was not the first time she had seen it in her sleep, but this time it was real and vivid. She could smell the old van: the cracked leather seats, the musty sleeping bags, leftover food and wet anoraks. It was a memory, not a dream, but one she could not place.

Though her mind was fuzzy and confused about the van, which seemed a long, long time ago, it was startlingly clear about the blue car she had tried to intercept. She also understood her folly. The shadowy figure in the old blue car could not possibly be Pascal. It had nothing to do with him. It was true he had threatened her yesterday afternoon, but on the phone, and though he had not said where he was calling from, she guessed it was from his apartment on the coast above Saint-Cyprien. She remembered how the old blue car had been watching the house before she left for New Year in France, before she fell out with Pascal.

Martha was convinced the real car, the blue car, as opposed to the car or van in her dream, had something to do with Thierry, though she could not understand how or why. The worst thing was that if the man in the car knew something about Thierry, good or bad, then by confronting and scaring him off, she had thrown away her last chance of making contact. She squirmed in her bed, feeling the excruciating anguish of having cut her lifeline. She wanted to go back in time, undo her actions, and find a more sensible, non-threatening way of approaching him. But however much she willed it, she could not scroll back. The deed was done. Her loss was total. She had no way of knowing that at that precise moment, the man in the blue car felt exactly the same.

4

The meeting

It was a cold January evening. Martha was cocooned in her big house, keeping cosy in Thierry's study with a portable radiator. She did not know what to do.

She had returned from the office, where she felt comfortably in control. She was aware people slumped in front of the fire or the television when they got home, but she never did. She was still seeking order and purpose, and although she had a gaping hole of time confronting her, she was driven by determination it should not be wasted. After eating too many bits and pieces, she sat at Thierry's desk for comfort and looked at her diary. She read, for the hundredth time, "The Social Worker's Diary" in gold script on the green cover. It was the last one the department would provide for her. Appointments and schedules filled the pages for the first three months of the year and then... blank. If she walked in tomorrow and asked to withdraw her resignation, Martin would probably leap for joy, but only metaphorically. The poor man seemed incapable of showing any discernible signs of pleasure, or any other extreme emotion, come to that.

But she would rather face the void than retreat. Quitting her career was the only thing she was certain about. She had been too work-orientated, but the drive and purpose had gone, the flame of zeal she had carried was extinguished. It was connected to losing Thierry. With her bereavement she had lost the lust to pursue her career. She persuaded herself she was content with what she had achieved, but did not wish to carry on. She was drawn to do something different with what remained of her life. Thierry's death had shaken her into appreciating that life could be cut short at any moment and death was the only event which defied planning. It could happen without reason and rob anyone of their expected lifespan. She was only half alive without him, but felt it imperative to use any remaining time well, to live for both of them, if that was not just rationalisation. Her future was a murky cloud, an ill-defined nothingness which scared her, but from which she did not attempt to escape into the safety of the familiar routine. She longed to talk to Thierry, ask his advice. *What do I do now?*

She must have been staring blindly for some time at the blank year planner, with its neat empty squares; no more strategies, no more appraisals and best of all, no more meetings.

The phone rang next to her elbow, causing her to jump.

'Hello, Martha, I've caught you in.' Erin's familiar tone pleased her and at the same time caused her to feel lonely back home on her own.

Martha thought, *Well, I haven't been out much except to the office*, but she said, 'Oh Erin, I'm glad it's you.'

Erin did not respond if she detected the sadness in Martha's voice.

'Martha, darling, we've been thinking. That's Claude and I. We're not convinced you should make a complete life change so soon after Thierry's death… but it's lovely we are so close again and we don't want to lose you. Claude and Sébastien have been going through the architect's drawings for Cachette. They're really impressed, and wonder why you don't go ahead with the restoration in spite of the shit.'

It took her a few seconds to comprehend. 'You mean Pascal?'

'I prefer to think of him as the shit. He's been round here, as you predicted he would, but don't worry, he didn't get anything. He tried the sorry lost boy look, sad and misunderstood, but I told him I'd also been at Le Caneton Sauvage, and heard what he said about you, so he needn't try that one. He turned nasty then, showed his true colours I suppose, and said if we had his drawings we were in possession of stolen property, which I know isn't right 'cause you paid dearly for them. Claude heard and came out of the house and stood on the step beside me and said simply and strongly, "Fuck off," which is very unlike him, but shows how deeply he feels.

'There was a stand-off. I wondered what was going to happen with these two alpha males. Then Claude calmly walked down the steps and continued walking till he was up close, and said, "You're not welcome here anymore."

'I was worried because Claude's no youngster. Pascal's young and strong and aggressive, but he blinked first. He turned on his heels and staggered away, and I'm told he stumbled into Chez-Madeleine and asked for a cognac, and just as he was about to drink it, Madeleine came up and took it out of his hand and told him he was banned from her place forever. "Out!" she commanded in that booming deep voice of hers, and he hasn't been seen in the village since, so, you see, it's quite safe here.'

Martha laughed for the first time in days.

'Oh, dear, everyone knows how stupid I've been with him.'

'You can't stop village gossip, but the sympathies are all with you.'

'Oh dear, poor Pascal, drummed out of Saint-Cyprien. I bet he's furious.'

'For heaven's sake, don't be sympathetic to him, Martha. Everybody's linked together to exclude him on your behalf. Don't be the social worker and take the side of the underdog. He deserves no sympathy. He's a shit.'

'I do appreciate your tenacious support, dear. You've quite bucked me up. You mentioned Madeleine. So, I guess the restaurant is open again? How marvellous, I miss it. How's Philippe?'

'Recovering. Because it's so quiet at this time of year, January, February, Madeleine's planning to shut up for a month and take him and Nadine away to the sun for a holiday.'

'Nadine too? Goodness.'

'Yes. What you told her about being selfish and trying to keep Philippe to herself must have made an impression. I've never known anyone speak to Madeleine like you did.'.

'Oh, well, at least some things are working out for the best. I would love to come back soon. Look, Erin, you're not going to lose me, but I've no idea how to progress with the house. I suppose I've got to find a new project manager, new builders, new all sorts. I've no idea where to start, or even if I've got the energy at the moment. To be honest, I feel half dead.'

'That's what Claude and I've been discussing, and Claude has been sounding out Sébastien in case you're up for it. Now you've bought the old mas, it makes sense to carry on doing it up. You know Sébastien took a year off work to complete their house, and they've moved in now, and although there's some finishing off to do, he's got time on his hands and he doesn't go back to work till April. He's not good with time on his hands. He'd be willing to get things going at Cachette. He knows loads of builders, plumbers, electricians, craftsmen, you name it, the lot. He thinks the estimates Pascal gave you were way too high. And the firms chosen weren't the best. Money was being syphoned off.'

Martha could feel herself returning to life, her spirits rising. She was near to tears, again in unfamiliar territory.

'Martha, are you still there?'

'Yes, Erin, and yes, it would be wonderful. I'll pay him of course.'

'He won't accept that. You'll just have to give in for once and let somebody do something for you out of friendship.'

It was true. Martha found it difficult to accept help or gifts. She found it easier to be the provider. It was linked to the deep uncertainty in her psyche. She determined that, if Sébastien would not take payment, she would give it to Bené instead, and that way it would get into their household via another route. She did not say this to Erin.

When they had finished their conversation, and Martha had promised to go over soon, she wandered through the house which felt chilly, in spite of the central heating, with only one person living in it. She did not mind, in fact she felt warmer inside than she had done half an hour ago.

For some reason she opened the door of the main guest bedroom, the one in which she had first slept with Pascal. It was neat and ready for the next guest, should there be one, with no sign of its last occupant. Mrs Lyle, her cleaning lady, had long since changed the sheets and tidied the room. Martha was still caught off guard in her own room, or in the study, when she smelled the familiar and distinctive small of Thierry. It was less frequent since his clothes had been taken away. There was no hint of either Thierry's or Pascal's smell in here, just a floral fragrance, probably furniture polish.

She could not forget. She did not regret. She and Pascal had used each other for their own needs. She was honest enough to acknowledge that. It was over, finished, and some things had been very pleasant; well, she had to admit the sex had been. But Pascal's ugly, powerful alter-ego concerned her. He was capable of hurting someone very badly, brutalising them, but it would not be her. She had poignant and mixed memories of that night in this bedroom which had changed something in her, and brought her back from her numb and bereaved state. It had been full of guilt and had been wrong.

Mrs Lyle's tidying had not obliterated her recollections. She had re-arranged bits and pieces on the dressing table the way she did, believing them to be an improvement. Martha proceeded to put things back where they should be, and recognised Pascal's shiny pen in a silver dish. Mrs Lyle always put anything she found in a place Martha was sure to notice. It was strange, she thought, that she and Mrs Lyle always addressed each other formally, not by their first names. They had the same desire to keep each other in their proper place. Martha remembered Pascal being irritable when he could not find the pen in France, so she had lent him an ordinary ballpoint to add up the bill for Cachette. She fingered the smooth shaft of the pen as she took it down to the study, Thierry's study as she still considered it, and put it safely in a spare box on the desk.

She had options. Keep it because he owed her so much. Or she could throw it away, perhaps ditch it in the

Channel next time she took the car across from Portsmouth. *No. I'll keep it for him, and hope one day we may be able to talk, and he may even apologise, and I will give it back. Yes*, she decided, *that is the best thing to do*. She was never going back to him, to his life, not after hearing him talk about her so brutally to his deluded girlfriend in the duck restaurant. Their bodies would never make love again, but she would like the chance to see if he had learned anything from the episode. *God knows, I certainly have*. Then she wondered, *What exactly have I learned? Um... I've learned I can be easy prey. I let my heart, or body, rule my head for once, and it didn't work. But I don't want it to make me close up to the possibility of a relationship in the future. Apart from choosing the wrong man, it was far too early*. She was both thrilled and embarrassed by her feelings for Pascal. She was glad she was alone, so her ambiguity could remain her own deep secret. And she understood she would never have a heart to heart with Pascal. It just would not happen. The Pascal she had adored did not exist. There would be no meeting of minds. They had been together in the flesh, but separate in their dreams.

The phone rang again. It startled her into the present. Twice in one evening after so many silent days. She picked up the receiver apprehensively, not believing this could be more good news. In Martha's experience, whenever the phone went after nine, it was usually the out of hours service at work with a problem, or the nursing home to say her mother was unwell.

'Martha, hello, it's Rajinder. How are you?'

'Oh, Rajinder, what a relief it's you!'

'Sorry to phone so late. I called a few times earlier, but it was constantly engaged.'

'Yes, I was on to a friend in France.'

'Ah, okay, well I rang to tell you I've had another call from the young man who phoned before Christmas. I managed to keep him talking long enough to get a message to reception, and they noted his number. He wanted to know more about the accident, if that's what it was, in which Thierry was killed.'

'Wouldn't we all.'

'I suggested we meet, and he said he was not sure about that, and hung up. I returned his call, which surprised him, frightened him I think, because he didn't believe I could get his number. I persuaded him to be in a pub on the Embankment at six when I could get away from the office.'

'Was he there?'

'I doubted he would be, but yes, and we talked.'

'And? Oh, Rajinder, don't stop there, please!' Her heart was racing. What was he going to say? Would she like whatever it was?

'I think you should meet him.'

'Well, who is he? What's he like? Why did he know Thierry?'

'His name is Justin, and he's eighteen, coming up nineteen…'

'Oh, so he's the J we were looking for,' she butted in.

'Yes, and I think he must tell you the rest.'

'Will I like it?'

'I don't know, Martha, I'm not sure how you'll feel, but it's important.'

That was certainly enigmatic, but for her own peace of mind she needed to see him and soon. What had this Justin to do with her husband? She assumed it was a personal connection and nothing to do with Benton & Powell.

Her brain went into organising mode. Martha frequently had appointments in town, though none this week, and she had to meet this Justin before he changed his mind. She looked at her diary. Rajinder was right. Nothing was more important than this. She committed herself to re-scheduling in order to meet Justin with Rajinder at eleven the next morning. She would have to call work early and make excuses.

'I'll introduce you and depart so you can talk together alone.'

It was eleven o'clock the next day. Martha walked across the paved area heading for the Festival Hall. She took a deep breath before pushing open the heavy plate glass doors. The bitter cold outside met the stuffy warmth of the building. Once inside the foyer she glanced round looking for Rajinder. They had chosen the Festival Hall because it was large enough for people to meet and not be noticed.

She wondered where Justin had come from. Her mind had run riot since Rajinder's call, and she was apprehensive.

Justin must have been in some sort of relationship with her husband. It had never occurred to her Thierry might be having an affair with either another woman or a young man. On the train she had scrutinised other passengers, wondering whether anyone ever completely knows their partner.

She had been warned she might not like it when she had committed herself to unearthing the truth. Thierry had been en route to meet this young man the day he died. Walking towards him, away from her. What happened? Justin knew Thierry was dead when he made that first phone call to Rajinder. So what did he want? She knew what she wanted. If Justin was the last person to see Thierry alive, she might find out how or why he had been killed.

Rajinder was standing at the top of the stairs, waving to attract her attention.

He kissed her cheek when she got up to him.

'Has he turned up?' She scanned the room.

'Yes, over there. You're shaking. Breathe deeply. Come, slowly.'

Rajinder took her arm and guided her to a small, smart area of chrome tables and chairs. There was an illuminated polished bar with staff in chic black uniforms serving tea, coffee, cakes and drinks. She saw a young man in a short bronze leather biker's jacket and tight blue jeans leaning on the bar chatting to the barman with his back to her. He was of medium height with shaggy blond highlighted hair, and as he turned his head, he was grinning. It seemed to her he had a knowing grin. She drew back. She did not want to think of the bike boy with Thierry. She felt humiliated. How could she cope or compete with this streetwise stranger?

'Coffee?' Rajinder asked, regaining her attention.

'Yes. Strong and black, please.'

'I'll introduce you and then fetch it.'

He guided her towards a table where a different young man was sitting awkwardly, looking uncomfortable. He could have been nineteen or so, a clean, unblemished face in profile, thick brown hair and a pale complexion. He was in black cords and a dark check shirt. His duffle coat hung on the back of his chair, and he was busily playing with his phone. Her stomach churned as she recognised the tilt of the head, the hunch of the shoulders. For a moment she thought she was looking at the young Thierry as he had been when she first saw him.

He looked up startled and anxious, perhaps shy, and Martha realised the phone was just a prop to keep busy fiddling with something. He looked at her, and she saw his face full on for the first time. It was not quite Thierry's. She recognised the young man who had come to her house with the online delivery of coffee pods she had not ordered. He had looked familiar then, but she had not been able to say why. It had haunted her. Now she understood.

Step by step they arrived in front of him.

'Justin, may I introduce Thierry's wife, Martha,' Rajinder said, and then he turned to her and said, 'Martha, this is Justin—'

'I know,' she said, 'Thierry's son.'

'How…'

She was not the type to faint, but a cold, clammy feeling had risen up her body and gone to her head. She felt sick with either pain or relief. She must have looked as if she were going to fall over because Justin jumped up and he and Rajinder both caught her and lowered her safely into a chair.

'Are you okay?' Rajinder looked concerned.

Justin had lurched back after helping, as if embarrassed to touch her.

'Yes, thanks.' She tried to smile, but felt cold. The world had got darker and everything sounded far away. The three of them stayed like that, two standing and one sitting, unsure what to do. Rajinder only left to fetch their coffees when he was sure she was all right.

'You came to the house?'

'Yes.' He smiled shyly and shuffled in his seat.

'Please tell me why. You sought me out.'

'I guessed he was dead. I wanted to find out more about him.'

'Why didn't say who you were?'

'You had some guy with you. Wasn't expecting that.'

'Did that put you off?'

'He wasn't friendly… Didn't like me… Didn't know who he was.'

'So?' she said after a while. It was a question. She had lots of questions.

'I've done online delivering as a part time job so it was an easy excuse to get into your house. But I didn't know what to say, so I made out it was a mistake. I thought you'd just forget about it. It was kind of daft I suppose.'

He seemed reluctant to say more.

'But you were in the car as well, weren't you, the old blue car. More than once. That frightened me.'

'Yeah... Sorry... It all went wrong.'

She saw tears forming in his eyes, before he looked away and blinked. She thought she might be challenging him too hard.

'What were you trying to do?' She tried to soften her voice.

'Pluck up courage to introduce myself properly. But I kept thinking I should give up the whole idea and go home. I didn't know what to do.'

'You'd no right to stake out my house like that.'

'No. Sorry.' There was a silence. 'It's just that you were my last hope. When you ran across the road you looked so fierce... you grabbed the door handle. I panicked, I guess... I was worried I'd hurt you when I drove off.'

'I was hurt. My hand. You didn't come back to see if I was all right!'

'No, sorry. I'm really sorry.'

She took pity on him. He was young. If she carried on interrogating him aggressively he might run away. She suggested they drink their coffee which Rajinder had put on the table before leaving them alone.

This was Thierry's son! Was that better than his gay lover? It was complicated in a different way. It spoke of another love.

'You wanted to contact me because I'm your link with your father?'

'Yeah. If that's all right.'

'And I wanted to meet you because you're the only one who may be able to explain his death.'

'I had nothing to do with his death. Only…'

'Only?'

'Well, I mean, if he hadn't been coming to meet me, he might not have died? I don't know what happened, but I feel responsible.'

'You can't be responsible. You didn't do anything to hurt him, did you?'

'I never met him.'

'Oh, I'd assumed…'

'I was supposed to meet him. We'd agreed on the phone to meet on the steps of the British Museum… to talk. He never turned up. I stayed on in case I missed him. I thought, he's stood me up.'

'So you never met him?'

'No. That was the first time we'd arranged to meet. I felt he'd walked out on me again.'

'Again?'

'The first time was when he left Mum pregnant with me.'

'Oh. Yes, I see. Did he know your mother was pregnant?'

'I dunno, do I? I assume he did. Mum won't talk about him, so I guess I've made up my own story.'

'I'm really sorry this has all been so awful for you. You mustn't feel responsible. You've done nothing wrong. But if your mother won't talk about your father, how did you find out about him?'

'I eventually got her to tell me his name and Googled it. She said he was an accountant. Didn't know if he was still in London. With a name like Thierry Jolivet, he wasn't so hard to find. She didn't want me to contact him. It was weird hearing his voice answer the phone. I'd expected a hard sounding business man, but he wasn't like that…'

'No, he had a nice voice.'

'Yeah. I'd told the receptionist I was his son. She put me through. He didn't believe me at first.'

'I can imagine. How did you persuade him?'

'I mentioned Mum's name, said, "I'm Lauren Beck's son, and I'm nineteen."'

Lauren Beck. Had Thierry ever mentioned that name?

'And he started to sound less suspicious,' Justin was saying. 'And he said he couldn't believe it, but he obviously did. He asked me lots of questions and then said he wanted to meet me. I said yes 'cause there was so much I wanted to ask him, like why he walked out on us, walked out on Mum when she was expecting me.'

'And you're hoping I can give you some of the answers he didn't?'

'Yes. Can you?'

'No. Well, some, possibly, not all. I'll try. If you've finished your coffee, I'd like to take a walk. I'm desperate for some fresh air. It's early for lunch, but would you like some later?'

'Err.' He hesitated, not prepared for this.

She wondered if he found her intimidating. He must think she was smart, perhaps over-dressed. His clothes looked poor, but then he was a teenager and she thought they all dressed like that. He was more articulate than she had expected, and was far from stupid, but she assumed he was out of his depth in this situation. Perhaps, in her usual way, she was taking charge too quickly.

'Can't. I've got to get to college for a two o'clock lecture,' he said as if it gave him an escape route.

'Where's that?'

'Gower Street.'

'That's not far from here, there's loads of time.'

'I can't afford lunch, not here.'

'It'll be my treat, my pleasure, I mean it, but let's get some fresh air first.'

They left the building together. He was well mannered and held the big glass door open for her. They exchanged something akin to a smile. Outside she led him along the Riverside Walk, past the South Bank theatres, with the Thames on their left. A busker was playing somewhere in the distance, and familiar words floated towards them about the sunset over Waterloo, appropriate feelings even though it was mid-morning. Martha thought the voice sounded good and caught the melancholy. Further along, brightly coloured acrobats were practising on the flagstones, attracting a circle of observers. Martha was captivated, not for the first time. *How alive London is.* Everyone they passed was different, everyone had their own story which she might be interested in. Justin dragged his feet, huddled up in his duffle coat, his hands in his pockets. He was uncommunicative again. She felt she had broken the spell of their earlier conversation, so she searched for a less emotional subject to re-ignite it.

'What are you studying?'

'Modern languages… French and German.'

'He was French. Is that why you chose it?'

'No. I didn't know about him when I applied… But it was going to college that started it.'

'Started what? What do you mean?' They had stopped. He had his back to the river, leaning on the railings.

'Mum made it clear the subject of my dad was taboo. Last year I applied to uni and had to produce my birth certificate, and when Mum finally gave it me, it had a blank space where my father's details should have been. That means… I'm illegitimate.'

'Go on,' she encouraged because he had dried up again.

'I suppose it's not a big issue nowadays, but it is to me.'

'Of course,' Martha said, trying to stay calm, determined not to tell him she shared the same issue, the same hole in her history. She put out a hand to hold onto the railings to steady herself. This was his story, not hers. 'You had it out with your mother?'

'She wouldn't look at me. I said I'd the right to know. We had a serious row. I left and went to a mate's for a few days, and when I came home to collect some clothes, she cried and begged me not to go away again.'

He was clearly affected telling his own story. They walked on and she wanted to touch him, hold his hand perhaps, but stopped herself.

'She told me she'd been in love with this French guy called Thierry Jolivet, and she thought he was in love with her. She said she might have been too possessive. Well, I can believe that! He met someone else and dumped her. I was born around the time he got married to this other woman. God, that's you, isn't it? She's always been in love with him... never got over him... always been madly jealous of this other woman, sorry, you.'

'Frozen in time,' Martha said, sad for Justin's mother and her wasted years.

'Oh, no! Not frozen at all. Far from it. Her feelings are still red hot and angry. She'll never forgive! She's not had anyone else, no one who lasted, and she didn't want me to contact him.'

He seemed to be thinking, working it out, so she waited to see where his thoughts were taking him.

'I don't know why... why she didn't want me to contact him. She could have used me to get to him, but she didn't. I guess she knew he'd been a success, and she hadn't. Maybe she didn't want him to know that.'

Justin was overawed by the good restaurants she knew and said he only wanted a pizza and a coke. She needed a glass of wine so they headed into the first pizza parlour they saw. Black and white floor tiles. Bright colourful modern art on white walls. They were ahead of the lunchtime rush so she chose a table by the panoramic window overlooking the street. They could take refuge watching passers-by, and he would not have to look at her directly if that was difficult. Each time their discussion halted it was hard to get him started again.

'You want to know about Thierry,' she said, acknowledging he had a right to some facts. 'What can I tell you?'

It was meant to be rhetorical, but he took it literally and asked what his father looked like.

'I'd have brought a photograph if I'd known who you are.' She remembered her fears about who she might have been meeting. 'He was quite like you, Justin. I can see that's why you unnerved me when you came to the house. He was only a few years older than you are now when I first met him. Like me, he was just about to take his degree. It was at a university film society. *Jules et Jim…*'

'Yeah, I know that film.'

'He was attractive. There was something… extra about him… a sparkle… especially in his eyes. He loved being in London and was very animated. He was with friends, and so was I. But we ended up together afterwards, and I agreed to meet him again, and that's how it started. I think I was aware he was, or had been, in a relationship, but was attempting to end it, and was having some difficulty doing so. Sorry, that's your mother.'

'I can believe it. She wouldn't let go easily.'

'For my own part, I'd never had many boyfriends. Perhaps I was a bit too studious. I was surprised he… how can I put it?'

'Fancied you?' Justin helped out.

'Well, yes, I suppose so,' she laughed. 'I said to Erin, who was, and still is, my best friend, I said he deserves someone who's sexy and extrovert, and she told me to have more confidence in myself. Well, young man, I've only just met you and I'm telling you things I wouldn't tell other people, but you have a right to know. I didn't know he left his last girl pregnant. I'm sure he didn't know. He wasn't like that. Why didn't she inform him? It's strange because, if she had, he may have felt duty bound to stay with her. Who can tell?

'But you want to hear about Thierry, not me or your mother. What can I say? He was bright and conscientious, but not flashy, which is why he got as far as he did with Benton and Powell and his work for the government. But more than that, he was introspective, and kind and had a quiet sense of humour, and was good at mentoring and tutoring young people. He would have made a good father… He would have loved you.' She came to a full stop, choked up, unable to continue.

Justin, who had been huddled over his pizza, leaned forward and poured her another large glass of wine. She thought she had better take it easy, but was grateful to him for his unprompted consideration. She asked if he would like a glass. He made a noise which conveyed that he was happy with his coke, and she resolved to leave the rest of the bottle untouched.

'You didn't have children,' he said. It was a statement. She knew he had looked Thierry up on the B&P website before it was taken down.

'No, no children. We were too busy being successful. I was ambivalent. He didn't push. I'm sorry now.'

'I didn't mean to…'

'To what? Open old wounds? Justin, that's so like Thierry. You haven't. Oh, I must stop making comparisons. You're yourself, not him. His death opened the wounds. His death ended all certainty. His death made me question the meaning, the purpose of our lifestyle. That's why I'm giving up my career and going to live abroad.'

'Shit, no! Oh, sorry.' He looked devastated, twisting his hands involuntarily. She had underestimated he would feel strongly about her going away. Another swift rejection? She regretted saying so much. It was unfair.

'Because of me?' he asked.

'No, oh no, no, no.' Then she thought that sounded dismissive of him, so she explained. 'I'd made my decision before I knew about you. But don't worry, I'm not going soon, and I'm not going far. We can stay in touch… if you want, which I hope you will. I'm going to live in France.'

'Because he was French?'

'Well, yes, that's part of it, I have to admit. I didn't consciously know, but you're right.' She saw how muddled her motives were. It would not help him to know how lost she was. He needed certainty. She was thinking how to clarify things when he said,

'Sorry. I've gotta go. Class.'

'Can we talk again?' She hoped she did not sound too urgent or clinging.

'Sure.'

'It's important for both of us. You know where I live. Why don't you come over when you can? I'd like to show you some pictures of Thierry, and some of his things, if you're interested. You could choose something.' She knew that she was bribing him.

'Okay.'

They exchanged phone numbers and he left. She was very alone. It was strange, she thought. *I didn't know he existed until a couple of hours ago, and now I don't want to lose him.* She might phone to remind him to visit. But it had to go at his pace. His needs were paramount, not hers. It was his choice whether he turned up or not, and she must hold back, hard as that may be. She poured herself the rest of the wine.

Martha drove down to Bournemouth the following Friday, planning to get there about ten thirty, which was coffee time at The Pines. May would normally be at her brightest. There was the possibility of a decent chat if she was having a good day. Martha had not yet informed the home about her move to France, which might, with luck, take place as early as Easter. The manager would surely know if, how, and when to break it to her mother. She planned to visit several times a year. She kept telling herself not to feel guilty.

As she drove she thought about that dream she had again last night, the one where she was very little in an old van or car. It was a long time ago. The air was still, and everything was eerily quiet. She was puzzled by the recurring dream which was happening more frequently lately. She associated the dream with her childhood. She wondered if it would mean anything to May if she were lucid? Had it drifted into her mind last night because she was seeing May today? Or did the dream recur more often at the moment because her life was in a state of flux?

The roads south were fairly clear. Most traffic was heading towards London. Martha did not particularly enjoy driving, but it gave her the chance to think.

Via email and phoning, using Erin as interpreter, she had enabled Sébastien to get work re-started at Cachette. He was pressing her to go over and meet him on site to discuss details, so she was using up the rest of her leave, going to see her mother this morning, then travelling directly to Gatwick, garaging the car and flying over to

Merignac for a few days, coming back on Tuesday to return to work on Wednesday. She had deemed it important to let Justin know she would be away, in case he was planning to come down to see her, although she judged it was too soon. She had left a message on his voicemail, and to her relief and surprise, had received a text saying he would contact her later.

Normally confident, she worried lest she had been a disappointment to Justin. He had one needy mother and did not need another. But the text confirmed, in her mind, she was significant to him. She warned herself to stop building up their relationship into something it was not. Only time and patience would confirm if it could develop.

Justin was a relief after the anxiety that Thierry might have been planning to leave her for someone else. Now she knew this was not the case. Thierry had discovered he had a son. That must have shaken him up. Surprise would have been followed by a variety of emotions. She guessed it may have made him proud, happy, disturbed, ashamed of his treatment of Lauren, uncertain as to how she, Martha, would react if or when he told her. More probably a mix of all these reactions.

It would surely have caused Thierry to review his own situations, both twenty years ago and now. Had it resulted in him re-evaluating his marriage. Was he happy? It must have accentuated the fact that he had no children with Martha. She could not recall him behaving differently in the days leading up to his death, when he was preparing to meet his son. Had she have been so wrapped up in her own concerns at work that she had missed anything? She honestly could not recall, which pointed to the fact she had not taken much notice. She was sad she could not undo her mistakes.

The jeans and trainers and hoody came into her mind as she drove. Surely, he was not going to meet Justin dressed like a teenager? No, he had gone out that last day dressed for business, and he had not taken that case so could not have intended to change clothes. But he had not been to work. What was it all about? He had prepared or used the clothes for something. Maybe it had nothing to do with Justin. Maybe he had two secrets. Meeting his son was one of them. Disguising himself and however he met his death could be the other. Her reasoning could get no further. She was no closer to the truth.

Since Thierry's death Martha had become painfully aware that they had failed to share their hopes and aspirations in recent years. She had to live with the knowledge. It would not help anyone for her to feel morbid or sorry for herself. It couldn't help Thierry.

She saw Thierry in Justin, in certain looks, in certain smiles. Justin was a lot less confident than Thierry had been, even at an early age. She had little idea what Lauren was like, but Justin had used the word possessive. She had been conscious at the start of their friendship that Thierry had been extricating himself from a relationship with somebody who exerted a hold over him, but was too sensitive to do it brutally. Thierry had not involved or confided in her, but had given hints. Martha had been happy, not only that he had chosen her, but also because he became freer and happier as this unknown woman receded into history. Martha did not even know what she was called or looked like. She banished her to the furthest recesses of her mind. With Thierry's death she had returned, unforgiving, with a son, and her name was Lauren.

She was nearing Bournemouth, managing both to reason and drive. Justin changed their history. She was glad Thierry had a son, conceived before they met. How sad and bizarre Thierry died on his way to meet his son. He was dead, but the loss was less final. She was starting to glimpse a future.

Martha's other connection with Justin was her own illegitimacy. Justin spoke about his birth certificate having no father's name on it. That resonated with the empty pit inside her. She had an adoption birth certificate, naming May and Stan as her adoptive parents. She did not know who her real birth parents were. She was too afraid to find out. It was the only instance where courage failed her. The gap in knowledge about her parentage was a bond with Justin, but one he knew nothing of. She could not burden Justin with her unresolved issues.

She hoped she could develop an adult relationship with Justin, and help him for Thierry's sake. She felt less confident about this as she arrived at The Pines to realise visiting May brought all her childhood feelings and conflicts to the surface.

The Pines was quiet, the garden bare in wintertime. The red brick house looked less attractive, naked and exposed, undisguised by foliage. Val, the deputy matron, always smiling, opened the front door. As Martha stepped across the threshold, she felt glad it smelled clean and fresh though the heat hit her, making her uncomfortable.

Martha had always been impressed with Val's efficient kindness in relation to residents who could rarely respond. Many were wrapped up in their unreachable inner world, usually in the past. Martha went into Val's office and told her about her move abroad, rather more abruptly than she had intended. Val could be interrupted by staff, or have to go and deal with an emergency, and Martha wanted her attention before this happened. Val patiently advised Martha she would have to decide whether the occasion was right and choose her words carefully. She said she must let her know if she had got the information through to May, so staff could monitor her reactions after Martha had left. It was exactly as Martha would have told a client.

May was in her room, which appeared dark and sombre, grey like the winter day outside. She had refused to sit in the day room after breakfast. There was a wan smile of acknowledgement which seemed to register who Martha was. She said a gruff, 'Thank you,' for the soft sweets she could suck. Martha had also brought some more notepaper, envelopes and assorted ballpoint pens and pencils. She recognised she was over-compensating as usual.

'I hope you'll enjoy using these,' Martha began, keen to know what May would write. She said "using" but thought it sounded as if she were implying "playing".

'Of course.' May's eyes looked hostile behind the distortion of her glasses. It signalled the end of that conversation.

A new young carer entered shyly with coffee in thick cups on a plywood tray with a corner missing. It provided a welcome distraction, and afforded Martha the opportunity to tidy the table beside May's chair to make room for the tray. She felt easier when she was doing something, even though she was really incapable of helping May.

Martha saw May looking at the garden through the window while she drank her coffee in silence. Watching with her, side by side, and talking about the garden might aid their conversation. She asked May if she was looking forward to seeing the spring flowers, and walking in the garden when the weather improved.

'You've got a garden, haven't you?' May asked unexpectedly, and then added, 'Remind me where you live?'

'In London. Well, the leafy suburbs really, Chislehurst, south east... You've been to the house, but not for a while. I've bought another house in France...' It was all too much. It sounded too grand.

'Terry came from there… France. I haven't seen him for a long time. Did you say he's dead?'

Martha untangled the threads of the conversation and explained about Thierry again, and about the house she had bought near the village where Erin lived. 'I've brought some photos,' she said brightly, but could see May was no longer listening. She had switched off with the overload of information.

They sat in silence for a while, each with their own thoughts. Even in past times they had not shared much empathy, and Martha found the silence excruciating. She was trying her best. Why did May cut her out?

'I don't sleep well,' May said, addressing the garden through the window, rather than looking at her daughter. Martha did not know if she was talking to her or thought she was one of the staff.

'Have you told anyone?' There was no reply.

After a while May said, 'I worry.'

It gave Martha the chance to ask what May was worried about. Instead, she offered reassurance.

'Don't. You've no cause to worry.'

'It all began with a misunderstanding… It's not right…'

'Look, you're not to get upset. If there's a misunderstanding let me clear it up with the staff.'

May slumped, looking defeated. They fell silent again.

'Mum.' Martha wanted to tell her what was on her mind. She preferred to call her May. It preserved their distance. May, once so proud, had accepted anybody could call her by her first name since coming to live at The Pines. Now it seemed more intimate for Martha to call her Mum.

'Mum, I don't always sleep well either. I have a recurring dream which frightens me. I'm very small. I'm in a car, maybe a van, with grown-ups, and it's very quiet. Nobody moves. I think we're in a ditch...'

'You don't remember that! You want to forget all about that,' May said sharply, light from the window glancing off her glasses, making her appear angry, before she turned away and said more softly, 'Oh, it's such a muddle.'

Then she looked out of the window and seemed to shrink, retreating into herself. She sat like a statue as if willing Martha to go. Martha left, saying she would come again. She knew she had sparked some memory and hoped the old lady might tell her about it next time, as long as it did not upset her too much. May sat staring straight ahead, and did not show she was aware of the exit until the door shut and then she turned to stare at the door which had closed Martha out and her in. Martha would have seen May was crying if she had stayed in the room.

'This is it! I can't turn back now!'

Martha was speaking to herself as much as to Erin. They stood together, keeping out of the activity, surveying the muddy building site surrounding the wreck of the old cottage. Erin had driven her over to Cachette on the

Saturday morning, following Martha's visit to her mother and her flight over to Bordeaux the day before.

'No turning back?' Erin repeated it as a question. 'Surely you don't want to? You've had plenty of opportunity to withdraw your notice at work, and you haven't done so. You could have simplified the plans for the old mas if you weren't planning to live here.'

She turned to look her old friend in the face. 'Do you know what you want, Martha?'

'I'm not really sure what I want, Erin. That's the one thing I've discovered about myself over these past few months. At least I recognise it now, though I don't know what to do about it. But renovating Le Mas de L'Ouest seems as good an occupation as any for the time being.'

'Anyway, you've found out something else about yourself. You've got a stepson!'

'I don't think that's legally the case, I don't think we've any formal relationship, because Thierry wasn't named on Justin's birth certificate, though Justin would like it if he was. Come to think of it, so would Thierry. I'd like to think Justin and I have a common bond in Thierry. At least I hope there is. He's young, I think he may be scared of me…'

'I'm not surprised!'

'They're not well off. I'm certain she's struggled. Lauren, I mean. I suppose bringing up a child on your own isn't cheap. Justin's not daft, but he's not confident…'

'Confident enough to meet you.'

'Rajinder engineered that, somehow persuaded him. Otherwise, it wouldn't have happened. I coaxed him into talking.'

'Yes, well you're practised at that. But he took the original initiative. He made those bold attempts to meet you, watching the house and so on. I know he botched it, and it was an odd way of going about it, but it showed determination on his part.'

'Determination yes. He's driven, obsessed to know about his father, which is understandable, so I'm sure I'll see him again. Well, I'm hoping. And I do feel a responsibility in Thierry's absence. Maybe that's my needs coming out again.'

'At least the mystery's cleared up. You now know where Thierry was going the day he died, and I can understand why he didn't tell you in advance.'

'Yes, so can I. Actually, Erin, I have to admit it's a relief to know he wasn't having an affair, a great relief, but the mystery isn't cleared up. I still don't know why or how he died. On his way to meet Justin. Coincidence or something else.'

'You may never know, but it makes it less likely that his death was anything to do with Benton and Power, or the government or whatever he was working on.'

'Powell, Erin, Benton and Powell, not Power, though come to think of it, Power's more fitting. Well, does it? If someone knew his plans, it was an ideal time to do it, don't you see. Smoke and mirrors. They were all too eager to suppose it was a freak accident and close the lid on it. Mind you, that doesn't rule out it being simply an accident after all. If so, it was stupid, so unlike him to be careless, such a waste... I'm no further forward. It makes no sense at all.'

'Calm down. Whatever it was it came to the same thing for Thierry in the end. He died, and hopefully quickly. It's those left behind who have to cope. Martha, you must leave it now. Move on, you can't help him any more.'

'I didn't help him then. I wasn't listening if he was trying to tell me something.'

'So, you're worrying about that now. You've always got to worry about something, haven't you? You've no evidence he was trying to say anything. The fact he'd got a son would be a shock, but when he'd adjusted to it, I think it would have been a pleasant shock. We know he wanted to meet his son. Until he'd done that, I doubt he was going to say anything to anyone, including you, Martha. Can't you see you have helped, and you are helping? Through your persistence and with Rajinder's help, you've found Justin. You've said you intend to do right by him. You can heal your remorse with Thierry by helping Justin, but for God's sake don't do your usual thing and take over. Just take it gently. You must accept you can't help Thierry himself any more. That's what I meant. You'll just continue to be stuck.'

'You're very perceptive, Erin. I suppose that's true, but I'd love to know what Thierry was thinking, what he was doing, when it happened. When would he have told me? How would he have told me? It may make no difference in the great scheme of things, but it would mean a lot to me to know. We all have to die, but I'd have preferred him to have had a good death, if you know what I mean, if he had to go then. The way it happened seems pointless. Demeaning.'

They had been huddled under a tree, looking at the cottage but not really seeing it. Their focus had been elsewhere, but a loud noise from the building brought them back.

'Is Sébastien enjoying himself?'

'Like a pig in muck. Yes, he's happy because it gives him something to do. He's seemed listless recently. Let's go and find him.' Erin took her arm and steered her round the corner.

'It was cruel that he was just about to see his son for the first time, and never reached him. I imagine he was happy to find out he had a son when he got over the shock. I know his death shook you to the core because you were totally unprepared, but it's you, the survivor, who has to deal with it all, the unresolved bits.'

'And Justin. He nearly met his father, but he was snatched away. How cruel is that? He thought he'd been abandoned again. He also thinks he's somehow responsible, that Thierry's death was his fault, irrational as that is.'

'Oh, Lord, he's taken all that on board and thinks he's killed his father, because it wouldn't have happened if he hadn't arranged to meet him. Poor lad! You'll have to convince him not to burden himself with that one. Now, about you, as I keep saying, time to move on. Put your energy into this house conversion.'

They had got round to the back of the house, still searching for Sébastien. They found themselves amongst piles of stones and bricks and building equipment. Although it was her place, Martha felt she had strayed somewhere out of bounds.

'Careful. I think we'd better retreat and go in the hole where the front door used to be. I'm looking forward to meeting Justin one day. You'll have plenty of space here. I take it you'll bring him over?'

'He's not mine to bring. To tell you the truth, it hadn't occurred to me. We only met the once so far. We don't even know each other well yet, and there are lots of barriers I have to break down if I am to get to know him. His mother might not like him associating with me.'

'He's nineteen. He can decide for himself who to associate with, and you are his father's widow. Just don't push too hard. Don't scare him off.'

'Thierry's widow. Such an old-fashioned phrase. That won't recommend me to Lauren. I stole him from her. Because I'm officially his widow she can never have him back. She must hate me, but that's not my problem. She'll resist my stealing Justin too, and she'll see my helping him as just that. Yes, I must take it at Justin's pace. I must do what's right for him… and what Thierry would have wanted me to do on his behalf.' This was an idea she found herself warming to.

'Sorry,' she said to a workman whose path they had been blocking.

'Give that some serious thought then,' Erin said, stepping aside too. 'Though come to think of it, you're a bit too serious anyway, so just go with your instincts. Do what comes naturally rather than plan it like a military campaign. Meanwhile, let's change the subject. You must unwind, have some fun. Treat this house as your fun. Designing it was the nearest I've seen you get to play, even if it was unfortunately with the shit—'

'Don't call him that, Erin. Even if it's true.'

'Okay, sorry, didn't mean to touch a raw nerve.'

'Just don't use that word. Okay, what he did wasn't nice, but he's not completely bad. The design for the house is the legacy he left me.'

'So, describe what it'll be like when you've finished playing with it. At the moment it looks as if they're pulling it down.'

'No. They're only demolishing the wall between the cottage and the stables. Oh, and the stairwell. And they have to open up the walls where the new windows will go, and dig up the earth for all the utilities, and lower the floor in places. Some of the roof has to come off. This mess is because the trees immediately around the building have been felled... Yes, I see what you mean. It gets worse before it gets better.'

'I'm sure it will get better, but it's difficult to see at this stage. I'll leave you now because I know you want to go through the plans with Sébastien. Ask him to bring you back to Saint-Cyprien when they all stop for lunch.'

Martha had to be honest and admit the house, even if completed, would not have looked at its best in the grey February half-light. Martha knew people back home in England imagine southern France is always sunny, but that is far from the case. This is a bleak time of year. Storms from the Bay of Biscay lashed the coastline. Inland, leaves dripped in the forest in spite of there being no obvious rainfall. There was a fairly continual drizzle, and a dense mist rising in the mornings as the ground warmed up. When it was not dripping, it was cold and murky. The pines, planted for protection just back from the shore, looked sad and dreary. Last year's bracken was brown, dry and brittle. It would be months before fresh green emerged from the undergrowth. This was not how the English pictured France, but it was the naked reality Martha had to get used to.

Erin had left to drive home, wondering if Martha was in her right mind investing so much of herself and her money in Cachette. Martha trudged through the mud and found Sébastien in a temporary hut, carefully measuring a plan with a man who turned out to be the joiner who would be making the new windows. She waited patiently while they discussed technicalities. Sébastien introduced her and asked her to confirm she did not want the windows prepared for painting.

She shook hands with the joiner, and said how pleased she was to meet him.

'That's right. I want them natural, not painted, finished in yacht varnish.'

Sébastien walked her around the house, pointing out what had been done and what was to be done.

'It's good to have you here, Martha. I can make a lot of decisions, but I want you to make some. I dreaded you coming back and saying, "I don't like that, it wasn't how I imagined it." '

'I won't. Anyway, tell me what you need me to comment on. And by the way, how's Bené?' she asked, taking his arm.

She noticed a pause.

'I think he's all right.'

'Only think?'

'Well, I don't see a lot of him at the moment. He's working hard and I'm out here much of the time.'

'I didn't mean to take you away from him.'

'It's not you or Cachette, Martha. Perhaps we're just going through a difficult patch. I'm sure every couple does at some stage.'

'Oh, Sébastien, please be careful. I've seen too many couples drift apart without meaning to. Thierry and I were starting, though I'm beginning to think we might have realised it in time and been able to retrieve the situation.'

'It would have given you a shock if he'd actually had the chance to tell you he had a son.'

'Yes, and a shock is precisely what we needed. It would have been good for us, shaken us out of complacency. I hope it would have brought us together again. Is that rationalising with hindsight? I'll never know. But you and Bené, you're too precious to me. Find out what the problem is before it gets too big.'

'I suppose so. See what you think of Bené when you come over this evening. And don't ask if you can bring anything, because it's all sorted. With the restaurant closed at the moment, it seems best to have a family evening together.'

'A family evening. I like the sound of that.'

Martha could not put her finger on it. Everything was perfectly prepared that evening, but the evening was not right. The atmosphere was strained and forced. Despite what Sébastien had said about Bené being busy, he had evidently had time to shop and present a beautiful meal for herself, Claude, Erin and the children. Sébastien acted the convivial host, but they were not relaxed together. They did not touch. There were no endearments. Martha wondered if they were using having guests to avoid each other. She was careful not to read too much into the situation, having been forewarned, but then she noticed that Erin was unusually edgy, perhaps subconsciously reacting to the atmosphere. Bené was superficially effusive, but actually evasive, wasting opportunities for confidences with her. On departing they all declared loudly the evening had been a great success, and Martha went to her bed troubled.

She had decided it was best not to interfere as she lay in bed thinking. Whatever Sébastien and Bené were going through was their own affair and only they could sort it out, she reasoned.

Only Claude was up when she came downstairs.

'Is Erin sleeping in?'

'She was awake in the night worrying, but as she was in deep slumber this morning, I got up quietly because I wanted to let her sleep as long as she could.'

'Was she worrying about Sébastien and Bené?'

Claude looked up sharply.

'No. Why?'

'Oh, sorry, nothing.'

'She's concerned about Niall as a matter of fact. That's why she was a bit withdrawn yesterday evening. Did you notice? There's some sort of telepathy between those two. She reads between the lines if he writes, and gets anxious if he doesn't.'

'I can see that.'

'As we're on the subject, she told me about her uncle and how you helped her to come to terms with what he'd done, and talk about it. You were right to leave it up to her to tell me. She thinks it's left Niall with more problems than her. He hasn't worked through them. He gets depressed.'

'I'm sure she's right. I'm sorry I missed him at Christmas,' Martha said as she helped herself to a croissant, and Claude poured her a mug of tea.

'It may have been for the best, for you I mean, that you didn't come out. It was a busy Christmas, frenetic in fact. There wasn't much time for anyone to talk about anything important. I don't think Erin and Nail had much time to chat, and that may have made things worse. That may be why she's anxious about him now.'

'And if I had been here, it would have been even busier. Perhaps you should encourage her to take a break and go and see him in London.'

Martha was tidying the kitchen around him.

'I don't think that's practical. His flat is smaller that this room. By the way I appreciate your attempts to bring some semblance of order here, but it won't be tidy once the brood come down.'

'No, but I'm going out, and I'm only responsible for it up to that point. I feel better leaving the kitchen clean.' She said as she left, 'Erin can come and stay with me if she wants to visit her brother, but she'd better be quick or I'll be living over here. I'm off to visit the boys now. I may be back for lunch. I'll phone and let you know.'

With that Martha set off briskly walking the country route. She had only seen the land in summer and early autumn before, hot and dry, densely green, visibly dying of heat.

She was learning to appreciate the seasons, even these darker winter months. In a way she could not express, the change of seasons through the year helped her put Thierry and his death into perspective. She wanted Thierry's approval for what she was doing. But they would not be moving to France if he was alive. Or would they? Was Thierry getting to the point where he wanted a change, a new direction? Her thought patterns and moods changed unexpectedly and she had no control over them. She learned to supress feelings when people were around. She found it comforting walking outdoors on her own, and sometimes gave in and screamed or shouted when there was nobody else around. Not the calm Martha people saw. The release felt good. For a time then she felt calm, and even laughed at herself.

This land between the Atlantic and the Gironde was more varied than she had been aware of at first. To the west lay the ocean and the ever-changing beach including Cachette. Inland there were trees, initially pines by the coast and around Saint-Cyprien, and then the more interesting oaks like those in the woods surrounding the eco-house. She disliked the packs of hunters in the woods in winter, dismayed they invoked no protests. The vineyards and then the estuary, where people fished for mussels, lay to the east, places she had not yet had the time to explore. The few vines she came across here glistened, bare, twiggy and brown at this time of year, cut back with no sign of new growth. The intriguing chateau at Saint-Aubin was over in the direction of the estuary. She was looking forward to spring when nature would wake up and she might be able to move forward with it. By the time she had settled out here in the summer she would have seen the land through the cycle of a whole year.

The future was taking shape in her head as she walked on hard earth down the rough dirt lane towards the startling house of wood and glass which housed two people who meant so much to her. She had decided during the night not to interfere, but this morning she was entering their garden. She had no idea what she was going to do or say when she met her friends.

At that very moment Sébastien lay in bed with his arm round Bené who was apparently asleep, looking innocent and dead to the world.

Is he that innocent, Sébastien mused? *He can be quite a tart, but I love him dearly all the same. I try to give him everything. I do everything I can for him. Is it enough?*

I can pretend there's no problem until he wakes. Then I'll try to talk about subjects which won't start an argument. If he says he has to go out I'll know he's hiding something from me. Where does he go? We used to share all our thoughts. What's his secret? Should I act as if I don't suspect anything? Will questioning push him further away? Is he going off for excitement? He clearly doesn't find me exciting.

I'd certainly be serious and sad without him. He makes me laugh even when he's being naughty. Those funny faces! I miss them. God, what would I do without him? I built this house for him and if he left it would be an empty shell, valueless.

Oh Bené, what are you dreaming of? Not me, I'll be bound! There's a frown on your face. What's on your mind? You're here, but you're not with me. How do I win you back? How do I show you there's more to me than you think? I'd like to tell you I'm strong, but not without you. I'm sensitive, but you don't want to recognise that. I get tired and probably don't give you enough sex, but then you don't always seem interested these days. You used to like sex so much, we were both so complete when I was buried deep inside you. That brought us together. Can I win you back that way?

Bené stirred as Sébastien bent over to kiss his mouth. He was awake. He nuzzled into Sébastien's chest, called him Doudou, then coughed and said hoarsely he needed a pee. Sébastien watched his back recede into the bathroom. The intimacy of the moment was over. The room felt colder. This was not going to be the day he hoped for, not a day spent together, even if they were both physically in the same house.

Bené came back into the bedroom. Sébastien dared not move. He saw Bené move over to the floor length window and lean on the bar, looking out. Sébastien watched the enticing curve of his naked back which he knew so well, and waited to hear what his lover was going to say. It might be significant and he dreaded it. He wasn't ready. He would rather hear nothing than hear Bené was walking out on him.

'There's Martha! What's she doing in the garden at this time in the morning?' He opened the glass doors.

'You can't go out with no clothes on,' Sébastien told the receding figure, but Bené was already out on the balcony.

'Hi!' he shouted down.

'Oh, hello.' The voice drifted up into the bedroom. 'I'm sorry to disturb you. I was just passing.'

'A likely story! I'll come and let you in,' Bené called down, and Sébastien caught him running past and handed him a dressing gown to put on.

They were in the hi-tech kitchen drinking coffee together among the debris of last night's dinner when Sébastien had dressed and gone down to join them.

'Fancy a walk?' Bené asked him, but the look advised him to refuse. They wanted to talk and he was not welcome.

'No,' he said, tousling Bené's hair as he passed behind him to get the cafetière. 'You go and I'll get some breakfast ready for when you come back.'

Bené went upstairs to dress, and Sébastien sat down opposite Martha.

'Don't worry,' she said. 'I'll get to the bottom of it.'

He laughed. She did not see the joke. He almost told her not to get involved, but simply smiled because he knew Martha could get Bené to talk if anyone could.

Bené bounced back into the room looking for his trainers, which Sébastien pointed to, and danced a jig getting his feet into them.

'Ready. Won't be long, but I must show Martha the new vegetable patches and the irrigation system.'

'Yes, I'm sure she came round specially to see those. Don't trip, your laces are undone.' Sébastien said to the vanishing figures who made no sign of hearing him. He set to clearing the kitchen. In a way he was happy. He just wanted things to go on like this and not come to a crisis.

'You've worked hard on this,' Martha conceded, pointing to the ploughed earth and rows of canes waiting to support the plants which should soon be sprouting out of the ground.

'Sébastien mainly. I thought we'd finished the house but he keeps working on things. He's determined we'll be as near self-sufficient as possible in the end. It's as if he's building a haven for the two of us here where we can live sheltered away from the world.'

'And you don't want that?' she asked.

'I don't know what I want, Martha. That's the truth. I suppose I'm a hunter. I enjoy the chase. I'm not so good at settling down.'

'Bené, are you in trouble?'

'I can't say exactly.'

'That's a strange answer. You must know, and if you think you are in trouble you could try telling me about it, and I'll see if I can help.'

'Like big sister!'

'I didn't have a little brother. I didn't have any brothers or sisters, but I do sort of think of you as a little brother. Have you got involved with someone?'

He looked away.

'How deeply? Bené?'

'I thought it was something I could handle. I thought it was just a lark, a bit of fun, a toe, so to speak, in the water, but I'm up to my neck. It's getting out of control.'

'Well, who is it? Does he — I presume it's a he — does he know about Sébastien?'

'Martha, you're asking too many questions. It's bad enough as it is. I keep trying to break it off, I mean to, but it's complicated.'

'People make things complicated, when they aren't. You have to decide: Sébastien or this other person. Surely the choice is obvious. Who is it anyway?'

'You don't know him.'

'Fair enough.' She felt rejected. 'I wasn't sure what I came round to say, but I've said what I needed. Be careful, Bené, please be careful. Don't do something irrevocable you'll regret.'

'Okay, leave it now Martha. Let's go and see what he's got for our breakfast.'

Martha was cross. Bené was clearly blocking her out, but she did as he suggested. Sébastien was preparing eggs Florentine for the three of them, and the warm hollandaise sauce melted in her mouth. Soon afterwards she left them to their Sunday together and took her time wandering back through the lanes to Saint-Cyprien. She should have known she could not just walk into their lives and sort them out. It left her feeling unfulfilled.

'I've had a card from Madeleine,' Erin told Martha late the following morning, while they were taking coffee together. Peace had descended on the cluttered family home after Claude and the children had left for work and school. Erin was going to take Martha to Cachette on her way to the office. She was on a later shift this week which made things easier.

'Where is Madeleine? What does she say?'

'She's in La Reunion, with Philippe and Nadine.' Erin produced the colourful card, a tropical scene, with an exotic stamp of colourful birds and trees. The words were in a characteristically flowery French style, but written with a shaky hand.

'Madeleine's handwriting is very French. But I'd expected it to be bolder,' Erin continued. 'I'd not heard of La Reunion 'til I lived out here, and discovered how popular it is with French people. It was one of their colonies, you know, and although I don't quite understand, they seem to consider it, and Martinique and other places like that, still part of France. It's all one happy family so they weren't colonialists after all! That's the theory, anyway, though I'm sure it's got a dark side. Madeleine talks of coming back and reopening in time for Easter.'

'Open for Easter. That'll be good. I might be out here on a more permanent basis by then, though I can't see the house being ready.'

'You can live here 'til it is. We'll have to organise a special night there to celebrate the reopening and welcome Madeleine back. We've got experience now.'

'And to celebrate my move. There's lots to celebrate.'

Martha's mind flashed back to New Year at Chez-Madeleine, and Pascal making love to her on the beach when they were alone. He might be no good, as Erin often reminded her, but he was good that night, the night before everything disintegrated.

'Hello!' Erin waved her hand in front of Martha's face. 'You're far away somewhere. Come back! That's better. Where were you?'

'Never you mind! And before I forget, it's still some time till Easter. I'm going home to pack up at work and sort out the house. Why don't you come over if you can get time off? Claude told me you're worried about Niall. I don't know him well enough to help, haven't seen him for years, but you could keep me company staying at my place and see him in London. Bring him over to stay too if his little flat is getting him down. I've loads of space.'

'Yes, that might be a good idea. Out of season we're not busy at work. I'd feel better if I actually saw Niall. He's depressed, but whether it's something I can cheer him out of or whether it's more serious than that, I just don't know. He tries to make light of it on the phone to stop me worrying.'

'That's settled then. Don't write to warn him, just arrive. Come with me tomorrow if we can get another plane ticket. Then he can't tell you not to. You can sort it out with the office this afternoon. Claude and the children will be fine while you're away.'

'Stop, Martha, stop. I appreciate your advice, but give me time to organise myself, for goodness' sake. You go and I'll follow. I promise.'

-'Will you?'

'Yes, but don't steam-roller me. And be aware I can't necessarily sort Niall out by coming over. Life isn't always so easy to tidy up. It's simply important to let him know I care. I care about you too, and you probably need some help tidying up in a practical way.'

'I certainly do.'

As the BA flight took off from Bordeaux, Martha realised this might well be the last time she commuted from her new home which was being prepared, to her old home which was up for sale. She snuggled down, deciding to ignore the approach of the steward bearing coffee and sandwiches, and try and sleep for the short flight, or at least rest and daydream.

Her mind was drawn to Thierry and Justin. She still thought of Thierry several times every day, even when she was busy. She often felt lost without him and spoke to him, told him about events, and imagined what he might reply, but his voice was frequently silent and she was not sure what he would make of her life since he died. She had expunged Pascal. Thierry did not need to know about him. She would have valued his advice on other matters. She remembered the last weekend they spent together, when they had driven to Box Hill and had a walk on the Downs, not speaking a great deal, but content in each other's company, with no foreboding of the catastrophe about to unfold. She pictured herself looking at his profile as he gazed over the escarpment, the sun fully on his strong kind face. He did not know he was about to discover he had a son.

She thought again how doubly cruel it was. He missed seeing his son grow up. He set off to meet him and never arrived. She lost him, but he lost his past and his future. They knew nothing of what was about to happen when they walked on the grass up Box Hill last summer.

She turned on data roaming whilst waiting in the queue for passports. News headlines flashed on her screen: the continuing euro crisis and more government cuts to public services. More of the same. It was strange that while in France she felt disconnected from the news and all that worried her French friends and neighbours. She was on holiday. Would it last when she lived there?

The queue was moving slowly. She was putting the mobile back in her pocket when the sound of a Tibetan bell rang out, and the people in front jumped. It was her alert for voicemails. There were two.

The first was from the estate agent. He had taken prospective buyers to view her house and they had put in an offer. Strange how neutral she felt about abandoning the house she had lived in for so many years. It was not the same without Thierry. She was asked to call and give instructions. The second voicemail was Justin, and her heart bounced. She had not thought she would hear from him so soon. What was he going to say? Would it good or bad news? He sounded more confident and self-assured on the machine than in person.

'I can borrow Mum's car and drive down to Chislehurst on Saturday or Sunday if you're not busy.'

She was never too busy to fit him in. She doubted he would tell his mother where he was going. She knew she was supposed to keep a straight face, but felt delinquent and carefree, smiling inanely as she handed her passport to the bemused looking official.

5

Justin and Lauren

Justin was alarmed when the door opened to reveal a woman who was not Martha. He had sent Martha a text confirming arrangements. That had been the easy part. Texting was second nature. He found meeting people face to face more nerve-racking, and had mixed feelings about meeting Martha again. She was posh and had an invisible barrier round her. She came from a different world, a rich world, but it was his father's world, and he wanted to know everything about him. He had psyched himself up to see her, but a different posh woman had opened her door.

His mother was wary of him these days. She had been uncharacteristically uninquisitive when he asked to borrow her car, although she might have thrown a fit if he had said he was going to visit Martha. As he walked up the gravel drive and rang her classy porcelain doorbell painted with wildflowers, he recognised he was making a step change in going to see his father's widow, in her own home, and this time, by invitation. Justin had intuitively discerned she was not straightforward. He did not want to be bossed about by her. He sensed rather than understood he could be swept up into her world. He was not hostile to her, just cautious and a little scared.

He took a deep breath to calm himself. He had constructed the scene in his head as he drove down, and knew just what he was going to say, how he was going to play it. It was going to be all right. That was why he was caught off balance when another woman, not Martha, was standing before him smiling in welcome, at an advantage, knowing who he was and expecting him.

'Hello, Justin. Oh, yes, I can see the resemblance. You are very like your father.' She had a creamy confident voice.

She stood aside so he could enter, but feeling like a lemon he just stood stock still. He could not cope with these high-class women. They unnerved him. He had to admit this one was friendly, more approachable than Martha. She had unruly but attractive blonde hair which looked as if it could do with a good brush, or perhaps even a good cut. She was in jeans and a chunky nearly white sweater, the sort he had heard called Aran or something like that. Despite her casual appearance, she exuded confidence. She was secure, in control of her life; all those things his mother was not and could never be. He felt small and unsure of himself.

'Do come in,' she continued. 'I'm Erin, by the way, Martha's friend. She's had to go out.'

So this is Erin, he thought. He remembered Martha saying something to the effect that Erin had encouraged her, saying she was sexy enough for Thierry. If Erin had not boosted her confidence she might not have gone out with his father. History might have been different. Would his mother have been happier if his father had stayed with her, or would she have always been insecure, convinced she was going to lose him until she drove him away?

'She's had to go out?' he repeated, feeling stupid. It was strange. She had asked him down. Surely, she could not have forgotten, given how insistent she had been about his coming. This was not the business-like Martha he was beginning to understand. She confused him.

'Do come in and I'll explain. It wasn't her choice, she had to go and she asked me to look after you 'til she got back.'

This really alarmed him. He felt panic rising from the pit of his stomach, but allowed himself to be practically manhandled into the hall, which he had seen before on that aborted visit. He caught Erin's perfume as they stood close, a heady expensive floral scent. He had showered and splashed on a cheap aftershave in preparation for his visit, but still felt shoddy though she seemed not to notice. Smiling, she steered him through into an elegant front room which was bigger than their flat in Lewisham.

'I'll make some coffee,' Erin said, and then thought to add, 'She was sorry to have to go at such short notice. There was a phone call very early from the home where her mother lives. They asked her to come right away, some sort of emergency. She said she'll be back as soon as poss, but if she is kept down there she will phone and speak to you. Lunch is prepared, but I can't see her getting back for it.'

'Oh,' Justin managed, wondering why she had not called or texted. He and his friends did so all the time over the smallest re-arrangements, but older people did not seem to get it. Maybe the emergency freaked her so she wasn't thinking.

Erin left him, suggesting he relax, something he knew would be difficult. He began to inspect the room cautiously. This was definitely a drawing room rather than a lounge. Tall draped French windows framed the neat garden like a picture. A bay window on another wall revealed more garden on that side of the house. She must have a gardener; she couldn't look after all this on her own. He knew enough about plants to realise there were hundreds of flowering bulbs, making a carpet of yellow and white. Erin had shown him to a traditional chintz covered settee, the sort he saw on television in programmes involving well to do people's houses. As he sat, unrelaxed, his head did not even come fully up the back of it. The seats felt overstuffed and uncomfortable, not the sort you could slouch in.

He was embarrassed how shabby his jeans looked, and noticed for the first time one of his cuffs was frayed. He panicked, thinking he may have brought dirt in on his shoes. He had washed and dressed carefully, but in contrast with the room which smelt of flowers, he imagined the whiff of his own home on himself, the smell of unwashed blankets and a bare muddy communal waste ground where they played football. He tried to relax into the settee, though he had a problem getting comfortable with all the cushions, so remained vigilant and ill at ease.

His eye caught a photo on a little table, and after trying to make it out, he got up and walked over to it. A wedding photo. A young man and woman. He recognised young Martha, and was interested her style had hardly changed in two decades. Her hair was short and simple, like now. He thought her dress was classic. The face was rounder and more open, more hopeful somehow, but essentially the same. Younger obviously. She looked as if she were about to laugh, confidently gazing into the camera. She had won the prize.

But Justin was more interested in the man. Although he was fuller in the body and older than Justin, he recognised the resemblance to himself. His hair was fashionably long, reminding Justin of glam rock pop groups of that time he had seen on countless repeated streamed *Top of the Pops*. His double-breasted suit was dated by today's standards, and he had evidently spent time expertly tying his tie like former footballers used to do when commentating on TV, before they had moved into today's casual open-neck look. Justin guessed he had bought a new suit and tie for his wedding. He was holding Martha tightly by the hand, not letting go. He was also looking directly into the lens, but there was something shy about him. He was less challenging than Martha. *He's looking straight at me! Can he see me? What would he say to me across nineteen years?* Oh, how he ached to talk to his dad rather than hear about him through intermediaries. The loneliness brought a chocking sensation to his throat.

Thinking he heard a noise, Justin controlled himself and glanced towards the door, but Erin had not returned. He went and looked out into the hall. Where in this big house was the kitchen where Erin had gone? He hesitated and then plucked up the courage to open a door. It was a large formal empty dining room with mirrors and pictures and dried flowers in a bowl on the table. It felt chilly. He shut the door and tried the next one which revealed a tiled floor and brightly lit kitchen big enough to live in. It was warm, and Erin was over at the sink by the window.

'Do you need any help?' he asked, embarrassed his voice sounded tinny and quavering, amplified by the distance and emptiness between them.

'No, I'm fine, but come in here if you like,' Erin invited him. He ventured into the largest kitchen he had ever set foot in, the sort he had seen in *Ideal Home* magazines in doctors' waiting rooms, the kind that made him wonder what people kept in so many cupboards and if they used all these gadgets. He tucked in his frayed cuff.

'I was just about to bring the coffee through, but we could drink it in here if you prefer,' Erin said as she poured two frothing cups from a fancy machine with lots of chrome tubes. She set a cup in front of him on the slate breakfast bar, so he hoisted himself onto a high stool with a black leather seat. 'I always think kitchens are cosier, she added.

Cosy was not his definition of this one, but he preferred it to the drawing room because it would cause less damage if he spilt something here.

'Smart, isn't it!' he said, looking round and catching sight of an abstract mural — bold slashes of red and blue — on the one white wall not covered in cupboards or appliances.

'Yes, it is. You should see my kitchen in France. Make-shift by comparison! Martha attempts to tidy it when she's over. I think she really wants to tidy me,' she confided, and Justin thought maybe he could like Erin even though he was a bit afraid of her. He imagined Martha attempted to tidy everyone she knew, including himself. He speculated Martha had told Erin all about him, which did not bother him. It made matters easier.

'You've known Martha a long time, haven't you?' he ventured as a first attempt to steer the conversation in the direction he wanted it to go. She might tell him about his father in a more objective way than Martha.

'Yes, darling, I'm a really old friend,' she laughed, and he felt embarrassed again. 'We're old ladies from your point of view!'

'You can't be more than early forties,' Justin said, and then felt stupid. He had been warned not to be direct about women's ages.

'Almost spot on, young man, Martha and I were at university together, we're nearly forty.'

'So, she was twenty-three when she married my father. How old was he?'

'Two years older I think.' Erin stopped, aware he did not even know how old his father was then or would have been today had he still been alive. 'He was a nice man,' she added, unsure how much to say in Martha's absence.

'I only spoke to him once.' Justin looked down at his hands which he thought looked coarse and too big in this chic kitchen. His frayed cuff had come down again, He tried to hide it by twisting it round. He felt embarrassed and could not go on.

'You phoned him at his office,' Erin said quietly, encouraging him. Unlike Martha she had children and spent time getting them to express themselves.

'Yes...'

'That must have been a hard thing to do.'

'It was.'

'Brave. I'd be interested to hear about it... if you don't mind telling me.'

'I guess not... I thought about it a lot, and then one day I did it. I was about to ring off, but a woman with a very plummy voice answered almost immediately.'

It was a relief to talk about it. It was easier with someone he did not know.

'I imagined her sitting in a plush office with a cocktail glass in her hand.' They both laughed at this idea and the ice started breaking. 'Her office would be all chrome and glass.' He looked round the kitchen and saw it was all chrome and glass and brilliant white. 'But it would be purple, I don't know why, but it's a cool colour.'

'What did you say to her?'

'I'd rehearsed it, but I didn't think he'd be in or free or able to speak. There'd be security questions, and I'd have to make something up, but in fact it was dead easy. She just asked who I wanted to speak to, so I asked for Thierry Jolivet, and she said, "Who shall I say is calling?" and I said, "His son." It was the first time I'd said it, I hadn't meant to.'

'And you got through?'

'Yes. It was amazing… I mean his voice on the phone. Talking to me! Soft voice. I'd built up the picture of a businessman, but he was different. He sounded mild, and obviously wondered who I was. I worried what she may be saying to him while I waited. I thought she'd come back and say he had no son, so sod off, young man. Oh, sorry, didn't mean to be rude.'

'Don't worry. You should hear me swear! Like a trooper! Go on.'

He thought that unlikely, but it was nice she was trying to put him at his ease.

'I didn't make the call from home. I went out and made it from my mobile. I was sitting on a bench in the park where nobody goes these days except winos in the evenings. It was deserted. Kind of anonymous. Can they trace your calls? Would I be in trouble? Would I be arrested? It was quiet. I heard the distant rumble of cars while I waited.

'"Hello?" It was a man's voice. He said it like a question. He didn't sound French, no accent to speak of. I suppose he'd lived here so long. He sounded kind, if cagey.

"'Hello,'" I replied, and wanted to add Dad, but it wouldn't come out.

"'Who's calling?'" the man asked, again not hostile, but suspicious, I guess.

'Your son, your fucking son! I wanted to shout, oh, sorry, but I said, "Justin, Justin Beck, and my mum's Lauren Beck."

That must have clinched it, because he said, "Just a minute," and I heard a sound like a chair scraping, and a door shutting. When he spoke again his voice was shaking.

"'You say you're Lauren's son? How old are you, Justin?"

"'Eighteen.'" I was eighteen then in June 'cause I'm nineteen now.

'There was a pause after that. "Where are you, Justin?"

"'In the park. Near Mum's flat in Lewisham," I said.

"'The park. In Lewisham.'" It sounded like he was remembering it. Then he asked, "Do your grandparents still live there?"

"'In Hall Road, yes,'" I told him. "They've always lived here." I felt I had to prove who I was. I remember looking around at the broken railings and the dirty, scrubby trees lining the path. Lewisham. Different from The Strand. One world talking to another. Then he asked me things. Did Mum know I was contacting him? Hell, no! Was she married? Again no. She's never got over him, but

I didn't say that. Then he said, "Justin, I'd very much like to meet you." It was like he'd made a decision. It was going to happen! I told him I wasn't after money or anything. I wanted to get that straight. He laughed nervously, maybe relief.

"'I didn't imagine you were." Then we talked about where to meet, and I suggested, "What about the British Museum?" and he said, "Great! Good idea. I could meet you there. On the steps, outside at the front. I may not find you inside."

'Oh, I'll find you all right, I thought.'

'What made you chose the British Museum?' Erin asked.

'This will probably sound daft, but I've always loved it, ever since I was a kid.'

'Have you? That's fascinating, because it's one of my favourite places in London. When I was unhappy at college, when I missed my brother who was still back home in Ireland, I'd go there and lose myself in worlds I could dream about. Why did you love it? Was it like that for you?'

'In a way,' Justin said, aware he was talking a lot, revealing a lot, but feeling it did not matter with Erin. She was easy to talk to, and seemed interested in him. He had nobody else to talk to about any of this. 'When I was little, I drove Mum mad asking her to take me. I'd seen a programme on TV. "What the hell do you want to go there for?" she shouted, but Granddad said, "I'll teck 'im if 'e's interested in that sort of thing."'

'What do you like best?' Erin asked.

'The Romans. I thought it'd be great to be a Roman, if you were wealthy of course. I'd probably have been one of the plebs.'

'Don't put yourself down, Justin. Have more confidence.'

Like Martha told him Erin had said to her. This woman was good at supporting people. He noticed her looking at the clock.

'I'll put the lasagne in the oven 'cos I can't see Martha getting back soon. I'm feeling peckish. You can stay, can't you?'

'Um, suppose so. I'm surprised she hasn't phoned.'

'Well, I hope everything's all right. Do you want to carry on and tell me about going to meet your father? I'm really interested. I liked Thierry. Martha can't have been all that easy to live with, but he was always so calm and gentle. She gets totally wrapped up in things and wants everybody to be involved in what she's involved with. I think he was a steadying influence on her, and of course she's lost that.'

Justin felt guilty. He had been sorry for himself and what he had lost. He had not considered how much Martha had lost. He still saw her as someone who had everything.

'How did you plan to recognise each other?'

'Oh, this bit is funny! He said he was going to be by the main door with a copy of *The Big Issue*, and wearing a yellow tie with butterflies. I thought that sounded corny like a spy movie, so I sent him a selfie, much more practical, and he sent one back, but he'd not done it before and he caught himself from a funny angle. Not a good photo. Look,' he said and got out his phone, zipped through the menu and showed her a grainy, out of focus shot of Thierry. The only one he had.

'No, not a good one,' Erin agreed. 'I think Martha's chosen some better ones for you.'

The phone rang. It was Martha. Erin spoke to her and then passed it to Justin.

'Justin, I am so, so sorry. I'm still down in Bournemouth. I hadn't planned this…'

'No, of course not. Is your mother…'

'She's not too bad now. Sweet of you to ask. It's complicated. I'll explain when I can, but I presume Erin is looking after you?'

Erin heard and called out, 'Yes and we're going to eat the lasagne now.'

'Do that! So, Justin, many, many apologies, and let's arrange to meet again soon. Would you like me to send some stuff of your dad's to be going on with?'

'No, no, please. My mum wouldn't like it.'

'Yes, I can see that. Insensitive of me. More apologies. It's been a bit upsetting today, but you don't need to hear about my woes.

Martha did not want to face anybody, not even Justin. She hoped that by the time she got home Justin would have left and Erin gone to visit Niall. She could reclaim her quiet house. She had been keen to see Justin, but now, at the end of such a day, was not the time.

Her tiredness was more mental than physical. True, she had stayed up late last night listening to Erin and advising her on her concerns about Niall. But it was not staying up late, nor driving down to Bournemouth early this morning that exhausted her. It was hard for her to cope with May's deterioration on top of Thierry's death. She was ambivalent about May and that made it worse. She did not want another death, another close loss. But she did not feel the closeness she thought she ought to feel, hated the guilt, and knew deep down she would be more freed up for the move to France if May passed away.

She had been woken at dawn by a phone call from The Pines. The light was creeping around the edge of the bedroom curtain, slowly revealing the pattern of the carpet. This early sign of winter moving into spring pleased her, though the phone call was unwelcome. Veronica, the matron at The Pines, Val's boss, had sat with her mother most of yesterday evening. May had been restless and disturbed and had started rambling which was unusual. A doctor had been called and prescribed a sedative, but later the overnight duty staff found her wandering into another resident's room, and this had led to a minor disturbance. The staff had been on the cusp of calling an ambulance, but knew May was terrified of hospitals. All the residents of the home were. Martha agreed to drive down to Bournemouth immediately.

Martha dressed quickly and quietly in warm clothes, and only woke Erin when she was about to leave the house. She asked her to look after Justin until she got back. She turned the car round, headed off down the drive and out onto the road. It was so quiet she reckoned she could get to Bournemouth in an hour and a quarter.

Was May physically ill with her rambling and wandering? Was it a sign of dementia? Martha had a hunch she was worried about something particular. She had no real experience of geriatric care, or interest, she admitted to herself. If only she and May had liked each other they might have had more mutual understanding. The antipathy was reciprocal. Martha found she did a lot of her thinking whilst driving. She made reasonable time and parked on the gravel drive by the brick bay window of The Pines. She got out feeling uncomfortable, her emotions knotted in her stomach.

May was safely back in bed and a doctor was with her, so Martha sat in the tiny office, drinking a fresh brew of tea to warm up, keeping out of the way until he had finished. It was still only just after eight, but several residents were downstairs and the light, bright conservatory dining room was filling up for breakfast. The home ran smoothly. Many residents had complicated needs, but the routine appeared to pacify them. She assumed the cleaning and changing of their rooms would be taking place with practised precision while their occupants ate.

'She's a lot calmer now,' the doctor announced, leaning against the open office doorway. 'I've given her a course of antibiotics, and recommend she stays in bed today. She may not want food, but make sure she gets plenty of liquid to drink.'

'She doesn't usually like to drink much apart from tea.'

'That may be part of the problem. She's probably dehydrated. Get her carer to check her every two hours and persuade her to drink a small glass of water each time.'

Martha thanked the doctor for sparing May the trip to hospital. She said she would like to sit with her mother, and the doctor had no objection. He warned May might not recognise her or be up to talking.

'I'll just sit with her as long as I'm not in the way,' Martha replied.

It was dark and shady in the room. The vertical blinds had been angled so as to keep out the early spring sunlight which was gaining strength. The bed had been changed to an electrical metal one, the sort Martha had seen in hospitals. It could be adjusted to different positions, and May was propped with her head raised. Her bony hands rested on the pale fluffy green counterpane, but although she gave the impression of being asleep, they made small incessant scurrying movements across the blankets, and Martha knew she was worrying.

Siobhan, her personal carer, entered silently, and after checking May's pulse, lifted a drinking cup, the sort toddlers have with a spout in the lid, and with one hand on

May's back, helped her take a sip of water. May said something which Martha did not catch, and Siobhan went out as quietly as she came in.

Martha sat and wondered what to do.

'Can't speak much,' May said.

'Don't try, Mum,' Martha said.

'Just nice to know you're here,' and Martha almost cried, both upset and thrilled. Those were the kindest words she could recall May ever saying to her.

Martha waited, unused to acting as nurse. May fidgeted around, evidently trying to sit up. Martha went to her aid, but without any of the skills the carers had, her attempts to help her mother sit up made matters worse.

'Never mind,' May said, irritably. 'Have to tell you…'

'Tell me what? Look, you're supposed to rest, and if I'm disturbing you, I'd better leave.'

'No!' The voice was weak. Then she had a coughing fit, and Martha managed to put some water to her lips, and this helped ease her throat.

'Have you forgiven me?' the old lady gasped, grasping Martha's hand with surprising force. Her old hands were warm and knobbly, the skin paper-thin.

Martha had not been prepared for this. She sat on the edge of the bed and held her mother's hand. She could not remember doing such a thing since she was little, and had not particularly enjoyed it then as she had been afraid of her mother. She was not afraid of her any more, just unsure what was happening. She would probably have to go and get help, but first she had better listen to whatever it was her mother wanted to get off her chest.

'Forgive what?' she asked.

May made one or two false starts and Martha leaned close so she could smell the sweetish warmth of her breath. She encouraged her to take it easy and not over exert herself.

'I always loved you, Poppy. You were such a bonny thing…'

Martha waited. May had never given her nicknames, never called her Poppy. Was that how she thought of her?

'I knew… I knew you'd come back…in the end. Look Stan, it's our Poppy!' May had difficulty in talking. Martha continued to hold her hand, though she had turned to ice inside. May was confusing her with someone else, and this intimacy was directed at that other person, whoever she was, just when her heart was melting because she thought May was asking for her forgiveness.

'Thank you… for sitting with me… you see, Stan, she's here, our Poppy's come back.'

The old lady fell asleep. Martha put the shrunken hand beneath the woolly bedclothes, tucked her in and silently went out. She felt strangely detached from the body in the bed.

Veronica was sitting in the office surrounded by files. She showed Martha the current objectives with May and asked her to sign them if she agreed. Martha added encourage her to speak about her memories, then signed and dated the sheet.

'Has May talked about someone called Poppy?' she asked Veronica.

'Poppy? I can't say she's mentioned a Poppy. She often talks to a Stan when she's confused.'

'Stan was her husband, my father, well, adoptive father,' Martha explained. 'She thought I was Poppy'.

'We haven't got a Poppy here, either on the staff or as a resident.'

'No, I'm certain it goes much further back.'

'Don't worry. You should hear some of the tales they come out with! I'll be sure to let you know if she says more about… Poppy did you say?'

'Yes. And you'll call me if she needs me?'

'Of course. But you're moving away to France permanently soon, aren't you?' Veronica asked.

'Yes, but I'll always come back.'

That guilty feeling again.

'Justin dropped me off at New Cross on his way back to Lewisham. I caught the tube from there and went to see Niall.'

It was the following morning. They were having breakfast in the sunlit kitchen, catching up and filling each other in on the previous day. They were also indulging their tastebuds.

'How is Niall?'

'Well. You know. Niall's Niall, poor lost soul. I depended on him when we were children. Now it's the other way round. Oh, I love this bread by the way. In France they think there's no good bread in England, but of course there is.'

'I know. There are lots of misunderstandings. Oh, try this jam, it's home-made, not by me, but by Mrs Lyle. Regarding Niall, I've said before, you're welcome to bring him over here, you know. I'd like to see him. It's been a long time. I'm not surprised he's depressed if his bedsit's as cramped and oppressive as you say. He might be glad of a change of scenery. It sounds like he needs counselling and company, rather than spending so much time alone.'

'Maybe. I can try to persuade him, but can't force him. He's not suicidal or anything, I hope he's not, just locked in with his unhappiness and unresolved feelings…'

'And you believe he killed his uncle, your uncle.'

'I think so, and if he did, it was because of what Uncle Conan did to me as a child, and maybe to him as well. I keep thinking I ought to get him some help when he's ready, and I ought to go with him. Even though it's a long time ago, he isn't ready to deal with it all yet, and he has to be if it's going to work. I've come through that barrier, with your help and with Claude's. For now, I'll try to coax him to come over here, but if I do, please, please understand. Don't push. It's got to be at his pace.'

'It's sometimes necessary to push people, you know.'

'That may be true occasionally, Martha, but I think you believe every problem can be sorted, every stray end neatly tied up and concluded. People can't be re-arranged in order. I'm not going to bully Niall. I know him. He'll get there in the end.'

'Well, if you say so, but talking of pushing, it doesn't sound as if you had to push Justin too hard to get him to talk.'

'No, he's hungry…'

Martha looked at Erin, needing her to explain.

'I mean he's hungry to find out about his father, to know what he was like. He offered to drive me over to Niall's, but I said just take me to New Cross. The intimacy of the car is a great way of getting the feel of a person. He was uncomfortable when he arrived and you weren't in. I think he was intimidated by the house. Your world is all so strange to him. I suppose the car is his space. He's a bit embarrassed about it being so old and tatty, but I said you should see my old Renault. I suspect the poverty he grew up in, well relative poverty from our viewpoint, is… Oh, what am I trying to say… I think emotional poverty makes a person feel emptier than material poverty. That's it. He may have been poor but he had love. I think his grandparents provided stability. He didn't say much about his mum. I suppose he was trying to be loyal, but she's definitely flaky. It's lucky he's got the grandparents,' Erin continued.

'It's lucky for me he persisted in trying to find out about his father, otherwise I'd never have known about him,' Martha added. 'I'm realistic enough to understand he isn't interested in me, only as a route to Thierry. I've learnt a bit about young people through Justin. I had thought they were a species apart, with their own electronic communications, but they're just the same as us, trying to make sense of it all.'

'I won't tell your colleagues, and especially your staff, you've only just realised that,' Erin said.

Martha had the grace to laugh at herself. She poured them both another cup of tea.

'Earl Grey. I get it from this man in the market. I've got stacks to take to France.'

Breakfast and conversation were worth savouring.

'Yes, I can see his grandparents may have compensated for… for what?' Erin strove to explain. 'I drew him out as much as I could without being too overt. His mother sounds steeped in her problems. I gather she takes drugs, prescription drugs I mean, but rather too many of them, Justin feels. She may have either not loved him enough, or smothered him with too much, or been inconsistent. Some people can't give, they haven't enough to give, they suck out. That's what I meant about emotional poverty. Golly, I must be catching this jargon from you! But you know what I mean, and that's why finding out about his father is so important to him. He has an emotional deficit, yes that's the word, that's unfulfilled. The shock of Thierry dying before meeting him must have been colossal. It made him feel irrationally guilty.'

Erin paused and was silent for a while, and then ventured, 'You still haven't made any attempt to find out about your actual parents?'

'No,' said Martha. It did not invite any follow up, but she persisted.

'You could go through official channels, or you could encourage May to talk.'

'May's got her own worries, but she probably knows very little about me before she adopted me.'

'You could ask.'

'I don't want to cause her anxiety. I don't get straight answers anyway.'

They were still lingering over the remains of breakfast, both looking to see if there were any goodies in need of finishing off.

'You could help me sort things out though, in a different sort of way. Preparing for the future, even if the past is a mystery,' Martha started, and Erin knew she was going to be organised into some activity. 'I seem to have a buyer for the house, some people who've made a formal offer, and for the asking price. So, this challenges me to actually do it. I have to begin sorting out. I've made a list. I've been through and disposed of a lot of Thierry's things since he died, but there's still the study, and so many cupboards. I've been ruthless, I don't keep clutter, but even so I'm amazed at what we collected over twenty years. I need your advice. The key thing is what to take to France.'

'If you're talking about your furniture, most of it is too big, too English…'

'Oh, I don't mind English. But you're right, most of it's too big, too formal, it isn't going to fit in. I want to choose things in keeping with the scale and the style of the old mas. I want to take a few personal things I can't be parted from. I can sell bits and pieces, I can give things to people as mementos. I can raise some money for charity, and make myself feel better. But I need to start somewhere, and maybe you could advise me, get me started.'

Erin thought it was interesting Martha had difficulty starting to prepare to leave. She kept that to herself.

They spent much of the day dismantling the study and crating up books. Several boxes were destined for the charity shop, a small number were to be sold through an antiquarian bookseller, and the chosen few were packed up to accompany Martha to her new home. The solid square desk would be going over there too because she could not part with it. It was not an heirloom — neither she nor Thierry came from that sort of family — but they had bought it from an auction when they had barely been able to afford it, and treated it as their heirloom, albeit there were no children to inherit. Maybe it would eventually go to Lucy who was already taking an interest in that sort of thing. It was rosewood, eighteenth century, and she intended to sit at it, in Cachette, and plan out her future. It was the only piece of furniture from this room she would keep.

They talked about Justin and Niall while they worked. Then Erin confided how concerned she was that Sébastien and Bené were so obviously unhappy, though trying to cover it up as if they could not face the possibility of splitting. She thought Sébastien had conceived the eco-house as their contribution to saving the planet, and as their love nest, but Bené seemed restless, maybe smothered by Sébastien's care. Martha said she would have another go at getting them to talk when she went back to Saint-Cyprien, but Erin said it would only work if they both invited her to do so.

It was while Martha was telling her friend about the day the police had arrived and searched the study, including the drawers in the desk, that she remembered the false bottom in one of the drawers in the right pedestal and they began emptying them to see which one it was. No one would have guessed, but the floor of the middle drawer lifted out and there was a space big enough to keep private correspondence. Martha had to look twice. She shook it and heard a rattle. She was not expecting to find anything, certainly not a brand new A4 notebook. Erin stood back.

Martha said, 'It's Thierry's. Some notes by the look of it. He was always making notes.'

'Yes, but hiding them?'

Erin knew this was important and private. She left Martha with her find, making an excuse she had to phone Claude.

Martha's pulse was racing. This had to be significant, or it would not have been hidden. She had to know. This was Thierry's! She opened the book with trepidation and saw it was dated the day before he died.

Tomorrow I'm going to meet my son for the first time. It feels like the beginning of a new life. I'm full of nerves and excitement. Nothing has been the same since he phoned me on Monday. I have a son! Wow!

Rewind twenty years.

Concentrate. Re-live, make sense.

I'd come over from rural France, and was at university. I loved exploring London, swinging London. I felt truly alive, and wanted to stay here forever. Letters from Mama reminded me to go to church, not to get involved with girls, and come home as soon as possible. No chance!

I remember we were encouraged to spend second year out of college, away from our halls of residence. It was supposed to be especially beneficial for foreign speaking students like me. The truth was there wasn't space for everyone, so they kicked you out on the understanding you could come back for your final year and big exams. That's how I ended up at the Becks.

LAUREN!

What do I remember?

Oh, yes!

I tried to ignore Lauren at first. She had long blonde hair, lacquered and piled up. Too much make-up and slightly chubby. Curvaceous. Tarty, but friendly to me. She worked in a shop, so when she came home she left work behind. She took to hanging around my bedroom door, asking why I was always working. I explained, being French I had to learn so much more, and I was beginning to realise I was good, but would have to work at it. She would bring me coffee and stay until her dad shouted for her to get her arse downstairs. Oh, yes! No one talked in that house, everyone shouted, no one listened. I found myself arbitrating because I could see what they wanted and they didn't seem able to see it themselves. I think they were happier finding problems than solutions. It was good for my English, and I learned a ripe vocabulary.

Why had Thierry committed this history to paper? Did he want it to be found? No. Presumably he had used these notes to sort out his head. It was his habit. She was aware he wrote if there was a big issue. Methodical Thierry! Oh, how she loved him! He would probably have intended to shred them when they were of no more use. She was compelled to read on. This was the sort of evidence she had searched for months ago, and here it was, in her own house all the time.

It was Mark from the class who gave me the address and phone number of the boarding house in Brighton. Cheap. They didn't ask questions. Pretended I was going to France for a visit. Lauren was supposed to be on holiday with a girlfriend. Don't know to this day if her parents were deceived. Her mother wanted us to get together. She probably thought it best if Lauren settled down and I was a good catch.

The week with Lauren began as a game, but I grew bored and she grew serious. We were using each other, acting out different fantasies. I must accept responsibility. I enjoyed the sex. It was becoming addictive, and she knew she'd got me there, got me hot. I wasn't nice to her, I'm not proud of that. Maybe her mates were right. I'm a snob! I was planning my career, and didn't see Lauren as a soulmate for life. But dropping her was harder than I expected.

I went back to living in hall, but she wouldn't let go. Friends wondered what I saw in her. Well, they knew what it was all about, the joy of sex, but it wasn't joy any more. England is class-ridden, even among apparently liberal students. They said she was common. I deceived myself, thinking that if I distanced myself gradually it was kinder than dumping her. I just hadn't got the balls to face up and tell her that I didn't want to go on like this. I was making her unhappy by being dishonest.

Then I met Martha, and I knew she was the one, the only one for me.

MARTHA

It may have been a trick of the light, but the first time I saw Martha, I was captured by her simple beauty which was translucent, perfect and self-contained. We met in the foyer of the student union building and everyone else melted away. Thankfully, Lauren had not wanted to come, though I had asked her, so I managed to engineer our group so I sat next to Martha, and she watched the film and I watched her, and I thought her exquisite. In profile her nose tips up like a child's. She doesn't like that, but I find it enchanting. We all had a drink together afterwards, and she talked about the bond between the two men in the film, and I just agreed with everything she said. Then, as we were about to disperse, I asked her out in front of all my friends and hers. It was do or die. I couldn't let her go. I might never see her again. She hesitated, taken aback, and the group watched us, spellbound. I think she was about to decline, embarrassed, but her friend Erin pushed her towards me, and said, 'If you don't say yes, I will.' That was it. We became an item.

And Martha had a depth of understanding I'd never encountered before. We met and talked, and walked and talked, and I was floating above the ground. Was this love? Although I was two years older, my course was longer, and our finals were about the same time. I nearly missed an assignment. She told me off, and said she wouldn't fail her course for me! Oh, yes, we made a pact. We would help each other graduate, and get the best marks possible. It became our pact for life. We've encouraged each other to get to the top ever since.

I made excuses to Lauren. Martha realised I had an issue to resolve. She approached it obliquely, but her advice was clear. If I had another relationship I had to choose. So I did. I went to see Lauren and took her out to the park and confessed I was seeing someone else, and I asked her to let me go. She cried and said she wanted to get away from all this. She gestured hopelessly pointing out the mess, broken railings and debris from litter bins, and looked at me through tears and running mascara, like a broken doll, and cried I was her ticket to freedom. I walked her home, and said I wouldn't come in, and she said, 'Too bloody right, my Dad'll kill you.' It was the last time I saw her.

Martha was spellbound, but also full of cramp from sitting on the floor, reading his notebook. She forced herself to put it down for a moment. She went into the living room, poured herself a whisky and took it back to the study. She could hear Erin in the kitchen, but needed to be on her own. She shut the study door firmly, and settled down in the swivel chair at the desk to read on, the glass comfortably at her elbow.

I felt bad. Ashamed of leading her on and dumping her. Mark said she had brought the situation on herself. I said, no, we were both to blame, and I couldn't hide from that. But oh! The relief as I felt Lauren's fingers falling away. I was like an insect emerging from a larva. I was complete and free and alive and ready for Martha, and I wanted to blot Lauren out of my life for ever.

LIFE WITH MARTHA

Ah, now we're getting to it.

I've grown comfortable with Martha. She's still beautiful, in fact she's hardly changed in looks, just got rather more regal...

Shit, no, not that again. She heard Thierry's voice. She experienced a stab of pain at his description of her. Regal! She did not want to be, but could not help it.

...and she's successful at work, well regarded, in line for a top job in Social Services or Whitehall when and if she chooses to go for it. We have both negotiated the corridors of power without sacrificing our ethics or making too many enemies. No mean achievement. We

live well and support a number of good causes. I assumed we would start a family at some stage, but there was always time ahead and then it slipped from our radar. It was only after Justin phoned, and I started to accept he must be real, that I understood he was the missing piece, the future we had not succeeded in creating.

How will Martha respond to discovering I have a son?

There was a break in the text. It looked as if he had returned to it later. A different pen too.

Continuing. I wanted to check. Martha is hard at work in her study.

It will test us, but I don't want it to break what we have. I won't tell her till I've seen him. I must find out what he wants, what he expects. It was a shock to me, and it will be to her, but Martha copes, Martha adjusts. Once she gets over the shock, I rather think Martha will be inclined to take over and make plans. It's her way. I don't intend to give her a head start. She might plan to adopt Justin as a stepson. She won't want Lauren as part of the picture, though Lauren is the boy's mother. Martha can be ruthless. I have a hunch the problem won't be Justin, the issue will be the unresolved triangle from two decades ago

Lauren... Me... Martha.

I got the sense from Justin that Lauren hasn't moved on, hasn't found the sort of happiness we've attained.

Surprised? No. Guilty? Yes.

It's all come back to haunt me. As I deserve.

Do I still have strong feelings for her? No, but I do sense a bill to pay. I don't mean just a financial bill, I mean a moral one, and I'm prepared to pay. Lauren is my past and Justin is... could be... my future. How do I resolve that? But I'm getting ahead of myself. One step at a time.

Do I love Martha? Yes, with all my heart. I don't want any of this to destroy our feelings for each other, but it will take some working through. I will come clean to her as soon as I've seen him. We may be the better for it in the end.

Does Martha love me, or just take me for granted?

Martha was overjoyed and sad in equal measure. He knew her so well, and he loved her all the same. That was the most important thing she needed to know. It was such a relief. But did he die unsure she loved him? That was terrible! And she couldn't change it. She wanted so much to reassure him and make it all right.

So, tomorrow I'm going to meet my son for the first time and it feels like the beginning of a new life. I'm full of nerves and excitement and hope this won't be a crushing disappointment for either of us.

What will he be like? He's taken the initiative to find me, seemingly against his mother's wishes, and had the courage to actually contact me, speak to me on the phone. He's still living at home, though about to go to college. I suspect he's ready to move out into the world. I must help him, but not against the wishes of his family.

I took some old clothes in a case to work yesterday, and bought a grey hoodie as well. I took a long lunch break and caught the tube to Lewisham, and changed in a public toilet. I walked down Hall Road and went in the park. It was much as I remember though there had been attempts to smarten it up, blue painted railings. The same but different, time had moved on, and my connection with it was tenuous. I changed on my way back to the office and wondered why I had done it.

I'm trying to act normally. I was shaking as I shaved this morning, in danger of nicking my chin and giving it away. I managed to steady my nerves, get dressed and look as if I was going to Benton's for the day. I don't think Martha noticed anything. She was preoccupied. After my excursion to Lewisham I confided in Rajinder that I am taking tomorrow off for personal reasons. He's the only one there I can trust. I almost told him why. He would have understood. Maybe I treat him a bit like a son. I didn't because it wasn't right to tell anyone before Martha. I reasoned with myself that when the time comes to share the information, she should be the first to know. I reasoned that's the best I can do.

I don't want Martha to suspect a thing. She's preparing for work tomorrow, and thinks I'm working here in my study this evening. I'm going to have my time *with my son, and nothing must stop me. Fallout or consequences will follow. I'll confront my errors, faults and responsibilities later. I am going to meet my son. It's as simple as that.*

Who else will I have to tell?

My mother!

Oh, God, won't it be a surprise to ma mère that she has a grandchild. I expect she'll be displeased as usual; everything I do displeases her. 'Mon Dieu, Thierry! How could you!' I will never please her, so it's pointless feeling sad, even though I do and always will. A son wants his mother's approval, whatever his age. I've had to live without that and validate myself. C'est la vie. Maman, she's the loser, I'm sad to say.

As long as Martha accepts me and my new-found son, the rest doesn't matter.

Just a few hours to go now. I'm ready!

Within eighteen hours of writing these thoughts, and preparing himself to see Justin, he was dead.

Martha vowed to help Justin as Thierry would have wanted. She erased Lauren from the story.

Justin came round the following weekend. She had put a number of things aside for him. There were photographs of Thierry going back to his student days. As she handed each photo to him she told its story. She had written dates and notes in pencil on the back of each one.

She offered his Rolex and his Parker pen with Thierry's name inscribed on the barrel.

'These are for you, Justin.'

'I can't take them, not now. Not till I've left home. Will you keep them for me, Martha?'

He looked through everything, touched everything, asking questions.

'I wish there was something…'

'What Justin? something what?'

'Something… this sounds daft! Something that speaks to me directly. Says what he was thinking when he found out about me. Stupid, I guess.'

She was touched that in spite of his gaucheness he was able to lay himself bare, unafraid to reveal his sensitivity and yearning. He was somebody she would not have met in the normal course of events, and here he was, revealing his vulnerability, being honest with her in a way she could not imagine many nineteen-year-olds doing.

In that moment she decided to break confidence with Thierry, for that is how she thought of it, and give him the one thing that revealed Thierry's last thoughts. She went into the study and returned with the A4 notebook.

'This is intimate. He had hidden it. It says things about your mum, about me, and your father, discloses his sex life in a way that was not intended for either of us to read. It talks of his excitement at finding you, or more correctly, you seeking him out. I wouldn't have it if he were alive, but in the circumstances… here, read.'

Justin took the notebook from her hand and she left him alone. Half an hour later he came to find her in the kitchen.

'Thanks,' he said quietly. She put her arms round him and he hugged her tight. It was spontaneous. It was healing. They both cried.

Justin called in at the flat to change his clothes before going to meet his mates for a drink. Radio Two was on as usual. His mother's music from the nineties. At least it was better than when she tuned into local radio, listening to inane phone-ins, or when Jeremy Kyle was on the TV. The flat looked tawdry after Martha's house. He was not ashamed of them being poor. His mother had not had Martha's advantages. It was the untidiness and disorganisation. His mother was defeated. She had given in. That was what annoyed him, and deeper than that, hurt him because he wanted better for her.

His bedroom door was open, and as he approached quietly, he saw his mother sitting at his desk, looking at the screen of his laptop. She shut it abruptly when she heard him.

'Oh, 'ello dear, just tidying up,' she said too loudly, smiling at him with wariness in her eyes, like a child caught red handed going through drawers in a parent's bedroom. Tidying up was the last thing she would be doing.

'What are you doing in here?' It was more a statement than a question.

'Sorry, love, sorry, would you like a cup of tea. I was just goin' to—'

He was in the doorway so she could not get past without manhandling him. He was in no mood to give way. He often felt sorry for her, often covered up for her, and often denied his own feelings so as not to upset her. It was as if he was responsible for her rather than the other way round. But today he felt let down by her and knew he had to make a stand.

'What've you been looking at? I don't do porn or drugs. You should know that. You should trust me.'

'I do, love, I do. Sorry, I shouldn't've looked…'

'I've been to see her, Martha. She gave me some of Dad's things.' It was blunt, sticking a knife in her.

She looked wretched for a moment. Then she recovered and started.

'I know you're seeing 'er, the stuck-up cunt. Behind my back. You do everything behind my back. Oh, you're so like your father, doing everything behind my back.'

He could have struck her. He had seen his granddad hit his grandma. He had witnessed his mother scream at them both. He had never screamed. He had never hit anyone. It was not in his nature and it made things worse. He remembered the last time he knew she had been in his room, looking through his things, reading his emails. It was the afternoon he had come home when he thought his father had stood him up. He got home and realised his mother had been home and been through his room. That was when he had picked up his chair and brought it crashing down on the desk. He had vented his frustration and anger on his room. He had gone for a long walk by the Thames, feeling suicidal. Even throwing himself in would solve nothing. No purpose in living, no answer in dying. He had slunk back into the flat and bleakly huddled down under the cold duvet. His mum had come in and held him. They had never talked about it. Now she had been doing her detective work again. She was jealous of Martha, whom she had never met.

'She's lost a lot too,' was all he could say.

'Oh yer. She's got the fucking cream, that bitch, and she wants you an' all. She's not takin' you away from me!'

'She's lost Thierry, like I've lost my dad, like you've lost... him too. Can't you just...' He could not find the word. Later he realised it was forgive.

'I'm going out. See you later.'

He had intended to shower and change before leaving, but he needed to get out immediately. He would see if he could clean up at Guy's house. Maybe Guy would lend him some clean clothes, let him crash for the night. Guy's mum liked him and seemed to understand matters without him having to say too much. He was grateful to Guy's mum. He felt his mother's swollen eyes boring into him as he walked out the door, but he left all the same without looking back. It was the most anger he would allow himself to show her.

Martha was looking forward to the clocks springing forward this coming weekend. The evenings would be lighter. Another sign of moving on.

The old blue car was parked in the road. That surprised her. She had not expected to see Justin again so soon, but was delighted if he had spontaneously decided to call. But why this evening and why so late? And why had he not let her know? She would have come home from work earlier if she had known, before it started to get dark.

She had reflected during the drive home that hers was the sort of job that was impossible to tidy up and hand over in an orderly fashion, because people brought new problems. New issues were cropping up all the time, and now they were due for an inspection at the most inconvenient moment. The farewells, the handing over — it had all begun. There was no turning back. She was still usually the last one to leave at the end of the day. The manner in which she bowed out was important to her. Some colleague might be jealous or critical of her cutting herself adrift, but she was determined to give no cause for criticism of anything that happened on her watch.

She came to a halt on the drive. Where was he? She had not given him a key yet, though she was intending to do so.

'Justin?' she called after getting out. She had parking under the pergola that doubled as a car port. She rarely used the garage, which was now full of packing cases.

The beam must have picked her out because the security light came on illuminating the dusk as she walked towards the porch. She inserted her key in the front door and then let out an involuntary shriek as she saw the figure, not Justin, but a woman wrapped up in a big coat. She felt silly, embarrassed by her reaction, but shaken as well. Was the woman related to work? Perhaps a client bearing a grudge who had managed to obtain her home address? It had happened before. She had shrugged it off in the office. It was frightening in the shadows on the drive.

'Who are you?' she asked in a voice she modulated, hoping it sounded non-threatening, trying not to betray her fear.

'You never met me. I bet you never think about me. I think about you all the time.'

Martha's hand strayed to the mobile in her pocket. She would try to get the emergency number up without actually ringing it. She would coax the woman to speak. She would not let her in the house, but neither did she did want to spend too long out in the cold.

'What yer got in yer pocket?'

She decided to play it straight. 'My mobile phone. I might need to call for assistance. It depends on who you are and what you want. What do you have in your hand?'

''S only a knife, in' it. Don't look so worried, it's not for you. It'd be better if I used it on myself don't you think?'

'It would be nice if you told me who you are.'

'Ooo, la-di-da. That'd be awfully nice,' the woman mocked.

Martha was unsure what to do. She remained still.

'You know who I am,' the woman said. Martha saw the very blonde beehive hair, the old-fashioned style, too-much make-up, sorry eyes.

The woman she wanted to erase from her life.

'Lauren?'

'Lost for words, ain't ya? Thought words was your thing. Words is how you're weaving a spell to take my Justin away, just like you took Terry all those years ago.'

'It's cold, you'd better come in,' Martha said. She moved to unlock the door. She had to turn her back on Lauren to do this, and knew this left her open to attack. The spot between her shoulder blades tingled. She was frightened and vulnerable. No blow rained down on her, and after turning on the hall light, she felt a little more normal. She held out her hand and took Lauren's elbow to help her in, but Lauren shook her off. Martha beckoned her inside.

Lauren looked pale under the glow of the electric lights despite her real or fake tan, and Martha saw the determination draining from her as if she had had enough. She doubted Lauren had thought further than coming here to confront her, and now she had done that she would not know what to do. Martha moved her into the sitting room, and urged her to take a seat. Without thinking she poured them both a whisky. She needed one, and as she gave a glass to Lauren, she hoped she was not on medication that the drink would counteract. It was too late to care. Lauren inspected the glass and then drank it down in one. Martha sipped hers, but knew she would need another. She rarely drank straight away on getting in from work, but did so now in an attempt to calm her nerves. Martha was no longer afraid of Lauren, and sensed the power had shifted between them once she had gained her home ground. She had to be careful. The atmosphere was unstable and unpredictable and she practically smelled the other woman's animosity.

Martha carefully looked for the knife, but could not see it. Lauren had banged her glass down on a side table and stuffed her hands in her pocket, so it was impossible to tell.

'You talked about doing yourself harm…' Martha began. She was unsure if it was wise to be so direct, but she was tired and wanted to cut to the chase. There were things to be said between them, and here and now in her house was as good as anywhere. She was considering how she would get rid of Lauren after they had settled affairs.

'Much as you'd care.'

She was about to offer a platitude, but was unprepared for what Lauren said next.

'I killed 'im.'

'Who? You killed Jus—'

'No! Tel. Tierrie as you call 'im. I loved 'im and I killed 'im. Been going mad inside. There. Confessed. You win it all. May as well kill miself now.'

Martha was usually quick to grasp things. She was rarely lost for words, but this was one of those times.

'He was knocked down by a van,'

''E was killed 'cause I called him, across the street, and 'e stepped off the pavement coming to me, straight in front of the van. It was my fault.' She was getting louder, defying Martha to contradict her.

'Why were you there? How did you know—'

'I went to stop 'em meeting, didn't I? I wanted to plead with 'im not to take Justin away.' She looked up at the ceiling, her head swirling on her shoulders. Her voice became softer, more remote. 'I 'ad to see 'im, see if 'e still loved me.' She slumped back in her chair, drained.

So, this was how Thierry died. He was caught off guard by Lauren appearing and calling to him from across the busy street. Martha felt sick. She loathed Lauren who had robbed her of her life with Thierry. She felt violent towards her. She wanted to hit her. She knew at that moment she was capable of killing her. She wanted to shout at Lauren to get out, but saw she was in no fit state to be put out. Lauren sat there looking defeated, looking unlikely to do Martha any harm, though she did not trust her, and was unwilling to leave her alone. Might she self-harm? Martha did not care, and thought with any luck she would kill herself. As she forced herself to breathe slowly, Martha's better-self intervened, and told her this was

313

wrong. She continued breathing deeply to calm herself and resolved to get Lauren home safely.

'Would you let me call Justin? See if he can come and collect you.'

'No! Don't want 'im to know I'm 'ere. Don't want 'im to know I came to confess to you. Don't want 'im to know I killed 'is father.'

She could have reasoned with Lauren, said he did not need to know all that, but she let it rest. She would have liked to have gone and got something to eat, maybe prepared a meal for the two of them, but she dared not leave Lauren alone, and Lauren seemed immovable. They sat in silence. Lauren was staring randomly at the ceiling, at the room or at the floor, seemingly lost in thought. Martha used the time to take stock. It was best if she encouraged Lauren to talk, to say how she felt, even if that meant hearing how much the other woman hated her.

'Did you think Thierry had changed much when you saw him in Guildford Street? You hadn't seen him for nearly twenty years.'

'What? Er, Guildford Street? Oh, yer, on the way to Russell Square. He'd filled out a bit, but then you do, don't you. Well, not you, you're as thin as a rake, probably anar... annax whatsit.' The animosity was still there, but she seemed to be fighting confusion or exhaustion. ''E still looked... lovely. 'E looked 'appy, smiling, like. 'E'd been such a serious young man when 'e came to live with us. Do you know, 'e came 'cause 'e wanted to improve his English, lodged in our 'ouse, what a laugh! We were

314

always shoutin' at each other or not speakin' at all. He musta been very confused! Took refuge in his room, with 'is grammar texts and 'is 'ccountancy books.'

'Would you like a coffee?' Martha asked. She felt more comfortable having got Lauren talking.

'No. Want another of these.' Lauren waved her whisky glass, and Martha took it to refill. She poured herself another as well. She thought they ought to eat something, but was unwilling to leave Lauren even to go and fetch some biscuits.

''E met you at that arty farty film, didn't 'e? I didn't feel at ease with his student friends. I said no to going to that film. It sounded poncy, not my thing. Story of a French boy and 'is German chum who end up on different sides of a war; I ask you! You went, didn't you? That's where he met you.'

'Yes.'

'I should 'ave gone. 'E met you and it was never the same again. Must admit 'e'd always been a bit cool. I'd had to do the chasing, egging him on. Used to take 'im dancin', with me mates. The girls thought 'e was a pet. The boys thought 'e was a poof. 'E was that gentle. Wasn't though. I got 'im out of his clothes, on the sofa, when me parents were out. Got 'im hot! Lovely body! Nearly caught once. That's why we went to Brighton. Parents didn't know we'd gone together. Even there 'e liked to go for walks, on 'is own, alone, on the downs as 'e called 'em. I could come, long as I didn't talk, but I wasn't welcome. 'E had to have 'is space. I said, "You should 'ave grown up in our 'ouse. No personal space there," and 'e said, "I know." Sometimes I planned out our future, but when I told 'im 'e said knock it off. Well, being French and posh-like, 'e didn't use those words exactly, but that's what 'e meant. I remember 'e didn't look at me when 'e said 'e wasn't ready for commitment. I've had lots of time to think about it, years, and I think 'e must a been planning to dump me, to get away, long afore 'e did.'

She was silent, contemplating. Martha waited, as Lauren's mood had gone quiet and reflective.

'Moved back to college. Said it were important for 'is final year. Wasn't right living under my parents' roof after what we'd done. Mum and Dad were glad, 'cause they could see it were becoming complicated, us all living together. They liked things proper. They asked for a girl student next time. Right dullard she turned out to be.

'We were still going out when he told me about the film, and I said it didn't sound interestin'. I wanted 'im to come dancin' with me instead. 'E started meeting you after that, didn't 'e? I think 'e'd seen you several times when 'e plucked up courage to tell me it was all over 'tween us. I remember we was sitting on a park bench, the dirty local park, it was, with litter all around. I felt I belonged there and 'e didn't. Looked too pure! 'E was s'posed to be my 'scape route. 'E walked me back to th'ouse, but wouldn't come in. My life was over. Cried for days.

'Mum and Dad weren't surprised when I said 'e 'ad a social work student girlfriend now. They said, "'E wasn't your type." They meant well, but it 'urt.

'Then of course I found out I was in the club. Bloody Brighton. Had to tell Mum when it started to show. Dad declared it was Mum's fault for taking in a foreign lodger. "What did you expect?" She told him not to be so bloody daft. I said it was nobody's fault. Dad was all for going up the college and doing something, don't know what. "He should be thrown off his course," Dad said. When it came down to it neither Mum nor Dad wanted to force 'im to marry me, so they didn't confront 'im, and I had the baby without Tel knowing. "Better off without him," Mum said.

''E was a lovely baby. Quiet. You've not 'ad a baby, have you? Suppose they're too messy for you. They're 'ard work, they take your time. Called him Justin, thought it was unusual name. Didn't know it was going to be so popular. There was three in 'is class. It's more Essex than French. Wished I'd called him some'ut else.

'Mum said we'd stick together and look the neighbours in the face, brave it out. So much for being proper. Proper daft. No one gave a toss. Found there was lots of unmarried mums round our way. Went back to work. Mum looked after Justin 'til 'e started school. 'E was a bit unsure of 'isself, but 'appy in 'is little way. 'E did well at school. I went to parents' evening, scared out of me wits, and the teacher said, "Now, about his academic performance…" and I said, "Oh, I see to it 'e does 'is 'omework," and she said, "Yes, he's very bright indeed and determined as well. He'll go far." Cor, you could have knocked me down!'

'Yes, he's done well,' Martha said.

'Yer, gone to university. Dad's got over 'is prejudice against students now Justin's a student. Without their help I couldn't 'ave done it.

'Got my own flat off the council. Dad helped me do it up. Justin went to Mum for tea and I picked him up after work.

'I know he comes across shy like, but if 'e wants to do something 'e does it. 'E's got some good friends. From college mainly, not from back home. 'E's had girlfriends, but won't tell me much about 'em. Only natural. 'Is little group, they're not a wild crowd. 'E works hard, and still lives at home, well most of the time.'

'He was certainly determined to find out about his father.'

'Yeh. 'E's ad this bee in 'is bonnet about finding 'is father. I 'ad to give him some details, 'e'd walked out on me once and I wanted to stop him going again. I thought 'e might be 'appy wi' what I told him and leave it at that. But oh, no. When I looked in 'is room I could see 'e'd been on the internet and Facebook and God knows what, tracking Tel down. I didn't know he was still in England. I got it out of him. 'E'd actually spoken to Tel as I called 'im on the phone and was going to meet 'im!

'E'd spoken to Tel!

'I'd wanted to speak to 'im for nineteen fuckin' long lonely years, and 'e'd gone and bloody done it, just like that. I was afraid if 'e met 'is dad 'e'd leave me. What 'ad I to offer? Tel and 'is posh wife, you'd steal 'im off of me. I guessed Tel was still with you. I knew your name.

Martha. 'E'd told me on that cold park bench, "I'm with Martha now, and I love her." 'E was honest, I'll give 'im that. You came from other side of the tracks. I thought of you as the ice queen. 'Aw I 'ated you. 'E'd fallen for you, 'ook, line and sinker. Tel always got what 'e wanted. 'E always kept what 'e wanted. That was you, not me. You must 'ave been very 'appy. Cat with the bloody cream'.

Now she had started she could not stop talking. Martha did not interrupt.

'Well. what was I to do? I thought if only I can get to 'im first I can explain Justin and 'ow 'e's my world. Even if I couldn't stop 'em meeting I could beg 'im not to take Justin away from me. If 'e took 'im away, what 'ad I left? I'd found out where they was meeting. If I knew 'im, 'e'd be early, and Justin would just about make it on time, you know teenagers. So, I took the morning off work and caught the tube. Planned to get to the British Museum, speak to Tel and get away before Justin turned up. Okay, sounds crazy, but I was beside myself and couldn't think of anything better.

'There 'e was, in the flesh, real as you or me. Beautiful. Always thought 'e was beautiful, and 'appy. Oh, Tel! Tel! Knocked the stuffing right out of me. I saw 'im first, on other side of the street walking in the same direction, looking purposeful. Smart suit. Not a student now. Jacket over his shoulder. I called out, and 'e turned. I'll never forget the look on 'is face. Surprise? Shock? Didn't look pleased. 'E wasn't expecting to see me. Twenty years, or nearly so, and we recognised each other just like that! All that 'istory, it doesn't go away, even though a lot's 'appened. I like to think 'e smiled at me. I'm not convinced, but I tell myself 'e smiled 'cause I want to believe 'e did. 'E came towards me. I suppose 'e stepped off the pavement. 'E was looking straight at me…'

Lauren was crying. She looked imploringly at Martha, but Martha would not respond, would not comfort her in her distress. Martha was horrified, finally understanding Thierry's last moments. Caught off guard by Lauren from the past. She saw it clearly now, the few seconds which ended his life and changed hers utterly. She could not comfort Lauren. She would love to kill her, but knew that was wrong and would undo everything that mattered.

''E didn't see the traffic. In my sleep I see the white van, hear the thud, white van gone. Can't sleep no more.' Lauren's voice got through to Martha and she tried to pull herself back from the scene in Guildford Street, back in the house, back in the present with Lauren making her confession. She wanted to talk to Lauren, to ask about Thierry's final moments, but no sound came out when she tried to speak. Lauren was looking round the room desperately as if she thought she might find Thierry hiding somewhere.

'No Tel. Where was 'e? People crowding round. Someone tried to stop the traffic. A policeman appeared with a walkie-talkie thing. I heard 'im say "fatal casualty". I came to, like it 'ad been a dream and found I'd been rooted to the spot since the moment I saw 'im. I turned and ran back to the station, falling down the steps onto the platform, sweating. My 'ead felt it was goin' to burst. A train was coming, whooshing down the track, blowin' cold. I was falling, falling onto the rails. Someone caught me, pulled me back. "Are you all right?" 'e said. I just saw a blur. "Yes," I said and got on the train. People was lookin', pointin', talkin' about me. I 'eard 'em say she needs a doctor. "I'll be okay," I shouted. "Sorry, sorry, sorry!" They thought I was saying sorry I'd frightened them. I was saying sorry to Tel. Sorry, I killed ya, sorry, Tel! Sorry.'

Lauren stopped and there was silence. Martha hated her. And bizarrely, despite all the stupid woman had done, she now felt sorry for her. Lauren had been the last one to see Thierry. Her meddling had brought about his death. She could not forgive that. People say they forgive. How do they do that? She also felt the other woman's pain and hopelessness. The room was strangely quite peaceful. What now?

'So, you've told nobody until me now?'

'Nobody. I puked up when I got 'ome. 'Ad to get myself together and clean up. But I couldn't stay in. Justin would be 'ome. 'E hadn't met 'is Dad. 'E thought I was at work. I sat in the park, yeah, same stinkin' one, more litter. They'd tried to tidy it with bits and pieces, sculpture they called it, but they were growing graffiti too. At last I thought it safe to go 'ome … the flat was empty. No Justin. 'E'd been in. 'Is room was smashed up. Papers 'e'd printed about 'is dad were torn to shreds. I picked 'em up. I picked 'is chair up, and then I shut the door on 'is room. Oh,

Justin, where are you? 'E thought 'e'd been stood up. 'Is father 'ad chickened out. 'E wasn't loved. My love didn't count. Not enough. Wanted 'is dad. 'E wasn't wanted. Where'd 'e gone? It was my faut, all my fault. I'd destroyed 'em both. I'd probably lost 'im an' all.

'When 'e did slink back into the flat 'e went straight to 'is room. I went in and 'e was on the bed 'owling like a baby. I 'eld 'im best I could. I was a fraud. I was responsible for this and 'e didn't know!'

Lauren seemed to remember her drink. She finished it in a gulp, banged it down on the side table, and then glared at Martha.

'So, what do I do now, clever Mrs Jolly… Joly-whatever? You're expert on people. Do I confess I killed 'is father? 'E'll never forgive me. All I want is to go back to before setting off for Russell Square. I say to myself, *Don't go, don't go. Let 'em meet. Let 'em be 'appy'*. But I did go, and I spoilt everything… as always.'

Martha could not contradict her because it was true. She waited to see if Lauren had finished.

'I let 'im believe 'is father let him down, didn't want to see 'im. You see I 'adn't the balls.' The silence was only interrupted by Lauren's intermittent sobs.

Martha was out of her depth because of her love for Thierry and her shock and sadness at how pointlessly he had died. She thought of Justin and realised she needed to protect him because Lauren was no longer capable of that. She had to make decisions and take charge of the situation.

'I have no idea what I would have done in your situation, nor what you should do now.' Martha spoke slowly, conscious of needing to use the right words. 'Let's concentrate on Justin and what's best for him. He knows his father was anxious to meet him,' Martha told her, though she doubted Lauren was listening. 'He doesn't think his father chickened out, he is now aware something happened and he just didn't get there. I may have inadvertently muddied the waters. I couldn't accept he may have been taken from me by a silly accident. So, I fed him the idea Thierry may have been killed deliberately. He worked on high security investigations, you know, corporate fraud, money laundering, that sort of thing. The police were initially interested and then they dropped the case like it was a red-hot potato. My imagination worked overtime, and Justin was quick to pick up on conspiracy theories. You know what kids are like, they watch too many movies...'

Martha realised she was rambling to herself, so she stopped. Lauren was glassy-eyed and silent. She was not listening. She would not have understood a word.

'I'm going to get us both a sandwich. I think we need to eat something and then calmly decide what's best, for Justin. You'll be all right for a moment, won't you?' Martha almost touched Lauren, but drew back. Lauren nodded and Martha was relieved. Lauren sat quietly while she left the room.

When Martha returned with a plate of bread, cheese, cold meat and chutney, Lauren was slouched over in her chair. The whisky bottle was open by her side, nearly empty, and a bottle of pills was in her lap, also almost empty.

'Shit!' Martha dropped the sandwiches on the couch, ran to Lauren and slapped her face hard. It was hot and clammy. She tried to get her on her feet. Lauren was too heavy. She grabbed the phone, dialled 999, and after a wait which seemed interminable, reported the situation as factually as she could. They told her to walk Lauren up and down, and make sure she got some fresh air. The ambulance was on its way.

She shouted at Lauren as she raised her from her chair.

'I'm not going to let you die on me, you bitch! Not here. Not in Thierry's house. I won't have it! Do you hear, you stupid bitch?'

She threw open both windows to let in a shock of cold air, then hauled Lauren roughly onto her feet as best she could.

'Walk, damn it!' She forced her to move forward. Lauren slumped over her, a dead weight. It was difficult to keep her balance. Martha felt panic. She let Lauren slide down onto the sofa. She reached for the phone again and pressed Justin's mobile number, which she had put in her personal contacts, and mercifully he answered.

'Justin, you've got to come. Your mother's taken an overdose... oh, at my house. I know, yes, it's a shock. No time to explain. Get a taxi and go to Saint Mary's A and E. We should get there about the same time. If you haven't enough money, phone and I'll come out and pay.'

Martha pulled Lauren up again and dragged her to the window to get her some air. Lauren collapsed on the windowsill and vomited all over the plants in her garden.

Justin was at Guy's house and they were both lying on the floor listening to music when he got Martha's call. The intimacy and tranquillity of the moment was shattered. Guy's mum gave him a lift to the hospital. He thanked her and told her not to wait, then headed for Casualty. The long white corridor reminded him of other hospitals where he had been to collect his mother. The receptionist directed him to an annexe where he would find the lady who had come with his mother. Yes, of course Martha was the lady. He did not want her here. She was out of place. She looked incongruous, sitting on an orange plastic chair. She was still in business clothes. It looked like an expensive suit. One to take on directors rather than deal with clients. He had heard of power dressing. He wondered when was the last time she had seen a real client. He wanted to hide this side of his life, protect her from all this. Pale and tired, she got up to give him a small hug. He felt her bones through the soft bobbly woollen material of her grey jacket.

'She's in a cubicle,' Martha pointed to doors definitely closed to non-medics. 'They're washing her stomach out. We can't go in. I don't know if she's going to pull through. They haven't been out to tell me anything.'

'It's okay. I've been through this before. She'll be okay. Well, she'll live, anyway.'

'I'm sorry, Justin.'

'What for? You've nothing to apologise for.'

He had not wanted his mother and Martha to meet. Different worlds, emotionally charged. He had tried to keep these two worlds apart. Why had his mother gone to see Martha? Probably to warn her off from seeing him. Why had she taken the pills? Maybe to attempt to kill herself in Martha's house. That would make her feel extra guilty.

'I shouldn't have left her. I didn't realise she'd do this, but I should have guessed. I only went to the kitchen to make her a sandwich.'

Justin flopped into a chair and she sat down again, this time next to him. Thankfully there was no one else around. He was staring at the floor.

'Are you okay?' he heard her ask. It was a silly question, but the sort of thing people ask when they do not know what to say. He was thinking his father was dead, and his mother had tried to kill herself. The important people were deserting him. No, he did not really feel okay, but he couldn't tell her that.

He had the urge to hold her hand. He wanted to be held, to be comforted, but they were still very new to each other and he did not know what sort of relationship they had. He must not rely on her. His mother was behind those doors. Martha was not his mother. He didn't need two.

'Okay, I guess,' he replied. 'Thanks for calling me.' After a while he continued, 'She's done it before, you know.'

'So I gather.'

He was tired. He stared down at his jeans and Doc Martens and felt shabby. He felt her hand move into his. He did not look, but accepted her touch. She squeezed his hand and held it. He fixed his gaze on the wall opposite. There was a sign requesting visitors to be quiet and saying violence against staff would not be tolerated. That familiar hospital smell. He had the urge to explain to her.

'She's always been... unstable. I had a funny childhood. Nan looked after me, and tried to look after Mum too. Later, when Nan was older and so was I, it was me who went to the police and the hospitals if she was missing. I found her in the park once. She'd been sick, she'd tried to...'

'Oh, I am sorry.'

She sounded like a social worker. He knew she would have experience, however distant, of people feeling wretched, needing her to take away their troubles.

'Each time I hope this will be the last time I sit in a hospital corridor while Mum's pumped out after an overdose... I'm sure she'll do it one day, and there'll be no one around to get her to hospital, so even if it's only a gesture she may die. Why was she at your house, anyway? She didn't hurt you, did she?'

'No, no. I'm fine. She came to confront me, tell me she didn't like me, and tell me not to take you away from her. That's what she's worried about, Justin, that you'll turn your back on her.'

'She goes about things a funny way, doesn't she! She brings about the things she doesn't want to happen. What a mess!'

'But she does have you, and you do understand her,' Martha said, probably meaning to comfort him. He realised it was true. Even though he disliked his mother's behaviour and crises, their blood bond existed. He would not abandon her.

'My mate Guy says I've been programmed to help her and there's nothing I can do about it.' He gave an involuntary laugh, but it was not funny. He felt it was unfair, life was unfair, and felt selfish and bad for feeling that.

They had a long wait. They both became intimately acquainted with the corridor, the non-matching notices which jostled for attention, the magazine rack with periodicals and newspapers neither of them was interested in, but which acted like magnets. The place looked clean, blanched hospital clean, and he caught a definite whiff from time to time. Disinfectant? There was activity. They could hear the drone of noise and the occasional voice from the A&E waiting room round the corner. There was a TV on somewhere. Nurses came and went down their corridor, fetching and carrying things, and disappeared through doors, but nobody came near them.

Martha put down the tabloid she had picked up to read with a look of let's see what the other half get up to. She looked bored, though he noticed she had read all about the celebrities she claimed not to know. Justin showed her a game on his phone. She told him she was not interested in games, but he persuaded her to try it and she grasped it quickly and said, 'It's quite addictive. I think that's what I feared.'

Finally, a doctor came out.

'Miss Beck has pulled through and is resting now.'

He addressed Martha.

Justin asked, 'I don't suppose she can be discharged tonight?'

'And you are?'

'Her son.'

'I'm just a family friend,' Martha explained, and Justin thought, that's not quite true, you're more than that. 'I'm afraid Justin has had to look after his mother a lot.'

The doctor said Miss Beck could not be discharged until she had seen a psychiatrist, probably not till tomorrow. 'That's normal procedure as it is not the first time.'

Justin almost said I know. Instead, he said, 'I'll phone tomorrow and find out what time I can pick her up.'

'I'm sorry you've got this sort of responsibility,' Martha said after the doctor had left. They were walking the long white corridor towards the exit. 'I followed the ambulance. I shouldn't have driven because I'd had a whisky, but I didn't think about that in the circumstances, My car's in the car park over there.'

'You're not going home straight away, are you?' he asked. Then he saw she looked exhausted and was probably hungry too. It was selfish to want to hold on to her. He certainly did not want her to drive him home. He did not want to show her their flat. It would be better if he drove Martha home in her car, then collected his mother's car and drove himself home. He summoned up enough energy to suggest it.

Martha looked done in, but grateful. He saw her struggling to find the right words, friendship words, his sort of words, not too intimate.

'Want a pizza? I'm starving.'

'You bet!' he replied.

6

The rendezvous

'I'm going to meet my son, the son I knew nothing about!'

Thierry has a spring in his step as he walks briskly down busy Guildford Street towards Russell Square. He is fit, healthy and unable to stop smiling and singing to himself. It is warm and he is beginning to feel sweaty, so he removes the jacket of his smart black business suit, and carries it casually over his shoulder. He had his hair cut by a traditional barber on The Strand, near his office. He is glad he had smartened himself up. He is not vain, but today he wants to look his best. Not disappoint.

Thierry has loved London ever since he had arrived as a student from France over twenty years ago and stayed on. It appears at its best on a day like today, a fresh morning in early summer. Even the jarring traffic with its noise and dust cannot spoil it for him. He would have been in love with London whatever the season, because of the turn of events in his life. Since Justin's phone call everything has taken on a new life. Sounds are more vibrant, colours brighter, shapes clearer. So much changed with that one call. He still loves Martha, more than she knows, he suspects. But he wants to like his son as well. *Will I like him?* he wonders. *What is he like? I'm supposed to love him, but that could be difficult. He's a nineteen-year-old lad and I've missed those nineteen years, unaware of his existence. I've been doing other things, working for Benton's, prioritising Benton's, married to Martha, jogging along happily with Martha. I don't regret those years. I only wish I'd known. I could have been part of his life even at a distance, instead of sending my nineteen-year-old son a dodgy selfie so he can recognise me. And of course, Martha will have to know about Lauren and how shamefully I behaved. Lauren! I haven't thought about her for nearly two decades. Help!*

He has been in an unusual state of excitement for the last two days, since committing himself to the rendezvous, but careful to cover his tracks and let no one suspect. His adventure is secret as this stage. He has written his thoughts down to make sense of it all, and carefully hidden the papers. He will tell Martha as soon as he can but he must meet his son first. She has a habit of taking over.

Because he is unused to subterfuge, he inadvertently said something to Raj, but managed to turn it into a joke, and Raj had mercifully caught his mood and agreed to cover his absence from the office. After that he made sure he did not slip up again.

Life is good. It has just become a hell of a lot better. He loves his wife and has a son. He is confident about the future. The meeting is arranged for the steps of the British Museum. Anonymity within a crowd.

A vision from the past interrupts his happiness. It watches him from across the other side of the road. The figure looks like Lauren. She is dumpier than the girl he remembered, but the figure moves and clarifies itself as the real Lauren. Her style has not changed a lot. Her hair is still vividly blonde and piled up in an old-fashioned style. He feels sick rising from his stomach to his mouth when he knows he is not imagining her. He did not expect this, but it is too far-fetched to be a coincidence. Is it a sting? A trap he has been caught in? Surely not. He does not know Justin yet, but he instinctively trusts him, and Justin said his mother does not know he contacted him. She has obviously found out and is determined to intervene.

He is so nearly there! She must not stop him. He has to reach the museum on time. He cannot let Justin slip away or think he isn't turning up. But he must confront Lauren first. He needs to say sorry to her. His heart is thumping. There is so little time. He must beg her not to stop him meeting his son. He will not take the boy away from her. Her face is sad, as if life has defeated her. He is the cause. The road is a chasm between them. She is beckoning. He steps off the pavement.

7

This Summer

And so, we have arrived at this summer, a year on from Thierry's death.

I'm here at last. I'm settled, Martha says to herself, tells the cottage, the cliffs and the beach. She has doubts about the word settled. Perhaps it is premature, but this is where she wants to be and she has made it. Legal details of her living in France still have to be finalised.

Asparagus grows wild at Cachette at this time of year. She was amazed to discover it, for it does not generally grow in these parts, and wonders if it was originally planted by whoever owned the farm, long ago, Or perhaps birds dropped seeds brought over from Kent. Either way it is a good omen. Asparagus can be found among the grasses on the cliffs leading down to the cove. Martha goes and picks bunches of lush green stalks. Only the best. She is careful to break them part way up so as not to pull up the roots. She is looking forward to cooking them for tea. Her French friends adore chunky white asparagus, the sort you buy in Sablette market. She considers it tasteless. They are astonished the English like the green. Cattle fodder, they say! So, the asparagus challenge is on. She has to prove green asparagus is truly delicious. She will serve it to them this afternoon.

She looks back at the old farmhouse, sheltered from the coastal winds by young firs, and is glad to be living here at last. It is the first house that is hers alone, chosen by her. Not her parents' place, nor the house she bought with Thierry. Her own. She has stopped trying to control her grief at his death. It cannot be controlled, and still swamps her in waves, leaving her empty, but her instinct tells her she is doing the right thing moving on, and he would approve. She knows the truth about his death and no longer feels insecure about it. She feels her way forward day by day.

How am I?

I couldn't describe myself as happy or even content, but I have come to terms with myself and my situation. It has taken a whole year to get this far and it's far from complete. She assumes there will never be final resolution. In one sense she does not want there to be. Her history with Thierry is precious and her love lives on inside her. She is sad he is not here to share life. It was cruel.

Outwardly a new chapter opened when she moved out here after Easter. She had a life before and she has this life now. Somewhere in the middle was a muddled period of flux, a messy time of partial knowledge. Her relationship with Pascal proved how out of balance she was. It was part of the muddle.

Things have changed since she moved two months ago. She thinks back to the situation in April. She arrived feeling elated and frightened in equal measure, starting over again. Alone.

The British, or more accurately the English and Welsh, had voted to leave the EU. Madness. It made her sad that just as she had moved out to France a vital connection was broken. She had signed her postal vote in the village post office in Saint-Cyprien, witnessed by a number of intrigued locals queuing for stamps.

'Nous resterons!' she had declared as she handed her envelope over the counter, and one or two clapped. She was alone at Cachette the morning she tuned into the BBC Radio 4 in the kitchen, as she did first thing each day, and could not believe the result. She had no one to cry or shout with. It felt like a second bereavement.

'What have you done?' Sébastien demanded in disbelief when he came round later to finish off some outdoor jobs he had promised. 'We need each other.'

'It's not my fault! I voted to stay in. It's a protest vote, most of it nothing to do with Europe. People will live to regret it.' Her sadness had changed to anger, but there was nothing she could do. It was not fair to take it out on Sébastien who had his own problems.

She was determined to go forward even if the world was becoming divisive and going backwards. She went shopping in the market in Sablette one Saturday morning soon after the final move. She parked her car, a new left hand drive VW, in a side road and weaved her way through the outer stalls selling fabrics, clothes and bric-a-brac, all flapping in the breeze, shaded by large umbrellas. She was heading for the farmers selling eggs and vegetables over by the big church when, silhouetted in a gap between awnings, she unexpectedly spotted Pascal. She had not expected to see him again. It sparked the thought of Thierry spotting Lauren across the street, and the parallel unbalanced her. She had erased Pascal from her mind and he was no longer connected with her or the old mas at Cachette.

Stopping dead, she caused a woman to collide with her, and they both apologised. Pascal was with Bené and a couple who looked English. She guessed that from their dress, the leather patches on his old but good quality sports jacket, his cap, her Laura Ashley style long frock and straw sun hat. Martha was too far away to catch what they were saying. They were examining local wines and the stallholder was very attentive, probably hoping for a decent sale. She saw the tableau in an instant, but Pascal was the only one who saw her. He turned to Bené, gesturing at something on the other side of the market, and Bené dutifully, moved the couple away in search of whatever it was Pascal had directed them to.

Martha no longer feared him, at least not in the open air on a Saturday morning. Should she ignore or confront him? She knew she should at least acknowledge him even if he did not want to recognise her. She held him in her sights and moved closer. He saw her approaching, said something to the disappointed stallholder, and cut and ran, followed by the others who must have been surprised. She decided not to pursue. It would only be embarrassing. It left her, however, with an uneasy feeling. He had been nasty and threatening when she dropped him. He had said she would be sorry, sounding like a schoolyard bully. Was that all bluff? Was the danger past? Why was he so desperate to avoid her now?

Why was it necessary to prevent her meeting Bené and the English people? He was like a scar on her brain, a self-inflicted wound. But of course, he had the right to be there shopping in the market. In such a small rural community she was bound to bump into him. Later, back home, in the cottage on her own, worries about Pascal got muddled up with residues of guilt at abandoning "home", her home with Thierry, and she realised her move to France had not been enough in itself to resolve her conflicts. There were still things she had not come to terms with.

She was also unhappy because of Bené and Sébastien's break-up. They were no longer speaking to one another and Bené had taken refuge living at Erin's.

'Let him be,' Erin said. 'The children like having him around, and he is fun for them. I don't know what's happening, but it's best not to interfere.'

Sébastien had overseen the restoration of her cottage, but was still spending time at Cachette. Martha thought he was spinning it out, unwilling to be alone at his own place. She did not mind and enjoyed his company, but thought matters should be resolved. He may have accepted Bené had left him. Martha had not.

Martha watched and considered the situation for some weeks. Then she made a plan and phoned Bené at his office in Sablette.

'Are you free? Good! Then I'm taking you out for lunch. Meet me at The Shack at La Dune at twelve fifteen and we'll eat while we watch the sea.'

It was the place he had collected her and Erin last summer when they had been cut off by the tides. Only last summer? She drove along the tracks, hard, dry and dusty again at this time of year, and reached the café before him. She asked for a bottle of local red wine, a carafe of water and some bread. They could order food when he arrived. She poured herself a small glass of wine and waited. He was characteristically late, and the bottle was a third empty by then.

He was in a sunny disposition and it felt like old times. She poured him a glass of wine, and called the waiter to take their order.

They engaged in catch-up small talk for a few minutes and then she looked him straight in the face and asked, 'Are you going to tell me who he is or do I have to tell you?'

'No. Martha, I told you, you don't know him.' The smile had gone from his eyes. He looked wary and pained.

'You know that's not true, Bené. Do you have the courage to tell me, or do I have to guess? It's not difficult.'

'Oh Martha, I'm so unhappy, and I've made Sébastien unhappy. I've messed up, big time.' He cradled his head in his hands as if to protect it. He was unable to look at her.

She could see he might break down and cry. This was no time for a softly-softly approach. She would have to be cruel to be kind, and after all, he had hurt her as well. He must see that.

'Stop feeling sorry for yourself, Bené. Go and tell Pascal to sod off back to the Dordogne and get the hell out of all our lives.'

He looked up, horrified.

'You know!'

'For God's sake! It's so bloody obvious. You're not just working together. Things fit into place. I'm sure Sébastien's worked it out. You've just confirmed my suspicion.'

'No, no, I don't think he knows it's Pascal. He'd be so hurt. He'd want it to be anyone but Pascal.'

'So would I, but it is Pascal, and I'm hurt. And Sébastien will be. Why has Pascal got such a hold over you?'

'He threatened to write to you and tell you he'd been two-timing with me while he was having his relationship with you. He said you'd never speak to me again.'

'Yes, I can see I would be justified in doing so. But he's wrong. It would mean my affair with Pascal was more important than my friendship with you and Sébastien. It would make Pascal more important than he is. He's so egocentric.'

'And he threatened to make sure Sébastien became acquainted with every sordid detail of what we've been up

340

to. He said Sébastien wouldn't take me back. It would destroy us.'

'Charming. He's viler than I thought. Well, I know you're having it off with Pascal, and Sébastien must have guessed, so what's the secret? Pascal's lost the only power he had, the power to reveal it. Tell him to get stuffed.'

'He's said he'll tell Sébastien things about me that he could only know if... well, you know.'

'Twisting the screw, so to speak! Okay, so he's blackmailing you. Hurting you and then being nice to you. Can't you see how he manipulates? Can't you see it as blackmail, a power thing, control? I can guess some of the things you won't say, like how he's a good lover, an adventurous lover, physically I mean. He can be so loving you want to forgive him the bad things, pretend he isn't a bully. Hold on to only the nice bits. I went through all that. I tried to make excuses for him. In the end he'll make you suffer. I suffered. I won't again. That much I know.'

He did not respond. She hoped he realised she was right, but maybe Pascal's grip on Bené was tight. She tried another tack.

'So, tell me. What does he want from you, apart from easy sex, of course?' She took a sip of her wine.

She thought she detected Bené actually blush.

'You don't mess about, do you?'

'This is no time to mess about, Bené. You've already done too much of that. We need to get rid of him, and limit the damage he can cause. Friends should work together.'

'And are we still friends, Martha? Despite the fact I, oh God, I'm sorry… I deceived you, and started an affair with him when I knew you loved him… then, I mean. And how fragile you were?'

'Quite! I hope you are ashamed.'

'It was so wrong… it is still so wrong. I miss Sébastien!'

'Don't be so pathetic! You've brought this on yourself. Now, to answer your question. Are we still friends? The answer's yes. I can forgive, but we can only be friends again if you behave honourably right now — to Sébastien primarily. And don't you ever be so stupid again!'

'I bit off more than I could chew this time.'

She could not help laughing.

'I'm sure you've done plenty of that in your time, darling.'

'Oh yes, I could tell you some stories…'

'No! Another time, maybe. Spare me the details, please. Let's eat, and consider, and plan.'

The cheese omelettes were rich. She took stock of the situation. At least he had come clean with her. She had feared he would remain in denial.

'I answered your question, but you haven't answered mine.'

'What was that?'

'I want to know what Pascal wants from you?'

'The contract for the restoration of the chateau at Saint-Aubin, of course.'

'Of course! That's your attraction to him. Mr and Mrs Evans rely on you.'

'They do. I'm getting it for him. It's all but signed. But he still needs me as a broker with the Evanses.'

'And then he'll drop you, Bené, when you've got him what he wants. Can't you see it? By the way, was that the Evanses, the Welsh people, in the market in Sablette with you and Pascal? I thought they were an English couple, and couldn't understand their connection with Pascal.'

'Welsh, English, it's all the same to us. They're very rich. Got their money from pharmaceuticals and want to plough it into bringing the chateau and vineyard back to life. Yes, we did take them to the market. I don't remember seeing you there. Pascal wanted to impress them. He asked me to invite them on a wine tasting tour, to experience the competition so to speak. We passed through the market and stopped at the Chateau Loupiec stall to compare their quality. But he suddenly got agitated and told me we were falling behind schedule. We had an appointment at a vineyard so I had to hurry them on their way. Did you see us then?'

'Oh, yes, I saw you all, and I saw Pascal usher you all out of the way before I could get to you though the crowd. He was desperate to get you and the Evanses out of the way before I caught up. So, Bené: you and Pascal, Mr and Mrs Evans and the chateau. What stage has it reached?'

'He's drawn up plans, chosen contractors, and the work's nearly ready to start.'

'Déjà vu. And are the contractors he's selected as crooked as the ones he picked to rob me?'

'I haven't got involved with that side of it.'

'Well, I suggest you do, Bené! The Evanses live in Wales. They only come over intermittently. They may be wealthy, but they're vulnerable to being ripped off. They trust *you*. You have a moral responsibility.'

'God. This is getting out of hand.'

Although fond of him, she was irritated as well. She nearly told him to grow up, to stop trying to run away, but thought additional conflict would not help.

'The chateau would be an enormous contract. Can't you see, Bené. The one he lost for my cottage was miniscule in comparison. He'd be laughing all the way to the bank... at everyone's expense. This would be his revenge. It's our mission to stop him.'

'He promised he'd take me to the Dordogne when it's all over. I am tempted. It seems like a good way out.' Bené was still finding excuses. He sounded pathetic.

'Bené, don't you see, it'll never happen! He's got at least one woman waiting for him there, and I'm sure he's promised others. I don't think he'll ever be true to anyone. He'll dump you as soon as he doesn't need you. I can't make you go back to Sébastien. You have to want to go home. Do you want to go back, Bené? Do you love Sébastien?'

'Yes, of course I do, more than anything or anyone in the world, but he won't take me back. I've ruined everything.'

'I know Sébastien loves you too. Too much, perhaps. And he needs you more than you understand. He wants you back, but is frightened to come and ask you, in case your rejection of him is final. I suggest you go and make your peace with him. You'll have to take the risk and make a full confession. You'll have to confess and grovel. You've nothing to lose. You've lost him if you don't.'

'God, this is going to be hard.'

'I hope he is hard on you. You may enjoy it!'

'Stop it, Martha. You're terrible.' He grinned though he was almost crying. 'But what are we going to do about Pascal?

'We! He's your problem, not mine! But I see you're depending on me to resolve this... Well, wait a minute, I'm thinking... Yes, perhaps I have an idea. Okay, you go and make your peace with Sébastien. Leave Pascal to me!'

Later that same day she forced herself to mount the concrete staircase. Pascal rented the apartment at the top which doubled as his office. It had seemed so simple and brave when she had decided to go and have a show-down with him. Now she felt dizzy and scared. Memories of previous visits to the apartment did not help. They had played at being lovers here. He had tried to control her here.

She had been on a high when she had told Bené she would deal with Pascal, relishing the anticipated confrontation. She wanted to get her own back on Pascal.

Now she had to calm herself and take deep breaths before knocking. It would be fatal to show the slightest weakness. She would have to play her cards brilliantly, and surprise was her main ace, perhaps her only one.

She knew he was in because he was expecting Bené this evening, but she had sent him home to Sébastien. She imagined Bené was not feeling too cheerful at this moment either.

She knocked. There was no spyhole and after a moment the door opened. Martha saw the look of alarm on Pascal's face, and this gave her confidence. She was the last person in the world he was expecting to see, and the surprise was evidently an unpleasant one. He had not engineered this and was not in charge. He began to shut the door again without speaking. She was quick and forceful and pushed him out of the way before he could close it. She saw her strength and purpose confused him, and he was left with no alternative but to meekly follow her into his own living room. He was wearing short black shorts and a sleeveless white tee shirt which barely came down to his waist. He was dressed for Bené. She would have said he looked young and vulnerable if she had not known him and his play-acting.

His apartment was immaculate, neat, modern and tasteful. Its beauty should have reflected his character, but it was the anonymous beauty of a catalogue. She noticed he had added a few more pieces of art since her last visit. She picked up a small bronze statuette of an African girl and examined it. She put it down carefully.

'Nice. You always had good taste.' She was acting her part, taking control from him. Control was his game.

'What do you want, Martha? You broke off our relationship and I didn't think I'd see you again—'

'You saw me in the market,' she broke in.

'Yes, and it must have been clear I did not want to meet you. Now, please leave, I'm expecting Bené, and I'm afraid you'll be in the way.'

'He's not coming. He's gone back to Sébastien.'

A second surprise. It flickered across his face. He was recalculating.

'Ah ha. Well, well. I wonder what he'll tell him…'

'He'll tell him the truth. How you seduced him for the Saint-Aubin contract, and what a shit you are.'

Oh, God, I've said that word at last, she thought.

'Just so Sébastien gets the full unexpurgated story, I've written a letter for him. I'll send it to the big man if the little slut does something silly. That'll be sure to break Sébastien's heart.'

She could not let him go on. She had to keep the initiative. She heard him say,

'So Bené had better do as I warned him, and that goes for you too.'

He was walking towards her, so she put up her hand to signal stop, the gesture of a traffic cop. It worked.

'Not any more, Pascal. You can save the stamp on the letter, because by now Bené will have told him everything. I wouldn't be in, if I were you, when Sébastien decides to pay you a call.'

Pascal miraculously stopped, turned and sat down slowly on the leather sofa. He crossed his legs and took his time taking a cigarette out of an onyx box and lighting it. He rarely smoked and his hands were shaking. She knew he was stalling, replotting his thoughts. There was a look in his eyes she did not like. It was his hunting look. She had felt uncomfortable with that look before. He was weighing her up, weighing up how to play it. She remained standing so she could look down on him. She moved a step forward and stood with her feet apart in a stance calculated to look relaxed. It had been the correct decision to wear trousers. She had to appear strong and calm and maintain the upper hand.

'Why did you have to pick on Bené? I'm not bothered whether you're gay, straight or anything else. It's your targeting impressionable people that I detest, leading them on, using them.'

'The English talk about leading people on. Leading them up the garden path is the expression, I believe. Well Martha, I don't lead people up the garden path, they lead themselves. I smile a lot. I've found that gets me a long way with most people. Gay guys fancy me because I'm sexy. I may be a bit suggestive, even a bit camp with them if it suits me, and that makes them think, um, possibly. They begin to dream. They get hooked. They trap themselves like moths. You might as well know I've done everything with Bené, all ways. He enjoys being a bottom, but occasionally he wants to be a top, and I cover all bases. You'd no idea we were up to it while I was with you. You can both be very demanding! Luckily, I have staying power and give satisfaction.'

She knew he wanted to hurt her. She hated him. It was a new emotion for her. She had felt many things in her life, but pure hate was something she had never felt for anyone before, not even Lauren. She wanted to bring the encounter to an end. She feared if he talked long enough, he might trick her.

'You lost me some time ago, and now you've lost him as well. So, to business, Pascal!' She paused before delivering her line with maximum force. 'You will close your affairs here immediately and leave.'

He snorted. He ignored her. She began to panic about what to do next.

'You're not as smart as you think, are you? Coming here alone. Goodness knows what I might do to you. The pleasure and the hurt! And who would know?'

'Claude. He's outside, and if I blow this,' she pointed to her pocket as if there were something there, 'he'll be in and you'll be in hospital.' It was the best she could do. She had no back-up, and realised how stupid she had been, but she reckoned Pascal might swallow her lie. He was not brave. He was certainly afraid of Claude.

'So, what is it between you and Bené anyway?' He was changing the subject. 'You've turned him against me. You can't have him, you know. He's not into women. He likes cock.'

'He's a good friend. He may be silly sometimes. He may act like a teenager who hasn't grown up, but I'm fond of him. I'm fond of them both, Bené and Sébastien. I like their courage to be themselves, together. I'm not sure you'd understand that. Liking other people for their own sake. I don't want or need anything from them, just their friendship.'

'How sweet! I'm so touched. Puke!'

'Pascal, we haven't got long. This is your last chance. Stop trying to divert me from doing what I came here to do. Claude will be in if I don't come out in ten minutes, that's our arrangement, and you won't like it. His message won't be gentle.'

She stood her ground, pretending she was relaxed, maintaining the pressure. She made sure he was not between her and the door.

'Are you going to pull out of the Saint-Aubin contract voluntarily. If not I will make the Evanses aware how you tried to rip me off, and are using the same tactics to defraud them?'

He laughed. 'Come on, Martha, where's your evidence?'

'All the paperwork you were so careless about. It must be your arrogance, your belief you are invulnerable. Claude and Sébastien kept it secure and safe for me. The double accounting. The bills you were going to present, and the figures you actually planned to pay contractors. Then of course there's the damming record of your phone conversation to me at the department when you admitted fraud. I have the tape, safe, and if I were to disappear it will be released. You'd be out on your ear if Mr. Evans heard it. He'd no doubt contact the police.'

'You're bluffing,' he challenged. He had gone very pale, though his eyes looked dark and suspicious. She was bluffing, but he could not be sure. She had to keep her nerve and get him to panic first.

'And if I go back to the Dordogne, you'd let me have the papers and the tape?' It was as if he was forcing himself to laugh, making light of it.

'Don't be stupid, Pascal. I'll keep them, just in case I get word you're up to your tricks again, or on your way back here. However, I do have something I intend to give you though...' She moved closer and saw him flinch. Surely, he did not imagine she was going to hit him. That was more his style. She produced his elegant pen and laid it on the sofa beside him, within reach.

'You forgot this. I found it after you left. It's yours and I like to return things to their rightful owners.' She stood back carefully.

'I probably dropped it in the bedroom where we'd been fucking. You could give it to your next lover.'

'That shows how little you understand me. Right! Enough! I'll give you three days to wrap up your business here, or I'll contact the Evanses. It's all prepared.'

He did not try to prevent her leaving. He looked sad as he turned his head to watch her go. She had an idea that she had in some way won his respect. *He's definitely weird and unpredictable.* As she walked out of the apartment, down the stairs and out of building, she thought, *I got out. I'm safe. It's over, I've done it!*

She unlocked her car and got in. *How my life has changed since Thierry died. Up to then, apart from at work, I never acted alone. I followed Thierry, lived around Thierry, like a satellite around a moon. I adored him. I shall always miss him, but I had to become my own person, and I've done it. Today I did it! I shamed myself with Pascal but now I've redeemed myself.*

She knew what she had said to Pascal about friendships had not always been true for her. She had not felt the need for friends when she had been half of a couple. She wondered if she had restrained Thierry from being more sociable.

She no longer assumed she was self-sufficient. She must talk to Claude about her own security, recognising she was vulnerable out at Cachette if there were people like Pascal around.

Martha was shaking and exhausted now she was out of danger. Her hands could not stop trembling as she turned on the engine and looked to see if it was clear to pull out. No sign of Pascal. She calmed down as she drove. A few kilometres on she met a car coming in the opposite direction from Saint-Cyprien. The car flashed its lights and pulled in. She recognised it was Sébastien and Bené and stopped.

Sébastien leaned in the window she had wound down.
'Are you alright?' were his first words.
'Yes, yes, I'm fine, thanks.'

Bené appeared behind him, subdued.

'I told him everything,' Bené said.

'Good.'

Sébastien had regained his strength and looked energetic. He was staring up the road towards the apartment block as if Pascal was his target. She thought he would like to give Pascal a thrashing, so it was just as well she had completed her business.

'Bené told me you were going to confront Pascal. That sounded dangerous to me. We came to make sure you're okay. Did he touch you?'

'No. Thank you. I'm alright.'

She was grateful to them. She thought she had probably been stupid challenging Pascal on her own, but their coming over like this made it worthwhile.

'I was a bit stupid going on my own. But it's done. Leave it now, Sebastien. Pascal's not worth getting in trouble for. Take Bené home instead and be thankful.'

'We could all go to Chez-Madeleine?' Bené interrupted.

'No, thanks. Not tonight. I need to go home. It's like after-shock. I need to be on my own.'

'Drive on then and we'll follow you. We'll see you back to Cachette, and then if you're not up to company we'll leave you in peace.'

Now Martha carries the bunch of asparagus back up the hill. There is no gate into her property, only a gap in the row of bushes Sébastien helped her plant in late spring. It had been the pollen time, when the trees burst open covering everything in a fine yellow dust. They had both coughed for a week. It had been hard satisfying work digging down until they reached the earth below the sand. They filled the holes with rich terreau, a nutritious compost made chiefly of loam. Then they had fixed the shrubs with thick staves hammered deep into the ground. It had made their knuckles sore and calloused. It would take a few seasons for them to establish roots deeply enough to reach their own water supply and then the plants would take off. They will grow healthy and strong and not bend against the wind. The bushes include photinia and yellow forsythia and were chosen to blend with and glorify the countryside. This is not Chislehurst with its roses. She is creating a wild garden and laughs at the contradiction.

Now, Martha takes the path to the front door, newly carved in oak. It is a pattern she saw on a barn whilst out walking and drew in the notebook she always carries. She lays her bundle down on the floor in the corner, out of the sun, not in the fridge where it will wilt and shrivel. She is sure it will be all right until she cooks it this afternoon.

She pours herself a glass of cold water for a change, and takes it into the conservatory which is also her study. She spends a lot of time here, cosy inside but with glass on three sides it is like being in the garden. There is still no sound from above. He must be sleeping late. Or maybe she got up early. She will not wake him.

As it is warm, she slides open one of the glass doors before settling into a chair and picking up the bundle of papers. She has read them many times, but not shared them with anyone. She will let Erin into the secret eventually, but for now she is trying to absorb it. She reads the covering letter again to make sure it is true and not another of her dreams.

Veronica had phoned at the beginning of June to say she thought her mother had not long to live. They seemed to know that sort of thing in The Pines. Martha flew over, collected a hire car at Gatwick, and drove to Bournemouth. May had revived in the meanwhile, and was sitting up in bed uncharacteristically sipping a sherry.

'I was worried,' Martha told her.

'You gave me some worries when you were little,' May replied. Not unfriendly.

She seemed on good form; her eyes seemed to follow Martha as she gently straightened the bedclothes and moved the chair so she could sit close. She wanted to make sure May recognised her, and did not confuse her with anyone else. The only way to be certain was to take a risk and ask, 'Who's Poppy?'

There seemed to be a look of alarm in May's eyes, and Martha was concerned she may have miscalculated.

'Poppy…' The old lady started, and took one hand from under the bedcovers to grasp Martha. Martha wondered if May again mistook her for Poppy. She made soothing sounds and told her mother not to exert herself. May shook her off as quickly as she had taken hold of her, and fell back against her pillows.

Martha considered calling for help, but May had calmed down. Then she spoke.

'I should have told you about Poopy. She was… a child of nature…' And she chuckled. 'Not a bit like you!' she added in a voice that was suddenly strong, but it trailed off and Martha tried to catch what she was saying. It was evident Poppy had existed, but presumably did not exist anymore. May was rambling. Martha caught odd words; 'bombing' and 'shelter,' 'poppies growing… among the ruins' and 'understand' before May looked at her intently and spoke.

'Poppy was my daughter.'

She looked exhausted, but also peaceful. She closed her eyes and appeared to go to sleep.

'I'd better leave you to rest,' Martha said, tucking the sheets around her. Poppy was her daughter. What did that explain? It did not make it easier.

She was creeping towards the door when May spoke again. Martha turned back and saw May watching her.

'Did you say something?'

It came in single words. 'Take… care… of yourself… Martha.' It was almost inaudible.

'And you, Mum.'

Martha had to compose herself before entering the office.

'She seems peaceful, almost tranquil now, but she became agitated about Poppy. Said she was her daughter. She was trying to convey something, but it exhausted her.'

'She's been like that, up and down, fretting about something. I'll see if Siobhan can find out more.'

'I've got to go up to London for a few days to clear up some business. My house is empty so I've booked into a hotel, but you can reach me on my mobile. I'll come down again, of course, before I fly back to Bordeaux, but if she wants me I'll come anytime, anytime at all.'

Three days later Veronica's deputy Val phoned her. Martha had just emerged from her solicitor's office where she had signed the agreement to sell the house in Chislehurst, and papers regarding a small flat she was buying in a new development near the South Bank. She had accepted Rajinder's advice in acquiring the flat. They had chosen one in range of both Borough High Street and London Bridge stations, a recently gentrified area. The rental money would be useful, and it would always be there as a bolt-hole if she decided to return. She knew in her gut she had done the right thing, but felt guilty she had come into so much money because of Thierry's death.

Her phone rang and she grasped the tone of Val's voice, modulated like a newsreader imparting bad news. May had slipped away. She did not say died, no one does these days. The absolute finality shook Martha. She was bereft. Lonely for Thierry, lonely for May. So many missed opportunities. So many sentences unspoken.

So Martha stayed on. The funeral had been a quiet affair, but Veronica, Val and Siobhan came from the home, and Martha was accompanied by Priya and Fran who both wanted to go with her though they had not met May. They went to support her. Rajinder could not get away from Benton's.

Despite the season, it was cold outside the chapel as the small group waited for a much larger funeral to end and disperse. Their short service was conducted by the clergyman who visited The Pines regularly. He said he liked May, though they knew she used to give him the cold shoulder, and on the one occasion he had asked if she would like to pray, she had told him, 'It's too late for that.'

He had asked Martha if she would like to deliver the eulogy and share her memories of May, but she was too full of questions to say anything coherent. She simply read a poem which meant a lot to her, but could hear May's voice in her head saying, 'Why are you being soppy?'

Martha acknowledged that funerals are for the living not the dead, a means of making sense of that which has no comfortable sense.

They had tea and sandwiches at a restaurant near the crematorium, and Val said Siobhan had looked after May in her final days.

'She has things to tell you,' Val said.

Martha and Siobhan took their tea and sat in chairs by the window.

'Thank you for looking after her. I'd like to know what she said, whatever it is.'

'She was a lovely lady to look after. It was a pleasure, Mrs Jolivet...'

'Call me Martha, please,'

'Okay, um, Martha,' Siobhan began hesitantly. 'You mother opened up to me in her final days, not long conversations, but bits and pieces now and again. She asked me one day if I thought she was bitter. I mean, she never came across like that to me. She said life had trod her down. She talked about her husband. Stan, she called him. She'd let him make all the decisions, that was expected, but bit by bit her life had gone and it hadn't been what she wanted, and she'd not been allowed a voice. I think she was trying to say she'd been frustrated, so she came across as angry, but that's not how she was inside. She said she'd...'

'Go on, Siobhan, please.'

'She said she'd not been able to get close to you, because Stan had been strict. She wished you'd understood her better.'

'Yes, it wasn't an easy relationship. It seems the wrong way round, though, doesn't it. It's usually the offspring wondering if the parent understands them. It was only after she had settled at The Pines she started to... to what? To soften a little, I suppose. Did she say anything about a Poppy?'

'She told me little by little. I wasn't sure if it was real, so I asked Val, and she said to encourage her to get it off her chest. It might help her face the end, so to speak.'

'Yes, yes, I can see that. Did she want me to understand about Poppy?'

'I think so. Once I thought she had got you and me mixed up, and she was talking to you, so I just encouraged her, until she was tired. I gradually pieced it together. They'd been told they couldn't have children, she and Stan. It was assumed the problem was her, she was infertile, barren she called it. She said it made her feel incomplete. Apparently, they both worked at the same factory until they got married and then May had to leave. Married women weren't supposed to work. When the war came it all changed. The factory was turned over to munitions, and they called her back. She said the war was hard but the friendships were fun. Stan was sent away to France, then North Africa. She didn't know if she'd see him again. Cannon fodder she called him. She did sound a bit bitter then, I admit. She said all this in bits and pieces over a number of days. She had what she called a Yankee airman billeted on her in 1944, while Stan was at the front. I don't know how much you want to hear?'

'All of it, Siobhan. Everything she told you.'

'It happened during an air raid. They didn't go down to the shelter. She told me they got drunk, and as she put it, cuddled up against the Nazis instead of taking shelter. She said not to be shocked. You never knew how long you'd got in those days. You had to live for the moment.

By the time Poppy was showing for all to see, the airman had gone back across the Atlantic and Stan had been demobbed, and was on his way home. She was scared. She thought he'd beat her up, chuck her out, or walk out himself, but he said, '"Seems like it was me who had the problem."

'She asked him, "What do you want me to do?"'

'"You're going to have the baby and we'll say it's ours. We'll consider it a gift."

'May said she was a beautiful baby in a torn world and they called her Poppy because poppies bloomed in the wastelands of London bombsites where houses once stood. She cried a bit then. I must say I was choked. I'd never heard her talk poetical like that.'

'Did she say what happened to her?'

'No, maybe if she'd lived a while longer she would have told me, but that's all I got out of her.'

'So, I suppose Poppy died and they adopted me to replace her.' Martha said, thinking aloud. 'They must have been broken-hearted,' the realisation struck her.

The letter had arrived later, when Martha had returned to France, delivered to Cachette by a woman in a yellow post van. It was addressed 'Please give to Martha' sealed inside a larger envelope from The Pines. Veronica wrote they had found it hidden amongst May's things. It had almost been overlooked.

Dear Martha,

You have to know the truth. I am your grandmother.

I have started this letter several times. Here's another go. God knows if I'll have the courage to give it to you. I'm still in my own home, but I don't know for how much longer. I've begun forgetting things, although I try to cover up. You think I'm not safe anymore and should be put away. I must write it down before it gets confused. I can remember the past as clear as day.

The most important thing I want to say to you is I THOUGHT I WAS DOING THE RIGHT THING. Please believe me. Maybe I was wrong. I'm not good at owning up when I'm in the wrong.

Let me tell you about your mother, Poppy. I should have done so years ago, but Stan forbade it. I tried to please him too. It's my own fault. I tried to please everybody and finished up pleasing nobody.

Poppy. She looked very much like you, but had a wilder temperament. You're more like me, awkward! You won't like that, but think about it!

Poppy. She bloomed. Oh, she bloomed and I spoilt her.

'She's a free thinker,' I said proudly to Stan.

'Too bloody free. You're responsible.' He wore me down.

It was like I died the day she died. 1976. There was a tremendous thumping on the front door. Sounded like someone was trying to break it down. Stan was up first, to deal with whoever it was. Delinquents, I heard him say. I wasn't far behind. I saw the policeman's uniform over Stan's shoulder, and a pain hit my gut because something was seriously wrong. I didn't know it was Poppy.

Then Stan wept. I'd never heard him cry. A car crash. It was an old van, and lots of them had been in it, too many, travelling back from a potlatch, or something, whatever that was, a hippy festival, so I'm told. A tyre had blown. The van went into the side of a lorry. Lots dead. Poppy dead. She had a baby, six months old, it survived. We didn't know she had a baby. That's how estranged we were. Stan said to the policeman, 'We'll tek the baby.'

You were a pretty thing. You didn't cry. You looked around as if you understood everything. Your birth certificate when it was found said you were called Martha. Poppy had given you a biblical name. Odd that. It didn't say who your father was. One of her hippy boyfriends, I guess.

The Children's Department were happy for us to adopt you, even though it was not necessary as we were your grandparents, your next of kin, anyway. Problem solved from their point of view. You got a new adoption certificate, saying you were our child, a second gift, we didn't deserve. It was going to be different this time. No mistakes with this second gift. We'd be strict. You weren't going to be allowed to grow up to be a free spirit. I wasn't allowed to spoil you like I'd spoilt Poppy.

May must have broken off at this point, because the next page was written on different paper and with a different pen.

I was frightened of you as you grew up. You didn't want cuddles, and later I couldn't do it anyway. You were self-contained. When you asked me a question, I suspected you knew the answer and were just testing me. You organised everyone from an early age.

You never asked about your real parents. I waited and you didn't ask. When I eventually had to give you the certificate, you looked at it and said, 'Oh,' like you'd expected it, and took it to your room and shut the door, shutting me out. We were ordinary, and you wanted to be special. The certificate proved you didn't belong to us.

I liked Terry. He loved and cared for you, and because I was your mother, he cared for me too and broke through with his gentle winning ways.

Martha recognised the third and last part was on the paper she had given to May when she was living at The Pines. The writing was less legible. May was now having difficulty putting pen to paper.

I kept this letter hidden in the broken lining of my handbag, secret! I'm proud of that. I'm now living in a care home. Today I'm having one of my good days. Thank you for the paper. You must know the truth. I want to talk to you but can't.

You changed when Terry died. He was your compass. You lost him and you are all over the place. You see I worry for you. I hope this move to France turns out for the best. I hope you find yourself again. If you have to go to do that, so be it. I can't stop you. I'm used to losing people. I'll miss you more than you think.

I tried to please both you and Stan, and do my best, but the trouble is, we forget about kindness. Life teaches us to grow hard and we forget to be kind. I've been hard on myself, hard with you, too hard. Martha, LEARN TO BE GENTLE AGAIN. Don't let it get too late as it is for me.

I was shocked when you told me your dream about the crash. I wanted to tell you, to clear up the muddle in my head, but you kept calming me and said not to talk. I didn't think you could possibly remember the van, you were so small. What put that into your head? Well Martha, now you know. You were the baby who survived, sitting there among all those dead grown-ups. Poppy was dead, still holding you, protecting you.

I'm tired. Haven't written so much for a long time, but it's a relief. I'm sorry for such a lot. I want you to get this someday and understand.

God Bless you my love,

Your Mum and your Gran,

May.

The writing gets shakier towards the end. How many times has she re-read the letter? She aches to tell Thierry. She misses May so much. Why had they not taken the opportunity when they had it? She has so many regrets, but forbids herself to continue feeling guilty. May had begged her to learn to be gentle again, and she was right. It is not a comfortable world. Perhaps she has done her best to insulate herself against reality by relocating to Cachette, but then, why not? Lots of people need her help; Justin, Bené, Sébastien, Erin, Madeleine; there is quite a list, but it is important she waits and is there for them when they need her, not when she wants to be wanted. May had written, "we forget to be kind". How old fashioned. How true. One day she might even require help herself. She cannot imagine how, but conceives it is possible.

Stan and May both loved her. She had not been certain. Now she knows and it enables her to face the future. Thierry loved her. She is blessed.

There is a thump. Someone is coming downstairs. Justin appears in only a dressing gown. She is full of private joy that he has come to stay with her for his summer vacation. She persuaded Madeleine to take him on as a waiter for the holiday, and she is as strict with him as she is with the rest of her team.

'Sorry, slept in. Is there any breakfast?'

'Yes.' She puts the letter away and stirs from her chair. 'Just you?'

'Yeah,' he said, looking shocked.

'You can bring somebody back, you know, as long as I know.'

'I'll hit the shower,' he says and is gone. Embarrassed. She must take things slower.

She prepares breakfast for him, and he re-appears clean in cut-off jeans and a white tee shirt. She sits opposite as he eats heartily, and she has another coffee. She is getting addicted to the stuff.

'Can you reserve a table for tonight?' she asks.

'Sure, how many?'

'Oh, let's hope the whole gang, say about seven. The boys are coming over here for a light tea first.'

'Is that why you've picked the asparagus, for Séb and Bené?'

'Yes, I want to know what they think of it. It's just a silly contest we are into. I don't think he likes being called Séb though, it's not very French. We'll meet the others there. I don't know what time, mid evening I expect. Will you be our waiter?'

'Sure,'

He clears away. He is good like that. Madeleine has trained him well.

'Martha, can I ask you not to make this a really late Chez-Madeleine night, please.'

'Oh?'

'We want to close early if we can, that's me and the team. We're going to go down the beach with some fireworks and some booze afterwards. Don't worry I won't get drunk. Just the young ones are going.'

'Does Madeleine know?'

'She says it'll be all right as long as we clear up after the last diners. I'll probably stay in Saint-Cyprien because it'll be too late to cycle back here, but I'll see you tomorrow. They've done it before, gone down to the beach at night, but they've invited me this time. Sounds fun. Good for my French.'

He has his back to her, putting plates in the dishwasher.

'Yes, I remember it well.'

'Sorry. Didn't catch what you said.' He turns towards her.

'Nothing. I was just muttering to myself. Have fun tonight.'

He picks up his phone, his headset and a small backpack and smiles a goodbye as he moves towards the door, already living the day ahead.

'By the way, you haven't phoned your mum for a while. You must do so today!' she calls out to his receding figure. He gives her a departing wave, but she doesn't know if he heard.